Carousel
The Missing Years

Breaking The Chains of Abuse

by
Kimberley Rose Dawson

Bloomington, IN Milton Keynes, UK

authorHOUSE

AuthorHouse™
1663 Liberty Drive, Suite 200
Bloomington, IN 47403
www.authorhouse.com
Phone: 1-800-839-8640

AuthorHouse™ UK Ltd.
500 Avebury Boulevard
Central Milton Keynes, MK9 2BE
www.authorhouse.co.uk
Phone: 08001974150

This book is a work of non-fiction. Unless otherwise noted, the author and the publisher make no explicit guarantees as to the accuracy of the information contained in this book and in some cases, names of people and places have been altered to protect their privacy.

First published by AuthorHouse 4/24/2007

ISBN: 978-1-4343-0377-6 (sc)

Printed in the United States of America
Bloomington, Indiana

This book is printed on acid-free paper.

Book cover art © Linda G. Gustafson

Photograph of Her Mother's Hat © Terra Corbett

Photograph of "Trail Nestled in the Bottom of a Stone Bowl" © Mike Hockley.

Based on the true story of Elizabeth Burgess' struggle
to stay sober and fight off her ever enticing Carousel

*This book is dedicated to the love of my life
and my soul-mate*

George "Edmund" Bales

born December 15, 1944

died May 18, 1963

Acknowledgements

I'd like to thank all the readers of my first book Carousel, for their constant praises of the book. Their words of praise gave me the courage to go on and write Carousel - The Missing Years. Comments about Carousel such as, "I couldn't put it down." "I just loved it." "When is your next book coming out, I can't wait to read it." "It reminded me of Angela's Ashes." and "I liked Liz." made Carousel - The Missing Years possible.

Kudos to Carol Chamberlain, a high school English teacher of Literature, and a dear friend who took the time out of her busy schedule to proof-read Carousel - The Missing Years so I could make the necessary emendments.

Thanks to my children for bearing with me and allowing me to go public with Carousel.

Thanks to my dearest friends, Val Smith and Nancy Wilson (Carol Simpson), for being there for me in my struggles to write about, and thus relive my sad, but triumphant story.

Carousel: A merry-go-round, repeating the same rotations, covering the same ground over and over again.

Liz's was a carousel of painted white steeds, garlanded with flowers and ribbons, with smiles on their faces. Promise of happiness and potential for love was contained in their beauty. As they turned, their smiles turned to sneers. Quickly as they go round and round, look, they are smiling, look again they are sneering.

Look again, these horses are drunk on their mad turning round and round. Look again? No! She's getting off.

In 1981 the drunk horses made their last turn, but still Liz's Carousel tugs relentlessly as she struggles to stay sober.

Prologue

"Well, she's not capable of making a decision for herself, Jim. I think the best thing to do is commit her to the Daly Pavilion."

"No!" Liz screamed and started to shake and totally panic. She had heard horror stories from other A.A. members about how the psychiatrist at the Daly was adamant about giving antiquated shock treatments. Dr. Trent's words had penetrated Liz's fog and terrified her. She started to cry harder and flail her arms totally out of control.

Dr. Trent hugged her close and said, "Okay, Liz, okay. I think this is really necessary. But I know how you feel about Dr. Ward. I'll tell you what, you'll be strictly under my care, okay? I will instruct Dr. Ward that you are my patient only. He will have no jurisdiction over you, okay?" She gently moved the hair out of Liz's eyes and wiped her tears.

Liz nodded slowly. Then Dr. Trent said, "You can take her now. I'll call ahead and let them know you're coming."

The trio left the Dr.'s office and headed to the pavilion in a cab. Liz felt like a sheep being led to the slaughter, but there was nothing she could do to help herself. She felt like a piece of lead. She couldn't even lift her arms.

On arrival, Liz was admitted, although she had no recollection of it later. Jimmy sadly signed the documents that would imprison the mother that he loved. His heart was crushed but there was nothing else he could do.

Liz was taken to the large central common room where she was lowered into an over-stuffed rocker. She cried and cried and cried, until, suddenly, she spotted a young girl pirouetting all around the room. Liz watched fascinated as the girl twirled and twirled ever closer. She was dressed in pink and her flaming red hair was all tangled.

Liz was startled out of her wits when the girl pirouetted right for her and plopped herself at her feet. The girl began to speak,

"Hi, I'm Margie! Can I borrow your comb. You see, I've just had a miscarriage and I really need a comb." Liz's mouth was agape. She didn't know what to do, and she started to panic just as the girl flipped up and disappeared across the room pirouetting away as quickly as she had come.

Liz hardly had time to gather herself together again when a tall gray-haired strange-looking man dressed in nothing but an orange hospital kimono wandered aimlessly towards her. His eyes were all glassed over and Liz realized, too late, that he was going to walk right into the chair that she was occupying. He hit the edge of the chair, faltered, fell forward and as he fell the kimono flew open and Liz found herself face to face with an eight inch penis.

"Oh, my Gawd!" She yelled and took off running. What had they done to her. She was petrified. A nurse grabbed hold of her and said gently, "Come on I'll take you to your room."

****

"Uh, oh, trouble. Here come the guards. Someone's going to the rubber room again."

Liz was terrified of the rubber room. If a patient got out of control and the nurses couldn't handle him or her, they would send for security and the guards would swarm and surround the person, jump him or her and then the whole entourage would struggle toward the room they called the rubber room. It was called the rubber room because all the walls were padded as well as the floor. There was nothing in there and the patient would be stripped completely before being tossed in. The screaming that would go on afterward haunted Liz no end. She constantly lived in fear of getting out of control herself.

Chapter 1
The Turtle Story

Elizabeth Burgess stands crying and shaking at a pay phone attached to a red brick wall, the outside wall of the large Safeway store on Second Avenue in Trail, British Columbia. She struggles with vibrating hands to put a dime in the phone slot. She stops to wipe her tears with the back of one hand so she can see better. Then finally the coin drops with a clink and she hears a dial tone. She dials. And abruptly a staunch voice answers "Dr. Trent's Office."

"H-hello. C-can I please speak to Dr. Trent?" Liz mutters.

"Dr. Trent is busy with a patient right now. Can I give her a message and have her call you back?" the cold voice echoes through the confines of Liz's troubled mind.

"You can tell Dr. Trent they can look for my body in the river," Liz spits out.

"Uh, oh, my, just one moment!" Then click and soft music plays, but it offers no comfort to Liz. Then another click.

"Dr. Trent here! Liz, hold on, what seems to be the trouble."

"Oh, Dr. Trent, you gotta help me. I'm just vibrating and I feel like I'm going to lose my mind. I'm not gonna be able to stay sober. I've got this horrible guilt. You gotta help me. I can't stand it. I'm going crazy. It's like ants are crawling all under my skin. I feel like all my veins are going to burst."

"Where are you?"

"I'm at the pay phone at Safeway."

"Give me the number of the pay phone and stay right there. Don't move. I'm going to make one quick call and I'll get right back to you. Promise you won't move."

"Yeah, I promise, but don't be long. I can't take much more."

Liz hangs up the phone and fidgets impatiently. Shoppers pass by with their carts full staring at her. She drops her head down and chants, "Hurry up, hurry up." Then the phone jangles, she jumps nervously and grabs it.

"Liz? Doctor Trent here. I called Mental Health and Doctor Durham will see you right away. Do you know where the health unit is? Can you make it there?"

"Yeah, but what'll I say? What'll I say to him?"

"Just go there, right now. He's expecting you. He will help you."

Liz hangs up the phone, hugs herself to try to stop the shaking and heads across the parking lot to Second Avenue, then crosses to McQuarrie Street to the health unit.

She enters through the front door and gazes around. She spots the reception desk and moves toward it. Standing in front of the desk in the front office, quivering, she is told by a pretty blonde receptionist to wait around the corner in the office at the end of the hall for Dr. Durham. She quickly makes her way down the hall and turns the corner. She sees his office door open, but reluctant to enter his private domain, she just stands outside in the hallway. Doctor Durham, a middle aged, nervous, but good looking man comes bounding around the corner and just about runs into her. He nearly jumps out of his skin and at the same time lets out a little squeal.

"Oh, don't do that! You scared me out of my wits."

Liz looks at him and frowns. *He's supposed to help me? He looks in about as bad a shape as I am with his nerves.* Then an unbidden thought penetrates, *He sure is good looking though,* but she quickly dismisses it. "Sorry." she mutters.

"That's okay. Please come in," he says, as he ushers her to a large, brown leather chair and starts picking up and arranging files on his desk.

He adjusts his gold rimmed spectacles and runs his fingers through his dark brown but graying hair as he starts to speak. "Now what seems to be the problem."

"I quit drinking two weeks ago and now I'm just vibrating. I can't think straight. I feel like I'm losing my mind." Liz breaks into tears and bows her head in embarrassment. Kindly, he passes her a Kleenex.

"There, there, I expect you're suffering alcohol withdrawal symptoms."

"I've quit drinking before for longer periods of time and never been this bad off."

"When people drink or do drugs they bury all their inner feelings and when they quit all those pent up feelings and griefs rush to the surface and it can be very overwhelming especially if you've decided to quit for good. How about telling me a little bit about yourself, your background, starting with your childhood."

"My childhood? I don't know where to start."

"How about starting at the beginning."

"At the beginning?"

Dr. Durham nods and leans back in his large office chair, stretches out his legs and crosses them at the ankles while he folds his hands across his chest. Liz notices he is wearing argyle socks and thinks to herself, *he's gotta have a wife. No bachelor's clothes ever look that good.* Her eyes travel to the third finger on his left hand where she sees a gold band. She lets out a long sigh. She would *never* date a married man. Then she begins.

"Well as far back as I can remember I never felt like I fit anywhere. My mother never wanted me, she told me so enough times. And my dad didn't care or at least it seemed that way. I'll bet if you took all the words he ever uttered to me in my lifetime, you could fit them in a half hour. And most of those words were yelled. Although I do remember when I was really small there were a few times when he was good to me. You know, it's a funny thing he bought me this kid's book one time and you know what else, over the years, I could never talk about that story without crying. Weird, eh?"

Dr. Durham pulls himself up with interest, "Tell me about that story."

"Well there was this little turtle and he wanted to romp and play like all the other animals, but he had this heavy shell and couldn't run free. And his mother told him if he took off his shell he would be in big trouble. But the turtle never listened, he took off his shell and ended up in a major..." Liz's throat started to close over with a large lump so she couldn't speak and her big fawn eyes filled with tears.

"See, I told you," she croaked. "I can't even talk, what's the matter with me?"

"I suspect *you* are that little turtle," Dr. Durham said as he reached over and patted the back of her hand.

Liz sat up erect, her long chestnut hair bounced as she swung her head around to look into the Dr.'s kind face. "Yeah!" she said. "That makes a lot of sense. I sure did make a mess of my life."

Liz's thoughts raced to Lenny, her common-law husband, who had shot himself a few years ago. She could hear his words as clear as though he were right in front of her. *I've done the worst thing you could possibly think of.* Her palms started to sweat. She screwed up her face and shuddered.

"What's wrong? What were you thinking just then?" Dr. Durham asked as he peered intently at her through his spectacles.

"Nuthin'. I'm just really upset right now.

Dr. Durham sighed, knowing she wasn't telling the truth and said, "Well I think I'm going to prescribe a very mild sedative to get you through the worst and we'll continue with this session and I'll see you regularly until you're feeling better."

Liz glanced at his handsome face and her innards warmed at his kind words. The Carousel tugged relentlessly, the Carousel inside her head that whirred with delight when she was in love. Then the warmth receded and the Carousel became still with her next thoughts. *No nice man would ever want me. I am black to the core now and any chance I ever had to have a good man is probably gone forever.*

Chapter 2
Drunken Ira Hayes

Liz did continue to see Dr. Durham, but she never did disclose to him the horrible black secret that she carried within so she never really made any great progress.

Liz's parents, John and Alicia, had decided to retire in beautiful Creston, British Columbia in 1978. Liz followed them, from Beeton, Ontario in 1980 where she had hoped to effect a geographic cure for her alcoholism. Then after getting arrested for impaired driving, she had left Alicia's harping to move on to Trail with her four children, Jimmy, seventeen, Stacy sixteen, Bonnie fifteen and Janie twelve. They had arrived in 1981 to a thriving metropolis that had very little rental housing available. Cominco, a large smelter, sat on a hill overlooking the city like a large mother hen watching over her chicks, and employed 6,000 men. The city was just booming so there were few rentals available. But Liz finally landed a large single room with a kitchenette at Park apartments which was barely big enough for her and the two younger girls, let alone an older Jimmy and a pregnant Stacy.

When Liz moved to Trail she had two addictions, alcohol and what she called her Carousel which meant, basically, an addiction to men. She had tried to slow down her drinking when she first moved out West in 1980, but had failed miserably. So, on arrival in Trail, Jimmy opted to move to Edmonton where Liz's close friends, Carol and Darlene had moved. They had left Ontario in 1976. Jimmy knew he could stay with Carol because she was like an aunt to him. He hoped to find work for himself there. Liz's social worker sent Stacy to an unwed mother's home in Kamloops to help out the situation.

After Stacy had the baby and was bound and determined to give him up for adoption because of Liz's drinking, Liz convinced her to keep him with promises of going to A.A., helping her with the baby, and moving to a larger place which they eventually found on

Columbia Avenue in East Trail. These events led up to her eventual visits with Dr. Durham.

Liz was faithful in keeping her promise to attend A.A. And not only that, she was seeing Dr. Durham on a regular basis to try to work out her problems. But after a Monday night A.A. step meeting when Liz was about a month sober, she was wracked with sobs. Everyone else was gone except Liz and two nurses, also A.A. members, who were trying to console her.

"It's no use, I can't stay sober," Liz blubbered.

"Why? You've been doing great. You've got your first month in," Erica stated with her very matter of fact attitude. She was a good looking woman, a few years older than Liz, with dark hair and eyes. She reminded Liz of her sister, Joy. But Liz was very wary of her because like some nurses she had a very brusque way about her.

Susan, on the other hand, was beautiful on the inside as well as the outside. She was one of those nurses who was full of compassion and she listened intently, saying nothing, as Liz went on and on in grief. And Erica argued back.

"You know how we have to make amends and forgive people, and all that stuff from the twelve steps, before we can get better. Well I just can't do that. I've got something in my past that you guys could never begin to understand. I mean you guys are nurses, professional people from good families." Liz cried, exasperated.

The two women laughed. "Maybe we're professional people now, but we weren't always. We were drunks with sordid backgrounds just like yours," Susan exclaimed. "I had to go to school for years after I sobered up to get where I am today. You wouldn't be talking about incest, would you?" Susan said with a very kind tone to her voice.

Liz's face went scarlet. *How did she know? Did it show on the outside?* Liz hung her head, not able to look them in the face. Lenny's voice echoed again, *I've done the worst thing you could possibly think of.* Intellectually, Liz was aware of what he had done to her daughter, but she had woven a thick shroud around her heart so as never to feel, or fully acknowledge the act because she didn't feel she could and stay sane. But she had to tell someone or die drunk so slowly, with her head still hung down, she started to nod.

"I knew it! Sons of bitches! Men! I hate every last one of them!" Susan cried. She put her forefinger under Liz's chin and lifted her head and smiled warmly at her. Liz looked at her beauty, her short dark well-groomed hair, her chocolate eyes, and her wide sensual but warm smile and knew instantly she had found a soul mate.

"When I was a little girl, my father raped my sisters and I repeatedly. Then when I grew up, a frightened, uneducated, naive girl, didn't I end up marrying an asshole, excuse my French, who molested my girls. So I know exactly what you're talking about. I'm not with him anymore by the way, and I'm doing just fine on my own. So you can make it too, trust me." Susan looked into Liz's big fawn eyes, her chocolate ones melting and Liz knew she had found a sponsor. Susan hugged her and Liz clung to her like a life-line.

"Will you be my sponsor?" Liz asked shyly. "I mean you'll understand me better than anyone." Liz said, excitement in her voice. Finally, help she could trust. Someone in her own boat. She had known she should get a sponsor, but hadn't been able to decide on one. Susan would be perfect.

"Of course. I'd be happy to be to be your sponsor. But you have to listen to me, if you want to get well. Agreed? I don't want you to fight me every step of the way. I have enough on my plate."

"Agreed!"

"Okay the first thing I want you to do is volunteer to help at the Bingo. It helps pay the rent on our clubhouse. Everybody who is serious about staying sober takes a turn at it. It's humbling and helps to get your mind off your own troubles. Besides you'll feel good doing something positive."

"You gotta be kidding! I hate Bingo! I can't do that! The last time I played Bingo I was three sheets to the wind. I kept laughing so hard because I couldn't keep up with all the cards I was playing. Everyone was shushing me. Then the two women sitting on either side of me started yelling at me because I was playing half their cards as well as my own. I caused such a ruckus, they kicked me right out."

"You agreed." Susan smiled.

"Well I'm not going to like it much, but I did agree. So when do I start." Liz was willing to stand on her head in a corner and spit nickels if they asked her to just so she could stay sober and keep her family together. It had been a rough haul after Lenny had threatened to shoot her and then had turned the gun on himself.

"Next Tuesday. See Gene and he will help you to get started."

"Come on I'll give you a ride home. It's late," Susan said as she looked at her gold watch which read midnight.

Liz hugged Susan and Erica and they all headed for the door.

The next day Liz was bathing her new little grandson, Jason, now four months old. She loved him so much. He was the whole reason she had decided to get sober. To her there was something really special about babies. She'd never drunk alcohol during her pregnancies or after she'd had her babies. She'd given them the best of care, even though her first husband, Brian, had deserted her and their three babies, a two year old, a one year old and a new born in 1966. And she was just twenty-one years old at the time, to boot.

Her life had been a terrible struggle ever since, and now, because of Jason coming into their life, that all had to change or she'd die trying. Hmmph, she'd even work at the stupid Bingo. She laughed to herself, picked a dripping Jason out of the baby bath on the black and white kitchen chrome table and set him on a fluffy white towel.

She looked down at him and he giggled back at her. She dried the tufts of honey blonde hair on top of his head and looked into his sea blue eyes and started to croon.

"They call him drunken Ira Hayes, he don't answer anymore. Not the whiskey drinkin' Indian who went off to war." Liz felt like drunken Ira Hayes and she'd certainly been through what seemed like a war. But she was going to answer plenty. Starting with that stupid Bingo!

And a stupid Bingo it turned out to be. Gene, a good looking, brown haired young A.A. member, who had chosen to take Liz under his wing, started her out the next Tuesday night by getting her to dump the ashtrays into a large empty coffee can. Liz looked out into the hall from the back kitchen doorway. The room was full of people, mostly old ladies and gentlemen. Ladies and gentlemen was hardly the right terminology, she soon found out. Gene grinned and his green eyes lit up with mischief as he watched her move reluctantly into the room.

Liz moved cautiously. Her nerves were shattered and without any alcohol in her system her shyness wrapped itself around her encasing her in a solitary cocoon. She smiled nervously as she emptied a few ashtrays. No one paid any attention to her. They were too busy watching their numbers as Johnny bellowed out, "U-u-u-n-d-e-r the B 5". She looked up at Johnny. He was so handsome in his black felt cowboy hat and his black leather vest, but she was afraid of him. He was as tough as old shoe leather and whenever he hugged her he would almost crush her rib cage, but she couldn't help but feel a sort of animal attraction toward him. It seemed that since she had quit drinking the tugging of the Carousel had become much worse.

Thinking all these things she began to relax and reached out absentmindedly to pick up a large wad of chewing gum and the wrapper that it sat on, from in front of a very large middle-aged woman with absolutely no make up on and hair all askew. Just as Liz touched the paper wrapper, the woman grabbed her arm in a death grip and Liz jumped spilling the can's contents all over the floor.

"Don't touch that!" the woman growled. "That's my lucky gum! I never throw it out. I won three weeks ago when I was chewing that gum. Never, never, never throw it out!"

The woman had grabbed and let go of Liz's arm without ever having moved her eyes from her cards. Liz pulled her arm back and bent over to clean up the butts that had spilled onto the floor and quickly retreated to the kitchen where Gene was bent over with laughter.

He looked enough like John Lennon to be his brother and Liz had grown quite fond of him, but at this precise moment she would have liked to wring his neck. Gene so enjoyed the antics of the strung-out newcomers at their first encounter with Bingo duty. He had a good heart and would bend over backwards to help a new alkie out, but he had this little bit of a sinister attitude that Liz wasn't quite sure about.

He gave her a gentle shove and told her to get back out on the floor which she did with her tongue in her cheek. She continued to work until two women hollered out Bingo at the exact same time. She ran immediately for the kitchen.

"Now what do I do?" she chanted at Gene.

"Well, you better go check their cards and see which one is the actual winner."

"Not on your life." Liz wailed. "Those people are crazy. They'll rip me apart."

Gene laughed uproariously as he swaggered into the room to take over for her.

When the night was over Liz felt elated. Susan was right. It had taken a pound of flesh with her frazzled nerves, but she did feel like she had accomplished something and she had a newly acquired sense of belonging in the club. Just as she was basking in these new feelings Johnny headed her way with arms outstretched. "Oh, no, I'm outa here." she yelled as she flew out the back door and started to head for home.

Gene stuck his head out the door and yelled after her, "Hey don't forget there's a hospital meeting Friday night. I'll pick you up at seven o'clock. The best way to stay sober is to help other people get sober. There's a lot of sick alkies at the Daly Pavilion so we need as many A.A. members to attend that meeting as we can get. Those guys really need our help."

"Okay." Liz hollered back, eager to help with new ones whenever she could. As a matter of fact A.A. had become her way of life. She was at the club twenty-four/seven. She had to be to stay sober, and it hurt her no end when the kids would say, "Why don't you start drinking again Mom, at least we saw you once in a while back then." She was told by other A.A. members that her sobriety had to come first, before husbands, kids, friends, whatever, because without it she would have nothing including all of the above.

****

Friday night Gene picked Liz up at precisely seven o'clock. She was dressed in a new chocolate brown turtle neck sweater which made her feel classy for the first time in a long time. She was beginning to feel better already, amazing what a new piece of clothing could do for a girl.

Gene smiled approvingly when she climbed into his blue half-ton. Then they drove up hospital hill. After Gene parked the truck in the parking lot, they walked through the front doors of the Trail Memorial Hospital past the reception desk, then around the corner and down the hall to the Board Room. Liz was impressed. There was a huge walnut oval table in the center of the large, beige-painted room with black leather swivel chairs all around it. She sunk into one of the comfortable chairs and stretched her legs out in front of her, "So this is how the other half lives, eh?"

Gene grinned and said, "Yup, pretty neat for a couple of old alkies, eh?"

Liz smiled warmly at him as a tall, red-headed, very attractive woman sauntered into the room.

"Hi, I'm Val," she said smiling widely. She chattered incessantly like a spin head as she was only a few weeks sober herself, but Liz instantly liked her. She was Liz's age, thirty-six, and she was dressed to the nines and carried herself extremely well. She also had a delightful sense of humor. Not only that, Liz felt an instant companionship with her because of their mutual length of sobriety. And Liz could tell by the way she talked that Val had a Carousel of her own to contend with even though she was married.

A few more nicely dressed A.A. members arrived and then the patients from the Daly began to come into the room looking rather shaky. The meeting started with Gene chairing and after everyone had a turn to speak it ended with the usual Serenity Prayer.

Then just as they were finishing a woman came through the door. Liz could smell the alcohol right away. The woman staggered slightly as she crossed the room. Her clothing was all askew. The elastic in her pink fleecy jogging pants was twisted around so the front seam was across her stomach diagonally and her blouse was buttoned up wrong, as though she had dressed in a hurry. Her hair was all tangled. She presented quite a haggard picture even though she didn't appear to be any older than Liz.

Immediately Liz's heart went out to her. It hadn't been that long ago that she had looked and felt the same. Liz walked across the room to speak to the new comer, eager to help in any way she could. The woman began to weep and threw her arms around Liz. "I need help," she muttered in Liz's ear and just wailed on Liz's shoulder, Liz clutched her tightly, feeling her pain. Then the woman started to raise her head and out of the corner of Liz's eye she caught sight of a long string of mucous protruding from the woman's nose and stuck to the shoulder of her new brown sweater. Her stomach turned and she glanced over at Gene. His eyes were just twinkling as she shot him a *please help me* look. Then the woman began to wretch and proceeded to upchuck all over the front of Liz's class-act sweater. She jumped back and shrieked and Gene couldn't help but chuckle. Val rushed to Liz's rescue with wads of paper toweling and rushed her to the washroom down the hall.

"Thanks, Val. It was nice of you to help me," Liz muttered, upset about her new sweater.

"You're welcome. Anytime. Us alkies gotta stick together. Hey, give me your phone number and I'll call you tomorrow night. Jake's night shift and I feel so lonely in the house by myself. I got teenage kids at home, but they're always out on a Saturday night. Fridays are okay because we have the hospital meeting to keep me busy, but I find Saturdays really hard. Friday and Saturday were always party nights for me."

"Yeah, me too. They're the hardest nights to get through. I got a pen and an old envelope in my purse. I'll write my number down for you," Liz said as they returned to the Board Room.

Later in the truck, Gene teased Liz unmercifully. "Well *you* told me in order to stay sober, we had to help others get sober," she muttered, disgustedly. Gene laughed. "It's not funny!" Liz cried.

"Yeah? You shoulda seen your face." He broke out in fits of laughter again, and he reached over and patted the back of her hand. She took a swing at him and he ducked, still laughing.

When he pulled up in front of her house, he said, "I'll give you a bit of good advice, *Never* work with a drunk, wait until they sober up."

"I'll definitely keep that in mind," she said as she climbed out of the truck.

Liz had learned a valuable lesson. She was to learn a lot of lessons in her sobering years. As she had been told by Dr. Durham, there is no emotional growth when a person is using drugs or abusing alcohol, and there would prove to be a lot of painful growing up for Liz in the future.

Chapter 3
A True Kindred Spirit

Jason was in bed sleeping, and the girls had all gone to the show. Liz was feeling a little melancholy when the phone started to jangle. While reaching to grab it, she glanced up at the clock. It was 7 o'clock.

"Hello," she said, wondering who might be on the other end. She hoped it was Val and she was right.

"Hi, how's it goin'?" Val asked.

"Okay, I guess. Are you finding it hard to stay sober?" Liz queried.

"You bet I am. But there's one thing that helps to keep me sober. Last time I was drinking I got so drunk that I almost killed myself."

"God, how did that happen?"

"I was home alone. Jake was night shift, and I started drinking early in the evening. I took a bath, with a bottle of wine in the tub with me then got out and got into my nightgown, one of those nice lacy nylon ones. A girl's gotta look good all the time. You never know who might show up," she giggled, like a silly school girl and Liz laughed on the other end knowing exactly what she was getting at. "Anyway I took a couple of Valium just to ensure a good night's sleep. I always feel a little antsy when Jake's night shift. But I guess I didn't realize how much I'd drunk because it sure hit me. I was lying in my bed and the room was just swimming. Then I started to hear voices, like someone was calling to me outside. Our bedroom is upstairs and there are patio doors that lead out on to a deck. Anyway I got up opened the patio doors and it seemed like a woman's voice was calling me and beckoning me to come to her just beyond the deck. I was so mesmerized that I started to climb up on the railing. It's a long drop off that balcony and luckily a horn honking in the neighbourhood jarred my mind and brought me back to my senses.

But it sure scared the crap out of me. The very next day I went directly to the A.A. club."

"Well, I quit because of my grandson. I got drunk and slept right through his two in the morning feeding while my daughter was working night shift. She came in at four and had a hell of a time waking me up. Jason had been crying the whole time. If there had ever been a fire or anything I would have killed him. Then I would have just wanted to die myself." Liz lamented.

"Wow, it's a good job you sobered up too. Did you feel weird going to A.A?"

"Yeah, I sure did. Who ever would have thought when I was young I'd end up in A.A. I mean there's such a stigma to it."

"You got that right. Anyway I'd rather be in A.A. than dead. Besides there's lots of cute guys there," Val crooned.

"And *you've* got that right," Liz blurted out. *I was right she is fighting her own Carousel, I knew it!* Liz thought to herself.

"I know I'm married, and I sure wouldn't want to hurt Jake, but I got this thing about men. I've had it all my life it seems. You see, I was molested when I was a kid and they say women either become promiscuous or frigid after being sexually molested. Well you can guess what happened to me. Ever since I married Jake I've been fighting it, but it gets harder all the time especially when he's still drinking and flirting and stuff."

"I knew you had a man thing going on. I could just sense it. I got the same problem, but I don't think I was ever molested when I was a kid. At least not that I can remember. I know my papa would never have done that." Liz said.

"Neither would my father. It wasn't him. I never ever told anybody and it still bothers me to this day. Yuk, it makes me feel sick every time I talk about it. Let's change the subject."

"Okay. Hey what do you think of that Johnny?"

"He's good lookin' alright, but you know what they say."

"Yeah." Liz answered and both girls quoted at the same time. *Don't get involved for at least a year after you sober up.* Then they laughed uproariously.

Then Val said, "Well did anybody ever figure out who *they* are, anyway? I'll tell you one thing, though for sure, stay away from Billy.

I know, I know, he's as handsome as they come and what a charmer, but he's married and he sleeps with *everybody.*

"You don't have to worry about that. I know who you're talking about and my sponsor warned me about him too. He is good looking alright, but I got this thing I would *never* date a married man."

"And you sure wouldn't want to get pregnant or something at this stage of the game." Val uttered.

"Oh, I can't get pregnant. Lenny and I tried for years and I went to the doctor to get checked out and he said my womb was tilted and I wouldn't be able to have any more kids. It must be true because it's been thirteen years since I had Janie and I never used any birth control since then."

"Well be careful, anyway. You sure don't need that right now."

"That's for sure. That reminds me. I gotta' go for a colposcopy tomorrow."

"What the heck's that?"

"My pap test came back weird and so I have to have a biopsy done. I hate that kinda' stuff."

"Yeah, me too." Val said.

Liz and Val talked on and on like two kindred spirits right up until the girls came home from the movie at 10 o'clock and then Liz said she'd better go because they had been on the phone for three hours, but they still carried on until midnight when Val said, "Well we really better go this time for sure. It's been five hours. I think I'm going to have to get the phone amputated from my ear. I've always been a real phone bandit. Hey, how about if I take you to the hospital tomorrow for your test and we can go out to Castlegar for coffee. The A.A. guys out there always go to the Marlane for coffee after work and there's tons of cute guys. I can't do anything of course, but it sure doesn't hurt to enjoy the scenery. Then we can have supper out, my treat, and don't argue, then come back to Trail and go to the meeting together. Make a day of it. Jake'll be sleeping all day and then night shift again."

"Hey that would be terrific," Liz crooned, ecstatic over the beginning of their relationship and the chance to meet some cute guys. She was purring like a sassy young teenager and emotionally that was exactly what she was.

The next day Val showed up right on schedule and she was a virtual Greek bearing gifts (with absolutely no malice intended). She had an array of lipsticks and eyeshadows, bottles of different kinds of perfumes, several sweaters and a wide 14 karat gold ring with a heart carved out in the front of it. A tiny diamond graced the center of it at the top of the heart where it dipped.

Liz stared down at the tiny diamond and her eyes misted over as her mind raced back to the "Everett years" when Lenny had held her captive in that frightening shell of a farm house.

Val's voice broke through shattering her nerves, "What's the matter? You look terrible. I didn't mean to make you cry."

"Oh, it's not your fault. Just haunting memories."

"Tell me. It helps to get it out. My counsellor says venting is the best way to rid yourself of those old ghosts of the past."

Liz got a dreamy look on her face as she started to speak, "I had a real nice set of diamond rings once. Brian, my first husband, bought them for me when we were courting. Trying to impress me, I guess. Anyway they were beautiful. When Lenny and I were in the throes of our drinking, we got just polluted this one weekend and drank up all our money. There was no food for the kids and Lenny convinced me I would have to pawn the rings. Emotionally, they didn't mean that much to me any more, and after all it was imperative to get food for the kids. We hitchhiked together to town and got dropped off in front of the jewellery store in Alliston. Lenny made me go in by myself. I was so sick, and so full of shame and fear, prickly fear. Well, that jeweller really saw me coming, I'll tell you. No! He didn't see me coming, he *called me in*. "Eight dollars for the pair," he stated firmly.

You gotta be kidding! I thought, but didn't say anything. I was too ashamed and besides he was a rich jeweller. I was nothing but a lowly drunk. Who was I to argue? I was caught between a rock and a hard place. I glanced out the window at Lenny shaking and pacing back and forth in front of the store. I wished he'd had the balls to come in with me. Lenny was a big brave man when he was beating me up, but a coward when it came to dealing with life.

He spied me and mouthed the words 'Hurry up! I'm dyin' out here.' I gulped, nodded my head and hung it in more shame as the jeweller put the eight dollars into my sweating palm.

Lenny and I went to the grocery store and bought two loaves of bread, a large jar of peanut butter and some milk to last him and I and four kids for a week."

Liz choked up, she couldn't talk about it any more for fear she'd break out in sobs.

"Quick tell me a joke," she chanted at Val as she tried to get a grip.

Val laughed and Liz joined her as a lone tear slowly wended it's way down her cheek.

"Come on, freshen up we gotta go." Val cried, "The guys are waiting."

Liz went to the bathroom to freshen her make up, and when she came out a big grin broke out on her face as Val sprayed her with Tea Rose perfume. "There now you're all set to meet the doctor *and* the guys."

****

That was yukky!" Liz whispered to Val as she came out through the big doors of the examining room.

"Oh, well, at least it's over. Now let's go and have some fun." Val said as she slipped her arm through Liz's and pulled her along.

And indeed they did. They went to the Marlane Hotel coffee shop where there were several good looking men and Val flirted outrageously while Liz, being a little nervous, observed with delight. Then they dined at East Gate Gardens on scrumptious Chinese food, after which they headed back to Trail to attend an A.A. meeting.

Johnny was there to greet them at the door and reached for Liz and gave her a big, bone-crunching hug. "Hey, when are you going to go out with me?" he asked. Liz squirmed out from under his arms, batted her eyelashes at him and said, "Maybe never."

Billy lurked in the background, confidence seeping out of his every pore as he winked at Liz. She blushed and hung her head, then looked up to see Karl coming in the door. Karl was as good looking as all the rest, but was happily married with two young daughters.

"Would you look at you two! You're gorgeous. Sobriety has done you both a world of good. There's something about you alkie women that drives a man insane. It's no wonder our wives don't like us hanging around the club too much," Karl joked.

Alkie women! Liz thought. It was the same with the men. They were mostly good looking and very charming, once they sobered up, that is.

Liz was basking in all the male attention and her Carousel spun with delight. Ever since her father had rejected her at the age of five, she had sought out male attention and all it ever did was get her into trouble. Now she could enjoy it and hopefully stay out of trouble at the same time.

"Hey, who's your friend?" asked a man Liz hadn't seen before. He reminded her of Elmer Fudd, but he had a kindly look about him.

"Oh, hey, Vern, this is Liz, Liz, Vern," Val replied.

Liz would grow to become very fond of Vern, but their friendship would prove to present Liz with some big problems.

Weeks went by and Liz attached herself to Val and vice versa as though they were made for each other. They went on tons of twelve step calls together. Twelve step calls being visits to sick people who had called the club for help with their drinking. Liz and Val had been eager to have their names put on the list of ones who were willing to go on these rescuing calls. Members were instructed never to go alone though, always in twos. So Liz and Val became partners in their new venture. All went well until one Thursday morning when they were hanging around the club and a call came in to go to a woman in Fruitvale.

They drove out to Fruitvale with instructions to follow a long lane back into the woods where an isolated fairly new house stood amongst beautiful white birch trees. The sun shone down through the branches illuminating the soft green leaves and the beauty warmed Liz's heart.

She hadn't noticed such magnificence in nature in years. All the years she was drinking so heavily it was as though she had died to everything around her. Now she was beginning to come alive again and was really enjoying it. Then Val startled her back to reality.

"Well are you ready?" she asked as she pulled up in front of the house and parked.

"As ready as I'll ever be," Liz answered, nervously. She loved doing this work, but they never knew what they were going to get into.

They knocked on the door and a woman peered out from the tiny space where she had pulled the yellow gingham curtains aside. Her eyes looked wild and her hair was all askew, but she opened the door and welcomed the girls in. She introduced herself as Faye, then directed them to a beautiful oak dining set and asked them to sit down.

"You're just in time. I have a big pot of soup on. You'll stay for lunch," she insisted.

Then as she got bowls out of the cupboard and began to fill them with soup she started to talk about her life. At first she made sense and then she started to drift and talk a little crazy. Liz and Val looked at each other and raised their eyebrows as she set the soup down in front of them.

"Aren't you going to have any?" Val asked, nervously.

"No, I'm not hungry. You girls go ahead. It's good soup. I made it myself."

She continued to talk, "You know, I get so confused sometimes. I love to sew. I love cutting out the fresh new material especially with new *sharp* scissors. They're always so shiny." The woman's eyes started to glaze over. "Like when I was cutting out the material for my new drapes. The scissors just glided through the material as though they were cutting butter. It's funny, you know, sometimes I can't tell the difference between cutting up my curtains or cutting up my family."

Liz and Val looked at each other, looked at the soup that they had started to eat, and Val squeaked out, "You know what? I don't feel too hungry myself." She put down her spoon. And Liz immediately followed suit.

Val slowly rose from her chair, reaching in her purse for some pamplets. She dropped them on the table, and she and Liz made for the door, slowly backing away. Their eyes never left the woman as they safely passed through the opening and quickly retreated to the car.

"Oh, I don't feel so good," moaned Val as they pulled out of the yard.

Liz laughed and said, "You've just got an overactive imagination."

"I thought I'd die when she said what she said about cutting up her family," Val said. "I was scared to eat that soup."

"Yeah, me too, but I'm sure we'll be alright," Liz cracked up with laughter and Val joined her as they drove merrily on their way back to the club.

Liz's new sober life with Val was fraught with all kinds of adventures as the months passed by quickly. But Liz had one big worry on her mind. Her colposcopy test had come back pre-cancerous. Liz had gone for a D & C, but the follow-up colposcopy test had proved to be pre-cancerous as well, and the surgeon, Dr. Trent had sent her to, had advised her that if she wanted to have any more children she better plan for it soon because she would have to have a hysterectomy. She told the surgeon she certainly didn't wish to have any more children, and he said they would perform one more colposcopy before he went ahead with the hysterectomy.

She was beside herself with worry because she was only three months sober and she felt she just couldn't deal with major surgery at this precarious point in her life.

****

"Hi, Val, can I ask you a big favor? I have to go for my last colposcopy tomorrow. Can you give me a ride. I don't feel like walking up the hospital hill. I'm just sick about this. I don't think I can go through major surgery right now. My nerves just started to settle down and now I'm a wreck again," Liz cried as she talked to Val on the phone.

"Sure I can take you, no problem. But you know what, you should pray to your higher power about it," Val answered.

Liz hadn't prayed in years. All the heartache that she had been through and then her spiral down into the depths of alcoholism had left her pretty much a skeptic, but she took Val's advice and said a prayer that night before she went to sleep.

The next day Liz walked into the examining room and climbed up onto the table garbed in a skimpy hospital gown. She winced as she put her feet in the stirrups. Like all women, she loathed the position she was forced to be in. The doctor began his examination with his bright light and all of a sudden he popped his head up between Liz's legs and cried, "There's nothing there! It's gone!"

Liz had no idea what he was talking about, but she was sure it was good news by the look on his face. Her prayer had been answered. She couldn't believe it. She thought there had to be some explanation.

So a few weeks later in Dr. Trent's office Liz asked her to explain.

"I guess the D & C must have cleared it up," answered Dr. Trent.

"No!" said Liz, "The colposcopy after the D & C showed pre-cancerous still.

Dr. Trent flipped through the records in Liz's file and said, "Yes, you're right. Hmmm, well just don't ask any questions," she put her arm around Liz and hugged her close as she walked with her to the door. "I am so proud of what you're accomplishing. Keep up the good work."

Liz was elated. She had experienced her first miracle. But how long would her good fortune last?

Chapter 4
Lotus

Liz lazily stirred the pot of Chili while she thought about how good her sober life was with her friend, Val, with all the girls at home and with baby Jason who was sleeping soundly in his crib in their cozy little Columbia Avenue home. She dreamed on, content with herself. *There's only one thing missing.* She thought. *Jimmy.*

Then her mind was brought back to the present as she heard the squeaking of the front door opening. "Who's that?" she yelled from the back kitchen. The girls didn't answer so she started to yell again, "Who's..." and then she threw the spoon as the dark haired figure came through the kitchen doorway. She rushed toward him and squealed with delight, "Jimmeeey!"

He grinned and grabbed Liz around the waist and hugged her. Now eighteen, he was the image of the handsome Irish rover, Brian O'Shea, she had once been married to. She couldn't help but swell with pride. "What brings you here? I mean, I'm so glad to see you. You're staying, I hope. This place is bigger than the Park apartment. Not much mind you, but we can always make room for one more."

The words were no sooner out of her mouth than a little head with long gleaming, coal black hair peeked out from behind Jimmy. A shy smile warmed her face as her slanted eyes lit up.

"Mom, this is Lotus," Jimmy said, proudly. "I met her at a hostel in Edmonton. She's all the way from Hong Kong."

Liz noticed right away that she was a few years older than Jimmy and when their eyes met Liz detected a street-wise look that made her seem a lot older in spite of her warm smile. Liz felt a little squeamish because of the hardness that lurked behind that innocent smile, but nonetheless she stretched out her arms in welcome. If this was Jimmy's choice, then she would accept her. The girl cautiously moved into the circle of Liz's arms and Liz gave her a warm squeeze.

"We can't stay very long, just a couple of days, but I just had to come home and see Jason and everyone. We have to get back though and look for work as soon as we can because we've used up all our funds to come down here."

"How did you get here?" Liz asked, scared of the answer.

"We hitchhiked. Got a ride most of the way with a trucker headed to Cranbrook. Then just a few rides from there and here we are." He stretched out his arms as he spoke.

"Well we'll just have to set two more places at the table. Bonnie can you do that for me?"

"Sure, ma," Bonnie yelled from the living room.

When the chili was finished, they all sat down to dinner, and Liz's face shone with joy as she surveyed the table. Blonde haired, green eyed, Stacy and copper haired, blue eyed Bonnie had turned into real beauties. They wore their long hair in the same style as Farrah Fawcett and Liz didn't feel there were models any more beautiful. And she could tell that Janie would be a beauty too in a few years with her dark eyes and chestnut hair. And of course, Jimmy was just as handsome as the girls were beautiful. The one good thing that her ex-husbands had given her was that their good looks had been passed on to her children. And Jason, now five months old, looked so angelic with his honey blonde curls and big blue eyes. She was elated to be sober and have her whole family around the table.

"So how is it that you come to be in Canada, Lotus?" Liz inquired, trying to make her feel welcome.

In very broken English Lotus answered, "I come on horiday, but," she said with a gulp, "my visiting visa run out."

Liz had no idea what that could mean, but she was to find out, to her dismay, in the future.

"So tell us a little bit about yourself," Liz continued.

"My famiry own a store in Hong Kong. Lots of gambling go on in store. The Chinese do lot of gambling." Lotus was beginning to feel a little more at ease and she flashed a wide grin as she spoke.

Her English was so hard to understand that, without realizing it, Liz started to talk to Lotus louder and louder until Jimmy finally interrupted, "Mom, she's Chinese. She's not deaf!"

Everyone started to laugh and Liz joined in their mirth. She thought her heart would burst with pleasure at having her family all around.

"Hey, I've got two questions for you," Bonnie announced. Do you have Chinese dogs in Hong Kong?" Everyone just roared.

"We got same kinda dogs you do," Lotus answered, giggling. "What's other question?"

"When you dream, do you dream in English or Chinese?"

"Chinese, o' course," Lotus said, giggling again.

And so went the evening, and Liz was thrilled. Over the next few days they toured Trail on foot to show Lotus and Jimmy around.

"It like living in bottom of well," Lotus commented.

"Oh, no," Liz answered. "I love it. I feel so protected with the mountains all around. We'd never have a tornado here like they do in Edmonton." She twirled around and the scenery unfolded around her. It was fall and the leaves on the trees on the surrounding mountainsides were mostly golden yellow with some crimson. In the distance she could see Red Mountain, already with a sprinkling of snow on its peak. The skiers would be getting excited. Liz had heard that skiers came from all over the world to ski at Red and she'd even heard that Robert Redford skied there. She wasn't exactly sure how true that was, but it was all very exciting living in the Kootenays, and she wasn't about to let Lotus poison her mind by calling it the bottom of a well.

Then came the big let down. Jimmy and Lotus had to leave. Liz so longed to have her whole family together. Jimmy was still so young and she would have liked to help him better himself with a good career. But she could tell he was smitten and would follow wherever Lotus wanted to go and right now she was eager to get out of *the well* and get back to the big city. So it was with great sadness that Liz said her goodbyes.

After they left, Liz was alone. Bonnie and Janie were at school, Stacy was at work at Boston Pizza, and Jason was sleeping. Melancholy wrapped itself around Liz like a cloak as a big crystal tear slipped down her cheek. What was going to happen to her children. The worst was over now, but because of her drinking and drugging she had hardly taught them any living skills. Bonnie was dating Darren, who had kindly driven them to Kamloops when Stacy had given birth to Jason at the unwed mother's home. He seemed nice enough, but she was awfully young. Liz would have liked her to pursue a career.

Then she thought back to Edmund, the love of her life who had died when they were both eighteen. She had been fourteen when she met him, and snuck out to see him. That is until her mother had beaten her to within an inch of her life and forbidden her to ever see him again. She had hardly thought about him in years because of all the sadness that had surrounded her. Now she thought about the way he had made the Carousel whir with delight and she cried all the more. Just then the phone started to ring off the wall bringing her to her senses.

"Hi there, good lookin'," Johnny crooned.

"Hi," Liz answered. Normally she would have blown him off, but because of the mood she was in she let him talk. And talk he did, until he convinced her to go to the drive-in with him after the Friday night hospital meeting.

The next day Liz's sponsor, Susan, called her and asked if she would mind serving at a funeral luncheon that was to be held at the club on Friday afternoon. Liz readily agreed, eager to help in any way she could as she was so grateful to be sober. Susan explained that it was the funeral of a Russian man who had died drunk, but his wife, a native woman, had been sober for ten years. Sometimes Liz would have a feeling come over her as though she knew something before it happened. She had never met this woman before, but somehow she sensed something about her and was looking forward to meeting her, even though the circumstances weren't the best. During the conversation Liz didn't mention anything to Susan about Johnny because she knew what she'd say. *No relationships until you're at least a year sober.* Well she was six months sober and flying pretty high so what the heck!

Liz didn't know it at the time, but the funeral luncheon and the date with Johnny were to alter her life in two different ways. One for the good and one not so good.

Chapter 5
"Her Mother's Hat"

It was going to be a full day, but Liz had discovered keeping busy was the best policy for staying sober. Stacy had the day off so she was free for the next twenty-four hours at least. She had walked over town and she had some time to kill before the luncheon so she wandered into the little antique shop that she loved to browse through. Not that she had any extra money to spend, but she loved to look.

The bell tinkled on the door as she entered, and she turned to hold the door for the person entering behind her. As she did her eyes were captured by the painting over the door and she gasped, "It's beautiful!"

The owner of the shop said, "It sure is. It's a Norman Hepple called 'Her Mother's Hat'.

Liz stared at the painting set in the old fashioned oak frame. The girl with the long blonde hair and green eyes reminded her of Stacy. She looked to be about fourteen years old. She was wearing a plain black dress and a black hat with pink and blue roses gracing the brim. Her arm was bent at the elbow with her hand on her hip in a defiant stance, but it was the expression on the face that the painter had captured that held Liz in awe. It was a look of feminine mystique. As she moved around the room the girl's eyes followed her. "I've got to have it!" Liz cried. "How much?"

"A hundred dollars," the owner answered.

Liz's head sunk so her chin rested on her chest. It might as well have been a million. It cast a dark shadow over her day. Had she sobered up to notice such beauty and never be able to have it? Her friend, Val, had gone back to school to be a care aide worker, and at that precise moment Liz decided that was what she would have to do too, if she was ever going to have anything. But it would have to wait until Jason was a little older. After all she had promised Stacy she would help with his rearing and a promise was a promise. She walked out of the shop with shoulders slumped, but with a determination that some day she would own that painting.

She made her way to the club where all the women were busy arranging sandwiches and began to help. The place was buzzing with chatter, and Liz picked up on stories of how the deceased had treated his wife so badly. He had beat her constantly and would not allow her to go to A.A., but she had stayed sober through it all on her own and Liz's heart went out to her. She was even more eager to meet her after hearing the tale.

Shortly after the lunch was all set out the funeral party arrived and eventually Liz was introduced to the grieving widow. She looked crushed and haggard, but Liz could see that beneath the haggard look there was a beauty beyond compare. She held her arms out to the woman not sure if it was the proper thing to do being as she had just met her, but the woman immediately moved into the circle of Liz's arms. As she pulled away after a very warm hug, their eyes met and it was as though Liz could see into her soul and she really liked what she saw.

After cleaning up, Liz left the club with a spring in her step. She was rushing home to have a quick supper and get ready for the hospital meeting. It wasn't the meeting that had her so enamored. It was the thought of a date. She was a little reluctant about Johnny's toughness, but she quickly dismissed it as she dreamed of what it would be like to be held in his arms. It had been a long time since someone had held her. Of course she'd have to tell him not to squeeze so hard.

Gene chaired the hospital meeting as usual, and after, he approached Liz. "What are you all aglow about?" he asked.

"Oh, nuthin'," Liz replied and looked sideways at Johnny with a grin on her face.

"You two aren't up to anything, are you? You know it's not healthy to get into anything until you're a year sober."

"Hey, Gene, lighten up a little will you," Johnny said as he threw an arm around Liz's waist.

"Never mind, Johnny, I know we're buds, but I don't want to see her get hurt."

"Lookit, you're only sober a year yourself and you were in a relationship already when you sobered up."

"That's different. I was married and we already worked out our differences."

"Oh, sure," Johnny said as he walked out of the board room with Liz on his arm.

They arrived at the drive-in and got all settled in with popcorn, Pepsi, and the works. Johnny put an arm around Liz's shoulders and she snuggled into his side. He looked down and she looked up and as their eyes met her heart was stolen away. They slowly drifted closer and the magnetic field between their eyes drew them ever closer until their lips met in a crushing, searing, hot kiss. She could no more have turned away than she could have flown to the moon. The Carousel whirred with ecstasy.

From that day on Liz and Johnny were an item. Susan wasn't very pleased, but she knew it was too powerful for her to tackle so she left it alone, hoping against hope that it would be alright, and if it wasn't, she'd be there, as Liz's sponsor, to pick up the pieces.

Johnny had been living upstairs in the Arlington Hotel since he had sobered up which wasn't a good place for him to be so Liz offered for him to move in with her to help him stay sober, and he quickly agreed before she could change her mind. Liz wasn't about to change her mind because she was head over heels in love and she didn't want him to get away.

Shortly after he moved in she said, "Come with me I want to show you something."

She dragged him down to the antique store to show him *her* picture. It was still there because the price was so high. She knew she would never be able to afford it and Johnny couldn't either, but she wanted to share her dream with him. Johnny worked at odd jobs around town and just made enough to get by on. Liz had secured a job with a cleaning company and she cleaned the City Hall and the CIBC bank in the evenings when the girls were home to watch Jason. Between the two of them and Stacy's earnings they made enough to keep the family going.

Things went along fine in the Columbia Avenue home and Liz was elated. She was beginning to think that the members were wrong about the *one year* thing especially when Christmas came. She had learned from Johnny that he loved eagles and so she had purchased a gold eagle on a gold chain for him to wear around his neck. She presented it to him while they were alone in the bedroom. She was pleased with herself *and* his reaction. Tears flowed down his cheeks. But, nonetheless, her gift was to fade in comparison with what he got for her.

After he dried his eyes, he walked Liz into the living room with her hands over her eyes and then said, "Okay take your hands away." There propped up on the couch was *her* painting 'Her Mother's Hat.'

Immediately tears formed in her eyes and she began to stutter, "B-b-u-t how? You can't afford this. You'll have to take it back."

"No, Liz. I'm sorry it isn't the real picture, but obviously it looks close enough", he said grinning, pleased with himself. Then he continued, " The shop owner sent to England for a print. It was only twenty dollars and I found this old frame. It was painted an ugly green color, but Gene and I sanded it all down in his shop and, voila!" Liz's heart burst with love for Johnny. He had done the impossible. She couldn't be any happier.

After the winter came the spring and Silver City Days. Trail was called the silver city because the smelter processed real silver ingots. Liz had attended Silver City Days the year before when she first arrived in Trail, but this year was going to be so much better with Johnny. At eleven o'clock in the morning would be the huge parade. Liz loved a parade and she wished she could be in the middle of it.

Her favorite part was the kilties with their bag pipes. The hair would stand up on the back of her neck when they went by and this year she knew the drummer, a handsome young man that they jokingly called Dr. Bob at the club. She was so alive with all the sounds - the pipe band, the brass band; the smells - cotton candy and fresh corn on the cob; the sights - a huge, colorful Carousel right in the middle of the midway. Liz's thoughts drifted back to the Carousel her papa had held her on and the warm feeling that she'd had being held in his arms and she leaned closer into Johnny trying to recapture that feeling. She had tried to forget her papa. But now the vision of the Carousel brought the loss of him to the fore again. So after the fair she asked her parents to come and visit now that she was sober. They refused and that hurt.

But then came the summer and with it swimming, camping, and more fun. Gene and his wife invited Johnny and Liz to drop out and visit their campsite at Beaver Creek for a coffee. When they arrived, Liz spotted Billy's car. "What's *he* doing here?" she asked feeling disgruntled. For some reason he always made her feel uncomfortable. He seemed to be able to see right through her.

"Oh, never mind Billy. He's okay as long as you don't let him charm you," Johnny said as he squeezed her close to his side. She looked up and smiled at him and thought, *yeah he's right what do I care anyway. Billy will never get near me. I hate guys like that.* Liz took a pride in the fact that she would never have anything to do with a married man. It was the last strip of moral fibre she had left, and she was bound and determined to hold onto it. She was proud that she had not succumbed to his charm, because, indeed, he could be very charming.

The time passed quickly with Johnny and Liz so much in love and when he finally asked her to marry him she consented, even though everyone seemed to be against it. Everyone that is except Val who Liz had asked to be her Maid of Honor. Val, having never been a Maid of Honor before was thrilled, and she did her utmost to make it an elegant wedding for Liz. She even purchased a beautiful, cream colored full-length, wedding gown for Liz, and paid for Johnny and Liz to spend their wedding night at a quaint little chalet. Val knew they had no money and she wanted it to be a special occasion for the two.

They were married in Val's multi-flowered back yard beside the big pool with the turquoise water sparkling like diamonds in the bright sunshine. Against his better judgment, because of the *one year* thing, Gene had consented to be the best man. Of course, there was a pot luck supper at the club where everyone celebrated, in spite of the fact that they were a little nervous about the union so early in the couple's sobriety. Liz danced the first dance with stars in her eyes and joy in her heart and after the festivities were all over they drove to the chalet in a borrowed car. Her wedding night was spent in ecstasy.

And when they returned home they embarked on their new life together with dreams of forever in their hearts. Liz felt very smug. She was sober and now she had the carousel under control as well.

Then all hell broke loose the next spring when Vern, who Liz fondly thought of as *Elmer Fudd,* came to ask her a big favor. During the first year of her sobriety, she and Vern had become good friends. Her first sober Christmas Vern had showed up on her doorstep with a plastic ice cream pail filled to the brim with nickels, dimes, quarters and pennies to help her with Christmas for the kids. And it had also been his habit to show up on her door step with huge amounts of jelly candies which he knew she loved. (Because there is a lot of sugar in alcohol, when a person sobers up they crave that sugar.) Liz had been advised, as other alkies had, that eating a chocolate bar or a handful of candy would help to calm down the nerves. So Vern had undertaken to keep her supplied. She was grateful for his friendship and willing to do anything to help him out. What she didn't know was that it was going to cost her big time.

What he wanted was to have her accompany him to his son's wedding. His ex-wife was going to be there with her new husband and Vern felt he was going to be humiliated. It wasn't a real date per say, just helping a friend in need and he even offered to buy her a new gown for the occasion. How could she resist.

"He wants you to what?" Johnny exclaimed when she told him. "My girl doesn't go with any other guy, you hear!"

Liz was taken aback. She had never known Johnny to be jealous. Of course nothing like this had ever come up before. She was angry with him for not understanding and she stood her ground. After all Vern had been so good to her. What could be the harm?

On the day of the wedding Liz was getting ready, fussing with her chestnut hair and slipping into the new full-length shocking pink gown Vern had purchased for her. She was excited.

"Zip me up, please," she said to Johnny.

"Please don't do this," he pleaded.

"Come on, Johnny, don't be so asinine. I'll be home right after the dinner. Vern just doesn't want to be alone at his son's wedding with his ex-wife and her new husband there. Have a heart for the poor old guy."

"You're my woman! I don't want you out with any other guy! I don't care how old he is!" Johnny yelled as he slammed the door on his way out.

Liz felt a little disturbed. She knew that anger was not a good thing for someone who hadn't been sober all that long. But still, it was Johnny's problem and he would have to deal with it. Everyone was responsible for their own sobriety, weren't they?

Liz came home right after the dinner was over as she had promised, but Johnny was no where in sight. As a matter of fact he didn't return all that night or the next day.

Liz had to work the Bingo that night so she left right after supper. Stacy was at work and Bonnie and Janie were watching Jason and there was still no sign of Johnny. The Bingo was going full force and Liz, not frightened in the least anymore, was busy in the main hall when Gene called out, "It's the phone for you. It's Bonnie and she sounds pretty upset."

Liz raced for the phone, "What's the matter, what's the matter," she shouted into the receiver.

"Mom, thank God. Johnny was just here and he's really drunk. I locked the door and he tried to break it down. He said he was going to kill you and he's headed for the Club right now. Don't leave the Club and try to walk home. We're alright for now," Bonnie cried into the phone.

"Okay, okay, keep the door locked. I'll think of something. I'm not alone here so I'll be safe. Gene will help." Liz hung up the phone just shaking.

"Oh, my God! Gene!" Liz yelled into the main hall. He came running

"What's up?"

"It's Johnny. He's really drunk and he's coming here to kill me. The kids are home alone. He's already been there and threatened them. I've got to get home right away, but I'm scared to walk. He might find me. You know how tough he is and when he's drunk he'll be out of control." Liz's mind flashed back to the times Lenny had beaten her to a pulp. At least then she was drunk so she didn't always feel it, but now she was stone cold sober and scared to death.

"It's alright, Liz," Gene said as he gathered her into his arms. "*A year*," he quoted as he shook his head.

"Alright! Alright! But what am I going to do now"

"I'll phone the police and get them to send a cruiser for you to go home in." The words were no sooner out of his mouth than Johnny slammed into the kitchen. Liz ran into the main hall.

"Where is she?" Johnny slurred. "I'm gonna kill that bitch!"

"Calm down, Johnny. The police are on their way. So if you know what's good for you you'll get outa here."

"I don't care about no police. I want *her*!"

Liz could hear a struggle in the kitchen as Gene forced a drunken Johnny out through the back door. She felt awful that two friends were fighting because of her and also that Johnny had lost his sobriety because of her insisting on going with Vern. Was she wrong? Should she have stayed home when he asked her? Self-doubt started to creep in and that was dangerous for her. She had worked very hard to build her confidence back up since Lenny and alcohol had torn her to pieces. Lack of confidence could mean a return to drinking

Gene phoned the police right away and they showed up shortly afterward. Gene gave her a disgruntled look as the officer escorted her out of the building.

The police took her home and then went to Boston Pizza to pick up Stacy so she wouldn't come home to an empty house. The police officers were taking the whole family to the city's transition house, a place of safety for abused families. The whereabouts of the house was kept a secret so Liz had no idea where they were going.

Stacy came in the house screaming at Liz, "What the hell's going on. The police coming into my work. Why do we have to leave our home. I'm not going anywhere. Jason and I are staying right here!"

"Trust Stacy to put on a dramatic show," Bonnie muttered.

Stacy settled down eventually and the police convinced her that she couldn't be left alone there with Johnny on the loose. But she was mad!

Liz was in a total turmoil too. She felt that a drink would sure go good right about now, herself. Her nerves were shot. But there was lots worse to come in her future.

"Her Mother's Hat"

Liz & Baby Jason - Silver City Days 1982

Chapter 6
The Gulch

The next day Liz and her little family went back home. They walked from the Gulch, which is what the Italians had called the section of town that ran along Rossland Avenue. Rossland Avenue was like Little Italy. All the homes were painted in pastel pinks, greens and blues. A lot of Italian men had come from Italy just after the second world war to find employment at the smelter. As Liz walked along the street, she reflected on one of those Italians, a man named Giovanni, who had found his way to A. A.

Liz was quite fond of him as well, and she thoroughly enjoyed his stories. He could certainly tell a tale that could keep a person spellbound. He told her about his arrival by train. Before reaching Trail, they had to travel through Castlegar, a Russian community north of Trail. Just at that time the Doukhobors were in the midst of a demonstration at the train station, and all the ladies were in the nude, which was their custom during a demonstration. Giovanni said he thought he'd died and gone to heaven. "What a country," he'd exclaimed.

He had also told her the tale of how he'd gotten appendicitis during the war when he was only eighteen years old. He was serving on the front lines. The hospital in the closest town was bombed and the doctor had to operate on him in an old abandoned building with absolutely no anesthetic in order to save his life.

Liz was totally astounded. She'd had her appendix out when she was twenty-five and the pain afterwards was excruciating. She couldn't possibly imagine going through the surgery without any anesthetic at all. Giovanni certainly won a medal for bravery in her books.

Giovanni had joined A.A. very reluctantly because as he said it was shameful for an Italian not to be able to drink the veeno. So he undertook to write to the A. A. headquarters to find out if there were any other Italians in A.A., and was pleased to find out there was, indeed, one other Italian member in Philadelphia in the United States of America.

Liz reflected on all these stories in order to keep her mind off Johnny. She wondered if he'd be home when they got there.

He was. He was passed out, sprawled across their bed. When he came to, he couldn't apologize enough. Liz was willing to forgive him with the stipulation that he *must* remain sober.

He tried. He really tried, but once the cycle of his sobriety had been broken he found it very difficult and so eventually he succumbed again and again until Liz was nearly crazy. She knew she had to get out, if she was to remain sober herself. She knew that according to statistics ten out of one hundred alcoholics would find their way to A.A., and two out of that ten would make it. Scary odds. She wanted to make it.

In the meantime one good thing happened. She befriended the native woman she met at the funeral luncheon she'd served at. Rose had, joyfully, returned to A.A. right after Peter's death. With him gone, nothing could stop her. She had a lot of friends in A.A. so she was eager to return. Because of the closeness she felt to Liz at the luncheon, the two had automatically gravitated toward one another and it was through Rose that she met Mary, who was married to Fred, also an A.A. member.

Johnny was out performing and Rose was coming to pick Liz up for a much needed meeting. Liz sat at the window watching for her when a huge black, brand new Lincoln continental with tinted windows pulled up out front.

"Whoa, would you look at that boat," Liz called to Stacy. Stacy came and looked out the front window.

Then the horn started honking like crazy. "I think it's for you, Mom," Stacy said.

"Me! I don't think so. I don't know anybody with a rich car like that."

Just then the driver's window started to go down. Rose, with a huge grin on her face, stuck her head out the window and hollered, "Well, are you coming or are you going to sit there gaping all night?"

Liz flew out the door exclaiming excitedly, "Where did you get this?" She had never ever ridden in a car like that before.

"It was Peter's. He always had to have the best. Of course, I never got to drive it before. He would roll over in his grave if he could see me now," she giggled.

"Wow! Would you look at this? Power windows," Liz exclaimed as she climbed in the front seat and sank down into the luxurious leather.

"Yeah, it's fully loaded. Neat, eh? I had a real fight to get it though. Just three weeks before he died Peter changed his Will leaving everything to the kids when they come of age, so I couldn't touch a thing. Everything is frozen in the estate."

"I used to work at the court house in Creston. You can contest the Will. He can't do that. He can't rule from the grave," Liz cried.

"I know, but it could take years and in the meantime I don't know what I'm going to do. The lawyers let me have the use of the car, but I can't run the business and make a living anymore. I've had to turn to welfare and the worst of it is when the estate is finally settled I will have to pay it all back. It might be years and who knows how much debt will have accumulated by then." Rose looked sad and then suddenly she lifted her head and said, "But in the meantime let's have a good time in this big boat." She giggled again.

Off they went to pick up Mary.

Mary was just as excited about the car as Liz had been, and when they pulled up at the meeting everyone came out with amazed faces to inspect the new Lincoln. Rose was very proud.

After the meeting the girls went to Canton's, a little Chinese Restaurant on Bay Avenue which Liz had frequented often in her drinking days. She felt slightly embarrassed in front of Simon and Benny, the owners, because they had seen her stagger in many times before in a drunken stupor. But nonetheless she was proud to be there now, sober.

Liz didn't want to go home right away because her nerves were shot. Johnny was out on the prowl again, and she knew he wouldn't be home until later so the kids would be alright. The previous night he had come home drunk. The kids were all in bed, but Liz was up waiting for him to make sure he wouldn't bother the kids. He never had, but after living with Lenny she was afraid. He came in drunk and put a pot of water on to boil. Liz had no idea what for, but when the pot finally boiled, he came into the living room and flung the boiling water across the room, yelling something about foxholes as though he thought he was in the war and defending himself. Liz was petrified. She ducked just in time. When she related the whole story to Mary and Rose, Mary was aghast. "You've gotta get outa there," she exclaimed abruptly.

"I know, but I don't even know where I can go."

Mary, being the motherly, care giver type took right over. "Listen I know a place for rent up the Gulch. It's got three huge bedrooms. It's fairly modern and really nicely decorated. It would be a lot better for your big family than the little two bedroom bungalow you're living in. Go to welfare and they'll give you the deposit and the first month's rent. They have to under the circumstances."

Liz's heart lifted. The girls had all been crammed in the one bedroom with Jason's crib as well while she and Johnny had the other small bedroom. It would be nice to move to a bigger place. Besides you could cut the tension in the house with a knife between Johnny and the girls. They hated him now. Liz didn't hate him. She understood it was the alcohol that drove him, but she could no longer tolerate it either. She still loved him, but she had to think of the kids. Then her heart sank as she started to think of all the details.

"That's okay, but what about furniture. I can't take everything and leave him with nothing."

"It's yours!" Rose said.

"I know, but I just can't leave him with nothing." Liz had known women who had cleaned their husbands out and left them with absolutely nothing, not even a chair to sit on when they came home from work. Liz wasn't that kind of woman and never could be.

"Well, I've got lots of extra stuff like dishes and pots and pans and blankets I can give you," Mary said.

"Of course the kids will have their own beds, but what will I do?"

"Hey," Rose said, "you can have mine and Peter's bed. It's brand new. I was going to burn it anyway because I just can't sleep in it anymore. Too many bad memories. That is, if you don't mind having it."

"Beggars can't be choosers. I'd be happy to have it," Liz replied with a big smile on her face.

Gene who had come in during the conversation and sat at the next table piped up and said, "And I've got a truck to move you! I got a double mattress that I've been wanting to get rid of too, if you can use it."

"Yeah, and I've got an old chrome kitchen set," Joan, another member, hollered out.

So it was settled. Liz would be moving into 908 Rossland Avenue in the Gulch. She was elated to say the least.

The day they inspected the apartment Liz was even more elated. She couldn't believe how beautiful it was. It was huge. A beautiful pink bathroom. Large bedrooms of pale blue, pale green and beige, and a cream coloured kitchen and living room, and carpeted throughout with plush carpeting. The counter top stove and wall oven would be a nice convenience. Plus the automatic washer and dryer were a real bonus. No more lugging bags to the Laundromat. Liz would be living in luxury.

True to his word, Gene moved Liz and the girls and Jason in lock, stock and barrel while Johnny was at work. At least he had held on to his odd jobs even though he was still drinking. Johnny was furious when he came home and found Liz, the girls and Jason gone. He went on a toot and stayed drunk for days. He started to stalk Liz at her cleaning job. Then when he found out where they'd moved to, he started to stalk her at home until she was nearly a basket case. He would pace back and forth outside the window pounding his fist into his other hand, and if he spied her in the window, he would shake his fist at her with a viscious, threatening scowl on his face. She phoned the police several times on him. He was more than furious. He wanted her back, but Liz held her ground. Then finally Gene talked him into leaving town so life would be easier on him. He opted to move to Williams Lake where he hoped to get back into the A.A. program and get sober again without the pressure of a relationship.

Liz wasn't sure how she felt when she heard he'd left. At first she was ecstatic not to be hassled anymore, but then she started to miss him and the Carousel started to give her trouble as it always had. She felt empty without Johnny, and the Carousel whirring with delight.

She was hollow again. Not only that, after she'd sobered up she was lost. It was as though she didn't know who Liz was. So, in essence, she had looked to Johnny to be her personality. Without him she started to feel like she was nothing, like she couldn't function on her own. Until finally, in the middle of the night she woke up not able to breathe. Her heart was almost beating out of her chest. She had pain down her left arm and a crushing pain in her chest. She was just shaking and right out of control with fear. She managed to dial the phone and got Vern to rush her to the hospital. She was checked out for a heart attack and then sent home with Valium. She'd had her first experience with an anxiety attack and she was *embarrassed*!

The next evening she started to have the same symptoms again plus she had the feeling of the ants crawling all under her skin as well. She had been sober for some time and didn't understand what was happening to her now.

She called Susan, who was just leaving to take her daughters to the aquatic center in Nelson. "Listen, Liz it's just your nerves catching up to you. We do a lot of damage to our nervous systems when we drink like we did. Tell you what, I promised the girls to take them swimming so I can't come over, but why don't you join us?"

"Oh, I don't know. I'm real antsy. I don't think I want to be in public. Not now! Besides I've got no clean towels."

"Come on Liz. It'll do you the world of good. Get your mind off things. I guarantee you'll feel better. I'll bring towels you just grab your suit. I won't take no for an answer and I'll be there in ten minutes."

Susan was absolutely right, Liz thought, as she glided through the water in the large pool. She had never felt so alive. The lights danced off the blue water like diamonds as she floated on her back. She totally relaxed. The water felt like warm silk as it flowed over her body.

Then Susan invited her to join her in the hot tub. As they sat relaxing Liz told Susan about her anxiety attack. Susan laughed. Liz said, "It wasn't funny."

"I know, I'm sorry. It's just that I was remembering my first anxiety attack. It was right here in this hot tub. I was pretty newly sober and I'd brought the girls swimming. I thought I was having a heart attack, just like you, and they called an ambulance and people were swarming around. I was sooo embarrassed." Liz warmed up to her for sharing that story. It made her feel a little more at ease.

"You know, Liz, I've been meaning to talk to you about what you're going to do with your life. Now that Johnny's gone the best thing is for you to keep busy. Have you thought about going back to school?"

"Yeah, actually I have. That's what Val did and she's going to be a geriatric care aide."

"What would you like to do?"

"I don't know for sure. The only thing I've ever thought about is how much I enjoyed the short stint I worked at the Court House in Creston."

"I understand the college is going to put on a Legal Secretary Course this year. What would you think about that?"

"Hey, that would be great. Jason is older now. Bonnie's quit school, which I didn't want, but I was too weak to fight her on it. So she could watch Jason while Stacy works. She's gotta do something."

"Then it's settled. Drop into the college tomorrow for an application. The course starts in September so get in there right away."

There were only four seats available through U I for the Legal Secretarial program, and Liz got one of them. Her college days were about to begin. And begin they did! With a bang!

Chapter 7
School Days, School Daze

It was September, 1982. It had been twenty years since Liz had left school, and now she was going back. The night before school was to start, Liz was getting all ready for the first day when the phone rang and interrupted her.

"Hi, Mom. It's Jimmy."

Liz was elated. She hadn't heard from Jimmy in over a year and she didn't even know how to get in touch with him. But her elation was soon turned to pandemonium.

"Mom, Lotus and I got married. She was pregnant so I married her. We have a little girl. Her name is Jasmine. She's just a few months old. Uh, the problem is I just lost my job and Lotus hasn't been able to work because of the baby. We've been staying with her doctor here in Edmonton, but we can't keep staying here. Can we come to your place?"

Liz was astounded. They'd gotten married. They'd had a baby. She had another grand child. They hadn't even told her! Her feelings were scrambled to say the least. Of course, she wanted Jimmy home and of course, she wanted to see her new granddaughter, but how could they do all that without even telling her? She was upset with them, but she quickly got a grip on herself and stuttering, she said, "Y-y-eah, I g-g-uess so, I mean what else can you do?" After the initial shock wore off, she started to get excited with the aspect of a new little granddaughter, and then she started to really rattle on.

"We've got a much bigger place now. The bedrooms are huge. You can take Bonnie and Janie's room and they can move in with Stacy and Jason. Oh, I forgot. I'm starting school tomorrow too, so you guys are going to have to look after yourselves.

"Oh, we will, mom. We'll be down in about two weeks. I have to wait for my U I to start coming in so we have the money to travel."

"Okay, I'll be looking forward to seeing you," Liz said with her tongue in her cheek.Three more in an already over crowded apartment? And, that was only the beginning...

Liz started school the next day dressed to the nines in new, navy blue high heels that were mostly criss-crossing straps, very sexy, a new powder blue, silk blouse with frills down the front, and new, navy blue knickers that came to her knees to show off her shapely calves.

The first day was hectic. With her initial glimpse of the course schedule, she got a real eye opener. They had to squeeze a one year course into four months because of lack of funding from the government.This short term was going to be excruciating. There were thirteen women, including Liz, taking the course. Some were her age, some were older, and some were younger.

A lot of the women were fun to be with, especially Colleen. She was always cutting up. After their first day of shorthand, she walked out of the class saying, "Hah! Shorthand, I can't read or write it, but I sure can speak it." She pursed her lips and began, "Frd sd i cn drv th rd cr." Everyone just roared, including Liz. She felt so good and clean and everyone accepted her readily. Of course, she didn't tell them she was an alcoholic. She was afraid if she did, they wouldn't like her anymore.

After a few days of classes and scads of homework she began to realize her mind wasn't what it used to be. She had learned in A.A. that alcohol kills brain cells and it takes at least a year to get all the alcohol out of your system. She was learning rapidly that fact was very true. With this liability she would need to fully concentrate and she would need quiet. So she set up a table in her bedroom for studying. She was all set to settle in for the duration.

After a grueling first week of school, she attended a very much needed Friday night meeting, and then went out for coffee after with the gang. She came home late to a very quiet, dark house. She knew Bonnie was out with Darren. She tiptoed into Stacy's room. She and Jason were sound asleep. She pulled a small quilt up over Jason and a proud smile lit up her face. Then she quietly opened Janie's door, and there were sleeping bodies all over the place.

"She must have her new friends staying overnight," Liz whispered to herself as she backed out of the room and quietly shut the door. Liz was so happy Janie had made some new friends in Trail. Liz was very easygoing and didn't mind that Janie, now fourteen, had asked her friends to stay without waiting for permission.

She was sooo tired from her hectic week that she didn't even bother to bath. She would shower in the morning. She threw on her full-length flannel night gown and sauntered to the bathroom. She was basking in the quiet and the solitude. *I've got to stop drinking so much coffee*, she thought. She didn't bother to turn on the light. She just lifted her gown and plunked herself down, and then she let out a shrill scream, and jumped up a lot quicker than she had sat down. She grabbed for the light switch and looked around at the toilet seat. It was covered with puke and there was an empty wine bottle on the floor beside the toilet. "J-a-a-ni-e-e-e!" she screamed. Janie came running while Liz was quickly cleaning herself up.

"You get this cleaned up." Liz yelled. " I'll deal with you in the morning."

"Sorry, mom," Janie wailed. "It wasn't me. Teri was so upset with her parents that she drank a whole bottle of wine. She's having a lot of trouble at home. I guess she musta got sick. I didn't know. Anita and I dragged her into my room and put her to bed."

The next day Liz had a serious talk to Janie and her friends about alcoholism. She explained to them how alcoholism is progressive. At first it's fun, certainly a social lubricant, which alcoholics need because addicts have a personality problem to start with. THEY DON'T LIKE THEMSELVES. When a person is stuck in a room with someone they don't like the first thing they want to do is get away. But when that person is yourself, how do you escape? ALCOHOL!

Liz believed alcoholism was definitely in the genes and passed from generation to generation. When she discovered that fact, it had helped her tremendousley. She didn't feel quite so guilty. An alky, she had discovered would drink to feel better, get into trouble while drinking, sober up, then feel guilty and lousy all over again. Thus the need to drink again until it became an established pattern and an addiction with no way out, at least that was the way it seemed. She had discovered there was, indeed, a way out, learning to like yourself.

But she was also discovering it was very, very difficult sometimes almost impossible. She didn't want these young girls to have to experience that. After her lengthy explanations, which she hoped would help, she undertook the huge task of three days of homework. When the day was done she was exhausted. So she had a nice hot, bubble bath and retired early.

The Gulch apartment was perfect for her family. But there was one drawback. It was right across the street from the Trail Hotel. The hotel was a very active establishment. On Friday and Saturday nights the place was hopping with live bands and young people coming and going all night long. And they weren't very quiet about it either. She tossed and turned trying to shut out the noise, but eventually she went off to the land of nod. Then about four o'clock in the morning she was rudely awakened by a shrill piercing scream. She came full up out of a sound sleep and ran headlong down the hallway where Bonnie stood shaking her hands up and down and screaming frantically.

"What's wrong? What's wrong?" Liz cried.

"Someone's trying to break in," Bonnie squealed.

And then Liz tuned in to the thunderous banging coming from the kitchen. The door was buckling in and out and the door jamb was about to pry loose.

At first Liz was scared and then she got real mad. She'd had enough of being pushed around. She grabbed a baseball bat from the hall closet and ran to the door.

"What the *hell* do you want?" she hollered through the door, temper rising by the second.

"It's Stew! Lemme in!" a croaky voice yelled from the other side of the door.

"You've got the wrong house. Get outa here or I'm going to call the police." Just as Liz said the words, Bonnie reached for the phone. But when the drunk knew someone was on the other side of the door, he resumed his tactics with even more vigor. Liz was poised and ready with the bat.

"The police are coming," she hollered again and that seemed to stop him up for a moment, but then he resumed again. Within minutes, though, the cruiser was there and they hauled *Stew* off to the brink.

Liz was exhausted as she sank down into the living room easy chair, "What's next?" she muttered.

By the next weekend all hell broke loose again. Janie had gone out with her new friends and hadn't returned. By three in the morning Liz called the police and was told that nothing could be done until twenty-four hours had passed and then they could file a missing person's report.

Liz was frantic. It wasn't like Janie to take off like that. Things were good at home. Weren't they? Then the phone started ringing off the wall. Liz grabbed for the phone hoping it was Janie. She was mad, but she would feel a lot better if only she knew Janie was safe. It was Teri and Anita's parents. Janie's friends, Teri and Anita were missing too, and their parents were looking for them, as well.

Liz felt a little better knowing that the girls were probably all together. She spent a sleepless night and the next morning Teri and Anita's parents called.

"The girls are all in Creston. The police called and we told them to lock them up in a cell until we get there. You know, put a little scare into them." Teri's dad stated, sadistically.

Liz was livid. Janie would be petrified. How dare they tell the police to lock her daughter up in a cell. What they did with their own kids was their business, but they had no right where Janie was concerned and Liz told them so.

By the evening Janie was dropped off on Liz's door step.

"Why did you do that?" Liz queried. "I mean I thought you had it good here. There's no hard and fast rules. I trust you. I thought we had a good rapport."

"We do, mom. You're my best friend. I didn't need or want to run away, but Teri and Anita wanted to get away because of things that are going on at home and I just went with them cause their my friends." Liz felt a little better knowing that Janie wasn't having problems at home, but she was still upset for the sleepless night her daughter had inflicted on her.

"Well, I'm certainly glad you're okay, but you sure scared the crap out of me. Don't ever do that again."

"Don't worry, mom, I won't. I sure learned my lesson. It was awful being locked up in that cell."

Liz cringed at the thought, but vengeance was served when a week later she heard that just a few days after the cell incident, Teri's parents had been arrested and locked up on suspicion of trafficking marijuana. Liz never did hear if it was true or not, but she figured justice had certainly been done. What goes around, comes around.

Then another few days later, Liz was sleeping soundly when she was awakened by a scream, at six o'clock in the morning. Once again she came straight up in the air and flew out of her bed and ran headlong down the hallway to find Bonnie doubled over with laughter and Stacy standing holding a freshly warmed glass baby bottle of milk and rubbing her sleepy eyes. She had a very disgruntled look on her face.

"What's going on?" Liz asked with the same disgruntled look.

Bonnie squeaked between laughter, "You shoulda seen her face! I heard Jason crying and crying, so I sneaked into his room while Stacy had her back turned, warming his bottle at the stove. I knew she hadn't seen me so I picked Jason up and held him up at the top of the door frame with just his head looking around the corner while I hid behind the wall. When Stacy turned around half asleep and saw that, she just screamed, and her *face* you shoulda seen her face." Bonnie just roared again.

"I thought he was possessed for goodness sake," Stacy cried. "You know, like that movie we watched the other night. I couldn't figure out how he got up to the top of the door frame. I never even heard Bonnie go in." Then she started to laugh too and took a swat at Bonnie. Liz was upset to say the least, but in spite of herself, she couldn't help but join them in their laughter. Life had been so serious and a little humor was certainly welcomed to break the ice.

Then, finally, to top it all off, Jimmy, Lotus, and Jasmine arrived loaded down with luggage. Liz was in awe of Jasmine. She was so beautiful. Her face was a pale olive color with huge chocolate eyes that weren't at all slanted, but still somehow had a slight oriental look. And her hair! She had masses of thick coal black hair that, when wet, would curl up in tight little curls as if she'd just recently had a perm. The curly hair was a throwback from Liz's side of the family. Liz fell instantly and hopelessly in love with her new granddaughter.

But the household became a constant go round of loud rock & roll teen music, girls quibbling, Liz yelling, and babies crying. Liz woke up to the realization that she had sobered up to a very dysfunctional family. And all while trying to graduate from college.

Every Friday afternoon at the college the students would have a break from the rigorous course to enjoy a lecture. At one of these Friday sessions the women were given a stress test to take. A high level of stress was calculated to be around 100 points. With all the separations, divorces, moves, accidents, and such in her life, Liz clocked in at over 400. The other students were stunned. "It's a wonder you're alive!" they stated.

Liz started to falter with this newfound information about her stress level, with trying to hide the memories of her sordid past, with the present house full of activity at home, and with the heavy duty course she was undertaking. She ended up at the club one afternoon after school, a total mess.

"Susan, I can't do this anymore!" she gasped with tears rolling down her cheeks.

"Yes you can!" Susan answered firmly as she wiped the tears from Liz's face.

Then more gently she proceeded to tell Liz about how she had gone through the same thing about half way through her nursing course, how she'd cried on her sponsor's shoulder, and how her sponsor had reassured her that she would, indeed, finish and she had, at the top of her class.

Susan was Liz's idol. She looked up to what Susan had accomplished. She was so full of confidence and so beautiful. She had Liz's full admiration and so Liz bolstered herself up to continue, and continue she did, in spite of all her adversities, to graduate at the top of her class along with three other women who also graduated with honors. Her school days were over, and the schooling she'd received would prove to be very beneficial in more ways than one.

After Liz graduated the household settled down somewhat so Jimmy and Lotus felt they could take a little vacation. They decided to take Jasmine to Creston to meet Gary and Susan. Gary had taught Jimmy at the alternate school in Creston and Jimmy had grown to love him like a father.

While there in Creston Lotus was served with a deportation order. On their return to Trail Jimmy and Lotus frantically informed Liz of the circumstances.

"But I thought that if an immigrant was married to a Canadian citizen, they could stay in the country," Liz exclaimed, feeling exasperated.

"The order was passed *before* we got married," Lotus muttered, with her head hanging down. "They just caught up to me now." Liz flipped right out.

"No way! No way! You will not be deported back to Hong Kong with my granddaughter." She had come to love Jasmine with all her heart and the thought of Jasmine being transported back to Hong Kong, which was destined to be returned to Communist China in the near future, made her shudder with fear. To never be able to see Jasmine again would break Liz's heart and to have her lost forever somewhere in China was beyond any facet of her imagination.

Liz was frantic trying to come up with ideas to fight with. The best thing she could think of was to go to the MLA which she did immediately. He listened compassionately to her story and said he would do all he could. He said he was leaving for Ottawa in a day or two and would plead her case.

The MLA returned within a week with bad news for Liz. "I'm sorry, but there is no way a deportation order can be rescinded once it's served. I sympathize with your situation, but there's nothing further I can do. Liz left his office with her head hanging.

"Bull shit!" she muttered to herself as she walked down Bay Avenue. "There has to be something I can do." She was ready to fight tooth and nail to save her precious granddaughter.

Upon her arrival at home she called to Lotus, "Let me see *all* the papers you received."

Lotus brought her everything she had been given, even the papers she had received prior to having to appear in court, before the order had been issued.

Liz pored over them for hours with a fine tooth comb and then cried, "Aha!" The words of her instructor in the legal course echoed through her mind and she repeated the words aloud. "Everything has got to be *signed* and *dated* always, always, always! This is crucial."

The line for the date and the line for the signature on the document advising Lotus of her right for legal counsel flashed on and off like a strobe light in Liz's brain. They were *blank*!

"Lotus! Lotus!" Liz cried out. "When did you get this document? Before the court case or after?"

"After."

"Are you sure?"

"Yes. I got that paper after the court case."

"Did you have legal counsel?"

"No I went to court by myself."

"Eureka. We're going to see a lawyer."

"I can't afford a lawyer." Lotus lamented.

"We'll get legal aid."

Liz grabbed the phone book. "Let's see, McGruen & Company sounds as good as any."

Liz called and got an appointment immediately for the next day.

****

Liz, Jimmy, and Lotus climbed the stairs up to the lawyer's office and sat in the waiting room. Mr. McGruen came out and shook their hands. "Look, I'm sorry," he said, "I am really bogged down right now so I'm going to give your case over to my younger brother. He has just finished law school and he needs a start. I'm sure he'll give you his best because he'll be determined to make a good impression."

They walked into the junior Mr. McGruen's office and Liz nearly dropped to the floor. He didn't look any older than Jimmy. *My god they've given me a mere babe.* She thought and felt frightened for Jasmine.

With no other choice available to them, Liz showed him the document she had discovered. He perused it, put it in a file folder and said, "That'll be fine. I'll get a date for a re-trial and be in touch with you." That was it! Her baby was in the hands of another baby. It was then she decided she would need to do a lot of praying.

The court date was set. The trial was to be held in Cranbrook! Liz had no transportation. Being as the date was a week day and everyone she knew with a car was working, she was frantic. Finally she secured a ride for all of them with Herb, a fairly new A.A. member who was not all that stable yet. She was beside herself with grief, but she would have ridden with the devil himself to keep that court appearance.

Jimmy, Lotus, Jasmine, Liz and Bonnie, who had come along to help with the baby, all piled in Herb's old, rickety station wagon. *Beggars can't be choosers.* Liz thought as she slumped down in the front seat.

They arrived at the front doors of the court house and were greeted by the young Mr. McGruen. "Good, Jim and Lotus, you come into the court room with me. The rest of you will have to wait in the lobby."

The time on the big black and white clock ticked by unmercifully slow. Liz could tell Herb was getting really antsy and it was making her a little nervous. He was a man of about thirty years of age, but she was sure his mind was only nine or ten. She wondered at what age he had started drinking. Then all of a sudden he jumped up, startling Liz out of her wits, grabbed the plastic baby bottle that was about half full out of Bonnie's hands and shouted, "Catch me if you can!" He took off running up the set of stairs that ran up through the center of the lobby.

Bonnie hollered out, "Hey, you idiot, bring that back!"

He ran all the way to the top where he could look down through the center of the three story stairwell and hollered, "Okay. Look out below!" and abruptly dropped the bottle right to the bottom where Bonnie stood looking up at him. Luckily, it never split open, but Liz was totally humiliated as people turned to stare at the sound of the bottle slamming onto the floor. Liz could have crawled in a hole, but, fortunately, just after the bottle dropping incident, the court room doors flew open and the young Mr. McGruen came rushing through. Liz knew instantly what the news was. It was written all over McGruen's face. His face was lit up like a neon sign. He had won his first case! But Liz took pride in the fact that in all actuality *she* had won his first case. Jasmine and Lotus would be staying in Canada!

She held Jasmine with tears of relief and joy streaming down her face. She felt satisfied. But little did she know, at that time, in spite of all her efforts, she would never see Jasmine grow up.

Jasmine

Chapter 8
The Indian Reservation

After the hectic school days and the exciting court case, things settled down considerably at 908 Rossland Avenue, and Liz was tossed back into the throes of severe loneliness. Ever since she had been a small child she had felt hollow in the middle. An all consuming emptiness that could only be filled by a man.

Because she had been so busy with life's adversities, the emptiness had somehow faded into the background, but now it was becoming severe again. She missed Johnny. She *needed* him. She started to wonder where he was, how he was. She had too much time on her hands. She needed a distraction, so she called Rose.

Rose and Mary were more than eager to help her ease her pain. Mary, because she had kicked Fred out for some deep, dark secret act he had done in the past. An act that she was very reluctant to disclose to her friends, and that she could never get over. And Rose, for no particular reason, she just loved to have fun. As a result the girls started frequenting the bars and the dance halls and having a high old time. Rose and Mary had been sober long enough to withstand being surrounded by alcohol and after being assured by Liz that she, too, would be alright in an alcohol environment, they invited her to join them.

Thus was the beginning of a series of wild weekends of dressing to the nines, dancing, flirting and partying til the wee hours of the morning, *sober*. But their wild weekends would eventually catch up to them and leave two of them in total despair.

But in the meantime the girls continued with the party atmosphere. And the highlight of it all for Liz was the grand A.A. ball held at the posh Coeur d'Alene Hotel in Coeur d'Alene, Idaho.

There was no way Liz could afford to go, but because Mary's parents were very well off and helped Mary out anytime she needed it, Mary opted to take Liz as her guest. So Rose, Mary and Liz set out to paint the town red and paint the town red, they did.

Liz was able to squeeze enough money out of her household funds to purchase a sleek, black evening dress for the ball. It draped diagonally across the bodice in a Grecian style. It was tight at her tiny waist, fitted over her curvy hips, and it dropped straight to the floor with a slit that came up to her knee on the front left side. She would be dressed to kill.

All the members were given name tags and Liz secured hers to the left side of the bodice of her dress. She looked in the mirror. Her makeup was perfect and her hair was piled high in curls. She looked like a movie star. She felt like a move star.

As she walked along the burgundy carpeted corridor to head to the banquet room she was stopped by a good looking young man, obviously a tourist, who seemed very eager to talk to her.

"Hi," he said shyly. "Why are you here? I mean, are you somebody famous? A movie star or something? I mean, if you are, can I get your autograph."

Liz was so flattered. She smiled sweetly and shook her head. "I'm nobody special." she replied. "I'm just here for a banquet." Of course, she didn't tell him what kind of banquet. She just walked away with her head held high. Everything was right with her world.

After the dance a large group of the members retired to the restaurant off the hotel lobby for the usual coffees all around and Liz, Rose, and Mary joined them. They looked around for a place to sit and it seemed there were no empty seats. As they surveyed the room, Liz's eyes fell on a large booth that was empty except for two men. Billy crooked his finger and flashed a charming smile as Liz's eyes rested on him.

She was feeling sassy and confident after the young man's comment earlier in the evening, and so she returned his smile. If he wanted to play games, she would give him a run for his money. She knew he would never win her heart because of her strong aversion to dating married men, but if he wanted to play, she'd play alright. She'd lead him on for the evening and then leave him flat. It would serve him right for taking advantage of new, vulnerable A.A. women.

So Liz flirted openly with Billy and played him right along. He was eagerly pursuing her, and she smiled sweetly, knowing full well what the outcome would be. Rose and Mary retired reluctantly not sure what Liz was up to. But they were tired and Liz assured them that she would be okay. After an hour or so of flirtatious bantering back and forth, Billy was sure she was putty in his hands so he made his move. He slipped his arm around the back of the booth behind her and sidled closer. "I've got a room all by myself and it sure is lonely up there."

Liz looked at him, smiled sweetly, took him by the hand and lifted his arm away from around her and said ever so sweetly, "I'm sorry I'm married and *I* don't cheat!"

When she returned to her room she was bent over with laughter. "What's so funny?" Rose and Mary asked in unison.

"Billy's face!" Liz sputtered, and then proceeded to tell them the whole story and they joined in her laughter. Liz had won that round, but Billy was mad, and it made him more determined to conquer her. Liz went home from that ball with glee in her heart and a newfound confidence in herself.

Then the next weekend Rose's relatives arrived from the Cree reservation in Saskatchewan. To celebrate their arrival the girls planned a trip to go to the White Bird Tavern across the border, at Northport, Washington where liquor was served and a person could dance the wee hours away, even on a Sunday. Trail was very close to Washington State, and they could easily zip across the American border at Patterson.

"Liz this is my Uncle Armin. His name means warrior," Rose chanted proudly as she opened the passenger door of the Lincoln. Armin sat in the driver's seat. *The name is well chosen.* Liz thought. He was very big, and very dark skinned, with coal black hair that flowed down his back. His features were incredibly strong from his wide stern mouth, to his straight, large nose and his firm brow. He never smiled, just gave a quick nod, then held his head erect with more pride than Liz had ever seen in her life. He was frightening and yet very appealing. The Carousel was tugging again. Liz had always been attracted to dark, strong, arrogant men, and Armin sure fit the bill. Even though he was Rose's uncle, he was not much older than Liz.

"And this is my brother George and my cousin Eric," Rose continued, looking into the back seat where Mary, with her white skin, blonde hair and blue eyes, sat squeezed between the two dark men. Their looks made quite a contrast. Even so Liz didn't notice much about George or Eric because she had been so enthralled with Armin. Rose got out and let Liz squeeze in the middle of the front seat pushed up close to Armin. Her face flushed and Rose giggled.

When they arrived at the border, the border guard stopped them immediately. He checked all I. D.'s very carefully and did a very thorough search of the car. Satisfied, he finally had to let them go. After they pulled away, Armin chuckled a deep baritone chuckle. "Heap big Indian drive big hot Lincoln. Sumtin' wrong wit dis picture." Armin muttered and then laughed. And the boys in the back just roared.

When they got to the White Bird, Liz danced the evening away with Armin and was in her glory, but because she couldn't have a drink, she never had the nerve to make a pass at him, and he never did make a pass at her so her enchantment with Armin was short lived. Just one evening. She never saw him again.

Rose's relatives, including her mother and father, stayed for two weeks. Liz didn't see much of Rose during that time, but Mary moved right in with the family because she became enamored with Rose's brother George, and he with her.

Rose was sober, but her family was not. And so she called Liz in a state of panic late one night. "Liz, I don't know what I'm going to do. I feel so guilty. Mary has clung right on to George and I warned her not to get too close to him because he drinks. She wouldn't listen to me, and now, she's started drinking again too. She and George got just polluted the other night. I don't know what to do. I feel so bad that Mary lost her sobriety. She told me she could handle going to the bars. It never seemed to bother her before."

"Oh, Rose that's so sad. She's been sober for a long time. But it's not your fault. I guess it's true what they say, *you're only one drink away from a drunk.*"

"I know and another thing they say is true too. *You pick up right where you left off.* Mary sure got drunk in a hurry, and she's been drunk ever since. But the worst of it is my family is leaving tomorrow to go back to the reservation, and Mary's going with them.

I've talked 'til I'm blue in the face and she won't listen. Can you try talking to her if I come and pick you up."

"Well, I can try, if you want me to." But Liz knew it wouldn't do any good. She recalled her experience with the drunk woman at the hospital meeting and what Gene had said to her afterward. *Never work with a drunk. Wait until they sober up.* Well, there was no time. She had to try.

Rose came right away and picked Liz up and the two sat up most of the night trying to talk Mary out of going, but to no avail. "She won't be able to handle it," Rose said. "She's not used to that kind of life. It's rough. There's a lot of drinking and fighting. That's why I got out myself. A white woman on the reservation is bad medicine." Rose lamented.

"Well, it's not your fault, Rose. You did everything you could. You know I've often wondered what happened between her and Fred. She told me one time that she just couldn't get over what he did and just didn't care any more. Maybe she was destined to drink again. They say that out of a hundred people with a drinking problem only ten per cent make it to A.A. and out of those ten only two stay sober. The odds aren't very good. It's really sad, but don't blame yourself or you may spiral down emotionally and be swallowed up again too. Please don't let that happen. You mean the world to me." Liz said and gave her friend a warm hug.

Mary did, indeed, go to the reservation with Rose's brother and she wrote faithfully to Rose and Liz like she had promised to do, and they wrote back. Until one day four weeks later Rose phoned Liz in a total state of despair.

"Rose, I can't understand you, slow down, get a grip and try again." Liz stated firmly to her friend. Rose was sobbing so hard that her words were inaudible.

"I-i-i-t's M-m-ary. She's d-d-ead. My b-b-rother killed her by accident."

"Oh, my God, No! What happened?"

Rose continued struggling with her words, "They were fighting. You know how head strong Mary could be. Well, she wouldn't leave it alone when George was drunk, and said he didn't want to talk about it anymore. He got really angry and hit her in the head with his fist.

She was rushed to the hospital with a brain hemorrhage where she died shortly after. Oh, Liz what am I going to do. It's all my fault for introducing her to my brother and taking her to the bars with me." Rose cried.

"No! It's not your fault! Every human being is responsible for their own life. If you had known what she would end up doing, would you still have invited her?"

Slowly Rose answered, "N-n-o."

"Well there you go. So you had no way of knowing. Mary said she could handle it herself. How were you to know she couldn't. You weren't inside her. Get a grip, or you're going to end up drunk yourself and I couldn't stand that, I love you too much."

Rose had been so good to Liz over the short time she had known her and she couldn't have stood to lose her too. Liz hated alcoholism and what it did to nice, decent people. She even felt sorry for George in a sense. Alcohol had driven him mad as well.

Liz had just gotten Rose to see that Mary's death was in no way her fault when Fred, who was still sober and still frequenting the club, started to blame Liz and Rose for his wife's death. He verbally attacked them at the meetings, a place of sanctuary for them, a place they needed to be. Liz began to hate him. She was smart enough and strong enough to know that in no way was Mary's death her fault, but Rose was so vulnerable because of the connection to her family that it almost drove her to a nervous breakdown. Liz started to wonder just exactly what it was that drove Mary away from Fred in the first place. She began to think that perhaps Fred was feeling his own guilt about the situation and wanted desperately to transfer it elsewhere.

Liz stood behind Rose every step of the way and they developed a strong bond that was to last a lifetime. Time heals all wounds so as time passed Rose finally came to her old self again.

"Would you look at this." Rose said, as she raised her eyes up from the Trail Times newspaper she was reading while she and Liz were having coffee at the club.

"What?" Liz asked.

"Kenny Rogers is coming to Pullman, Washington to put on a concert. Oh, God, I just love him. We've gotta go."

"I don't have any money for that kind of thing." Liz bemoaned. She hated being poor and so far she'd had no luck securing a job in a law office. It seemed to be impossible to break into that profession.

Just then Vern came in the door looking totally despondent.

"What's your problem?" Liz asked.

"My oil stove blew up and spewed black smoke all over. My house is covered in oily soot. Hey, do you want a job?"

Vern worked at Cominco and he had plenty of bucks. Liz was excited. It was exactly what she needed.

Then her elation drooped to the floor. She couldn't keep any extra money she earned while on welfare. She had to be honest to stay sober. If she was going to learn to like herself she had to respect herself. But at least she could help him. Helping others, she had learned, was another way to help her like herself and stay sober.

"Well, I can't accept any money from you, being as I'm on welfare, but I'll certainly help you clean your place. You've been so good to me in the past.When do I start?"

"Right now if you want. I'll drive you out to have a look and you can let me know what you'll need."

They drove to his house in Beaver Falls and Liz looked just as despondent as Vern had when he walked into the club earlier. The white walls were all black. Not just black, but *oily* black.

"Gee, I don't know Vern. I think it'll take more than a cleaning. You're probably going to have to re-paint and wallpaper everything."

"Can you do it?"

Liz wasn't sure. Her sister, Jane, had taught her to wallpaper years ago and anybody could wield a paintbrush, couldn't they? Anyhow, she undertook the task and got started right away the next day. She worked her fingers to the bone and Vern's house was like new by the time she finished.

First she washed everything then painted and wallpapered. Vern was so pleased he brought all the neighbors in to see what she had done. And after the neighbours left Vern had a very nice surprise for Liz.

"What's this?" Liz asked, as Vern handed her a white envelope.

"Open it! Open it, you silly goose!" he chanted.

Liz slowly pried open the envelope and screamed and jumped up and down when she pulled out a ticket to the Kenny Rogers concert. She was going after all and she didn't have to cheat to do it. Life was good!

****

Well, Liz and Rose were somewhat like Lucy and Ethel. Excited, all agog and confused. They ended up getting on the wrong tour bus. They were to go on the bus with the older sedate folks, but ended up on the bus with all the wine drinkers. The worst of it was their luggage got put on the right bus. So they ended up arriving in Pullman at their motel with no luggage. The bus driver had told them to hurry and change and that there would be no time for supper as they would be late for the concert.

Of course, the girls had to primp, but by the time their luggage was brought over from the motel where the other bus had gone, they had only ten minutes to get ready. They rushed as fast as they could, but a girl needs time when it comes to makeup and such. They finally climbed aboard the bus where a wine-drinking crowd serenaded them with their own composition.

Totally out of key they chanted, "We've been waiting for you, we've been waiting for you." Liz and Rose skulked onto the bus with very red faces. And that wasn't the end of their problems.

When they arrived at the University where the concert was being held, they were very disappointed to find that their seats were in the nosebleed section. Kenny Rogers was about three inches tall from their vantage point.

"How brave are you?" Rose asked, with a grin on her face.

"As brave as they come," Liz answered, readily.

"Come on." Rose said as she grabbed Liz by the hand.

They made their way down to the ground floor and went to walk down the aisle when a security guard grabbed Rose by the arm and said you can't go down there. Those are special reserved seats.

Rose shrugged, disappointed and proceeded to walk away until she saw the security guard disappear. Then she grabbed Liz by the arm.

"Quick, duck down," she whispered.

Liz quickly squatted down as Rose had done and the two duck-walked to the front of the stage so the guard wouldn't see their heads in the crowd . They sat in the aisle with stars in their eyes as they looked up into Kenny Roger's face and he sang to them. Liz was thrilled. Rose had made her day. Liz smiled warmly at Rose with the beautifully featured Indian princess face.

Then the next day there was more excitement. The bus driver! A new driver had been commissioned to take them back to Trail and he was absolutely gorgeous. The girls were totally awe struck. Not only was he good looking, he was a real gentleman. He stopped at the North Town Mall in Spokane and allowed the ladies to go for lunch and to shop for a couple of hours.

While browsing through a large department store Rose spotted a rack of beautiful fur coats. "Look at this!" she cried as she held up a cardboard sign that was hung on the end of the rack with a string.

"$5.00 will hold me," Liz quoted and then started to laugh uproariously.

"What's so funny?" Rose asked.

Liz took the sign off the rack and hung it around her neck. "Now I'm ready to get back on the bus. I'll just wiggle this in front of the bus driver as I get on."

Rose burst into fits of laughter and Liz joined her while other customers all around them turned to stare at them wondering what their gaiety was all about. The girls giggled all the harder at the people's stares. Life was good! Life was grand! But for how long?

Rose & Liz

Chapter 9
The Nutcracker Ballerina

After Mary's death Rose and Liz withdrew from the bar scene and became very cautious. They had ventured out to the Kenny Rogers concert, but as far as the bars were concerned, they kept a pretty low profile. So as a result Liz was once more hurled into the depths of loneliness. The Carousel showed no mercy. It tugged relentlessly on her heart strings.

"Oh, if only Johnny were here," she moaned to herself on a rainy, dismal spring day. She was still smitten with him. He was still her husband. She still needed him to quiet the Carousel, but he was nowhere in sight and she had heard nothing of him since he left almost a year ago.

Lost in her day dreams of the early times of her romance with Johnny, she barely noticed the tapping on the kitchen door. "Oh, who can that be," she moaned. "I don't want to be bothered right now." She had been feeling sorry for herself and had not cared to take the time to groom herself in days, as a result, she was at her worst and didn't really care to be seen. Nonetheless, with a great deal of effort, she dragged herself from the couch and headed for the door just in case it was an important caller.

In an aggravated state she flung open the door, and immediately her heart began to pound out of her chest. There standing large as life, right in front of her was her cavalier. The handsome wandering jew had come home. He looked at her with apprehension in his eyes. She looked back at him with a questioning look, not sure what to expect.

Then all of a sudden he scooped her up in his arms and almost squeezed the life out of her. "Put me down," she wailed. "Where have you been?" She was so happy to see him, but at the same time she was upset that he hadn't even tried to contact her in spite of the fact that their parting hadn't been on the best of terms.

64

"I've been in Williams Lake. Oh, Liz. It's been fantastic. I met lots of really neat people and things are going really good for me. For the first time in my life I feel really clean and good about myself. This has never happened to me before and it feels great."

Liz stood back and looked him over. He did look wonderful. There was something different about him. A glow that she had never seen before and she knew deep in her heart that he had finally got the program and he was going to be okay. Her heart soared. They could finally be a couple and her life would finally come together. She truly did love him and not only that she really needed him, as much as she needed breath and blood.

"That's wonderful," she said, laughing with joy. "So are you going to move back in right away. We are still married, you know."

"Well, that's the thing, Liz, I'm doing really well for the first time in my life and I'm a little scared of screwing it up. I do want to see you, of course, that is if you're willing, but let's take it a little slow. Relationships are the hardest thing in life to deal with and without a lot of living skills, I'm still kinda green."

Liz's heart sank, but at the same time she could understand what he was saying. He was fairly newly sober again and she sure didn't want to ruin it for him. So very reluctantly, she agreed to wait. But in the meantime, he took her to the Terra Nova where they rented a room so that they could re-consumate their relationship. Johnny took Liz to heights that she had thought she would never see again. She left the room to return home with stars in her eyes and joy in her heart. But on the way home she developed a nagging feeling of discontent. He wasn't coming home with her.

Johnny rented a room in the basement of an older A.A. member's house on Riverside Avenue. The woman he had rented from, Blanche, was not one of Liz's favorite people. She didn't trust her. There seemed to be something a little shifty about her even though she put on airs as if she were a great lady. Something just didn't ring quite true, and Liz was left feeling a little frightened. Johnny started to spend a lot of time upstairs with Blanche and Liz was questioning herself because she didn't like it. Was she jealous? No, it couldn't be. The woman had to be in her sixties. She was old and wrinkled with orange hair. No, it wasn't jealousy. It was fear. Blanche was poisoning Johnny's mind. She was filling his head full of all kinds of notions particularly the idea that being single again would be a lot of fun. He had worked hard to be sober and he deserved to have some fun. She flirted outrageously with him and encouraged him to think about himself.

She constantly told him how good looking he was and how he could really bring the ladies on. She encouraged him to buy sexy colognes, fancy clothes, and jewelry to primp with in order to feel better about himself. Johnny didn't need all that primping as far as Liz was concerned. He was just fine the way he was.

Then the proverbial you-know-what hit the fan when a new beautiful, blonde haired, green eyed younger woman, named Leah, showed up at the doors of A.A. Of course she was given all the male attention that Liz had received upon her arrival. It seemed to be a thing the men did to make a girl feel welcome and flattered. It certainly did help lift a drunk woman out of the depths of despair. Even Billy, who was still in hot pursuit of Liz, changed his tactics and began to chase Leah.

Liz had loved all the attention when it was her turn, but now she was green with envy. It wasn't that she begrudged the girl her turn to be flattered. It was Leah's reaction to Johnny that really bit into Liz. Of course, Johnny, not feeling all that good about himself and lacking self-confidence hadn't made any overtures towards Leah, but she sure did towards him, and she wasn't about to give up. Liz knew her kind. She wasn't the least bit interested in Johnny. She just liked to play. She was a female Billy. She would stand right in front of Johnny and bat her long black eyelashes and demurely look up into his face. He couldn't help but be flattered because every man in the club was falling at her feet and she chose Johnny.

Liz wanted him home! But he refused to come. It seemed that with Blanche's encouragement and Leah's pursuit, he was enthralled with his freedom. Liz was fuming. Then she blew her stack when Leah and Johnny walked in the club one evening with a pizza to share between them. They sat in the back and laughed and talked and ate pizza and totally ignored Liz. She was furious, but she couldn't bring herself to go and interrupt them. If Johnny didn't want to acknowledge her, she had too much pride to let him know it bothered her. Of course, Johnny denied having any feelings for Leah. "We're just friends," he would declare over and over again. "I'm just helping out a new member. You know I love you, Liz."

"Then why won't you come home where you belong."

"I'm just not ready yet. You trust me don't you. I need some more time. Trust me, Liz, please."

Things continued in the same fashion, with Johnny torn between still needing Liz and yet wanting his freedom, with Liz seething, and with Leah hotly pursuing Johnny, until one night while Liz and Johnny were in the throes of hot passionate love-making in Johnny's apartment, and the phone started to ring off the hook.

"Let it ring," Liz gasped.

"It might be important," Johnny moaned.

"They'll call back."

"No, I better get it. It might be a member in dire straits."

Liz moaned as Johnny got up with the sheet around him to grab the phone. She pulled the quilt up over herself waiting for him to return. She could hear his voice from the other room.

"Take it easy, take it easy," he crooned.

It didn't take Liz very long to figure out who was on the other end. The bed grew cold as ice on the other side as the minutes slowly ticked by. Johnny stuck his head in the door and stuck his forefinger up to Liz indicating for her to hold on.

She screwed her face up at him and mouthed the words, "Come on!" She was furious. How dare that woman phone at a time like this. Why didn't she call her sponsor or another female member. Why did it have to be Johnny. After a half hour Liz got up and despondently started to pull her clothes on. Johnny shook his head at her and shrugged his shoulders, but Liz continued to get dressed and skulked quietly out of his apartment broken hearted. He barely noticed her leaving.

Johnny was reluctant to move back in with Liz. He was enjoying his newfound sober freedom. He still loved her or wanted her, at least to some degree, but he was a bit miffed because he had heard all about Liz's antics with Rose and Mary from Fred.

But Liz had had enough. She refused to sleep with Johnny anymore. Let him suffer for awhile and then he would come running.

The tragic thing was he didn't come running, as a matter of fact, he was running in the other direction.

Liz was devastated. She *needed* him in order to exist. Without realizing it she had become dependant on him. Without him she was nothing. There was no Liz left. Her self-esteem hit an all time low. Not only that all the emotions from her past had started to severely surface all jumbled in one large mass of wriggling distress. There was Edmund's untimely death which she had never truly grieved. There was all the heartache of her marriage with Brian, the abuse from Norm and then the final, deadly blow, the incest with Lenny. She hadn't dealt with any of these things and they were whirring around in her sub-conscious mind at top speed. The alcohol and the carousel had kept them at bay, but now the alcohol was gone and the carousel had ceased it's delightful turns as well

Liz was coming unglued and very rapidly. Her anxiety attacks began to hit with a fervor. Then one Thursday morning she woke up in tears. She cried the morning away and continued to cry all that day, had a fitful sleep and continued to cry until the next afternoon. Lotus was very concerned about her. Liz was like a zombie. Lotus tried to talk to her, but Liz didn't respond.

Liz looked out through a pale yellow colored fog into Lotus' face. Lotus was leaning in close to Liz's face and calling her name. Liz could hear a muffled sound, but was making no sense of it. Lotus' face was all distorted as though Liz was looking at her through a concave mirror.

"Jimmy, Jimmy, come quick. Something's wrong with your mother," Lotus shouted. "She looks really weird. Her eyes are like glass marbles."

Jimmy ran to the kitchen where Liz was sitting at the chrome kitchen set and hollered, "Mom, mom are you alright."

Liz didn't respond. Jimmy called Dr. Trent, who said to bring her in right away. Liz could do nothing but cry, all the way to the doctor's in the cab, all the way up in the elevator, all through the waiting room. Dr. Trent came out immediately.

She examined Liz and tried to talk to her. No response.

"Liz, Liz, what do you want us to do with you?" Dr. Trent hollered.

That penetrated and Liz answered like a slurring automaton. "Jus' throw me in the garbage." And then she retreated back into her safe place -- the yellow fog.

"Well, she's not capable of making a decision for herself, Jim. I think the best thing to do is commit her to the Daly Pavilion."

"No!" Liz screamed and started to shake and totally panic. She had heard horror stories from other A.A. members about how the psychiatrist at the Daly was adamant about giving antiquated shock treatments. Dr. Trent's words had penetrated Liz's fog and terrified her. She started to cry harder and flail her arms totally out of control.

Dr. Trent hugged her close and said, "Okay, Liz, okay. I think this is really necessary. But I know how you feel about Dr. Ward. I'll tell you what, you'll be strictly under my care, okay? I will instruct Dr. Ward that you are my patient only. He will have no jurisdiction over you, okay?" She gently moved the hair out of Liz's eyes and wiped her tears.

Liz nodded slowly. Then Dr. Trent said, "You can take her now. I'll call ahead and let them know you're coming."

The trio left the Dr.'s office and headed to the pavilion in a cab. Liz felt like a sheep being led to the slaughter, but there was nothing she could do to help herself. She felt like a piece of lead. She couldn't even lift her arms.

On arrival, Liz was admitted, although she had no recollection of it later. Jimmy, sadly signed the documents that would imprison the mother that he loved. His heart was crushed but there was nothing else he could do.

Liz was taken to the large central common room where she was lowered into an over-stuffed rocker. She cried and cried and cried, until suddenly she spotted a young girl pirouetting all around the room. Liz watched fascinated as the girl twirled and twirled ever closer. She was dressed in pink and her flaming red hair was all tangled.

Liz was startled out of her wits when the girl pirouetted right for her and plopped herself at her feet. The girl began to speak, "Hi, I'm Margie! Can I borrow your comb. You see, I've just had a miscarriage and I really need a comb." Liz was agog. She didn't know what to do and she started to panic just as the girl flipped up and disappeared across the room pirouetting away as quickly as she had come.

Liz hardly had time to gather herself together again when a tall gray-haired strange-looking man dressed in nothing but an orange hospital kimono wandered aimlessly towards her. His eyes were all glassed over and Liz realized, too late, that he was going to walk right into the chair that she was occupying. He hit the edge of the chair, faltered, fell forward and as he fell the kimono flew open and Liz found herself face to face with an eight inch penis.

"Oh, my Gawd!" She yelled and took off running. What had they done to her. She was petrified. A nurse grabbed hold of her and said gently, "Come on I'll take you to your room." Liz had no luggage, not that she cared.

She was led down a hallway and around a corner to a fairly large beige colored room where there were two single beds with willow green spreads, two dressers and a washroom with a white sink and toilet. On one of the beds sat a blonde woman about thirty-seven years old. She was a handsome woman, not beautiful by any means, but striking nonetheless.

She held her hand out to Liz when they were introduced. Liz felt awkward, but she took the woman's extended hand. "I'm Greta," she said. "We'll be room mates."

Her aura was good and Liz felt safe with her. The woman let her settle in without talking too much. She seemed to sense Liz's condition, perhaps because she had been in the same condition when she had arrived a few days prior.

Liz crawled into the bed,exhausted and immediately fell asleep for seventeen hours. She awoke with a start, wondering where she was. Greta smiled warmly and said, "Hi, sleepyhead. Feel any better."

"My mouth feels like it's full of cotton," Liz moaned.

"I'll go and get you a nice cup of coffee. What do you take?"

"Cream and lots of sugar," Liz replied, gratefully.

Greta came promptly back to the room with Liz's coffee. She was accompanied by three other women. They were all clean cut good looking women, and Liz wondered what they were all doing in a place like the Daly Pavilion psychiatric ward.

"This is Joan. She's a nurse, but not from this hospital. She comes from Creston. This is Muriel, secretary from a Realty office, and this is Karen, an accountant. And I'm a loans manager from a bank in Nelson." Greta said, laughing. "Aren't we a fine kettle of fish. All in the Daly. What do you do?" She asked.

Liz was slightly embarrassed. Should she tell them about her alcoholism and risk their revulsion? The women all seemed so nice and they were here for their own reasons so with tongue in cheek she stated, "I'm a recovering alcoholic. I mean, that's not my occupation." The women all laughed. Liz was encouraged by their reaction and so she continued. "I guess everything has caught up to me and I've had a nervous breakdown."

"Same here," the women all chanted in unison.

"But what do you work at," Karen asked.

"Well, I haven't been working for awhile. But when I do, I do office work. I just finished the Legal Secretarial course at Selkirk, but I haven't been able to land a job in that field yet. I guess it's a good thing being as I ended up in here."

"I knew you were one of us," Joan said. "A professional person, I mean. We gotta stick together in here because there are some pretty sick people who don't make any sense."

"Yeah, I found that out yesterday," Liz lamented remembering the ballerina and the penis. She told the girls about the penis and they just roared with laughter.

"You'll probably be in our group," Greta said. "We do group counseling with Bart. He's really good and he's really kind. You'll like him."

"What do you do in group," Liz inquired, nervously. She certainly didn't want to disclose any of her horrendous background, especially the incest, to any of these fine women.

"We talk about our problems," Muriel answered, shyly.

"So what else do you do here?" Liz asked trying to change the subject.

"Oh, it's a hoot," Karen said, rolling her eyes. We're called up at seven o'clock to shower, then breakfast in the dining room, and then exercises, whoop de do! Then we have occupational therapy which is kinda neat. You can knit or embroider or do ceramics. Of course the men build things like picnic tables and such."

"Don't forget the bowling." Greta chanted.

"Oh, yeah, that's another hoot. Off we all go in the paddy wagon to the bowling alley. Like we really feel like bowling in the shape we're in." Karen stated.

"I like the cooking and baking," Muriel spoke up. She seemed to be not quite as sure of herself as the others, but Liz liked her, nonetheless.

The women sure seemed in a lot better shape than Liz was in, and their cheerful bantering helped Liz to feel a little more at ease. She was surprised to find such professional, sane women in the Daly. She thought everyone was a nut case and she was sure she was too.

"Alright, ladies, break it up. Time for your showers. Breakfast at 8 o'clock don't forget," a petite dark haired nurse piped as she stuck her head in the door.

Liz delighted in the shower. The warm spray caressed her tired aching body and soul. She was basking in the solitary confinement of the shower stall. Even though the women had cheered her up she was still teetering on the brink of insanity and making conversation was still difficult.

After a hearty breakfast that tasted like sawdust to Liz, all the patients retired to the exercise room. As Liz was entering she could hear the volunteer leader chanting, "Head and shoulders, knees and toes, knees and toes, knees and toes, head and shoulders, knees and toes, eyes, ears, mouth and nose." The woman touched each part of her body as she named it.

Liz gulped. It was a little ditty that the kindergartners played at school. Liz was shocked. They weren't in kindergarten. They were sick!

Just then Karen grabbed Liz by the arm and said, "Quick, in here!" Liz followed, as did Greta, Muriel and Joan, and found herself locked up in a huge broom closet. "Ssshh." Karen whispered. "We don't do exercises when that woman is here. She belongs in here herself if she thinks we're going to do that little number."

They had no sooner settled in the broom closet than a nurse who was scouting about for missing persons opened the door. "Well, well, what do we have here?" She questioned. "Alright girls if you're not going to exercise then no occupational therapy for you."

The women were disappointed and decided right there and then they were going to take this matter up in group. They hadn't wanted to rat on the exercise lady, but this was too much. Occupational therapy was the highlight of the day. When they related their story to Bart, he roared with laughter. "Tell you what I'll speak to administration."

"Please do!" They chanted in unison.

"Yeah," Liz said shyly. "I am about this far", she gestured an inch with her forefinger and thumb, "from totally losing it." If I have to do that exercise, I'm sure I'll be tipped right over the edge.

"That's right," they all laughed.

"Okay, let's get on with our session," Bart said smiling warmly.

Liz was very careful not to reveal anything about her sordid past. She did however focus on her marriage with Johnny. Bart listened very carefully. He had a plan that he would reveal to Liz sometime in the future.

In the meantime, Bart gave Liz a personality test to determine some of her personal assets and liabilities. She sat down in a small room beside Bart's office at a neat desk to answer some four hundred multiple choice questions. She determined to answer them as honestly as possible, if she didn't, of what benefit would it be to her? She answered questions such as, *Would you rather tidy your desk or kiss a nice looking guy?* There was no doubt in Liz's mind what the answer to that should be. Of course she'd rather kiss the guy. Finally, she finished after a gruelling two hours.

And then after waiting a few excruciating days, Bart called her into his office. "Hi, Liz, how are you doing? We have the results of your test."

"So what's the bad news. There's no help at all for me?"

"Oh, it's not all that bad. This is how it works. We have evaluated you in the different catagories on a scale of one percent to one hundred percent. One percent being way too low and one hundred percent being way too high. The fifty percent range would be perfect, but of course, no one would fit that, at least not in all categories. Now," Bart started, as he took a deep breath and stroked his chin with one hand, "Your need to be the centre of attention is at ninety-eight per cent."

Liz shrieked, "Oh, my gawd, that's awful, what a sicko."

"Hold on, it's not all that bad. Where do you think our movie stars and entertainers come from?"

With that comment Liz just beamed. Hey maybe, she belonged in the entertainment field. She always did like to play act and dress up when she was a child. "Carry on," she said feeling a little more at ease.

"I am a little concerned about your need to dominate. It sits at one per cent. You know what that means?"

"No."

"Everyone in the whole world is walking all over you."

"Well, I kinda like to keep everybody happy. I can't stand it if anybody is mad at me."

"Peace at all cost, eh?" Bart stated as he looked over the rim of his glasses. "We'll have to work with your fear of anger. The thing that concerns me most, though, is your need for men. It stands at ninety-nine per cent."

"I don't doubt that. I've always felt I needed a man. Isn't that okay, I mean there are two sexes and they go together."

"True, it's okay to want a man, but there's a difference between wanting and needing a man. There's a really good book out called *Why Do I Think I'm Nothing Without a Man?* It might be a good idea for you to have a look at it. I think there's one in our library."

Liz went away feeling good on the one hand, but not so good on the other hand. She wasn't as bad as she'd thought she was, but she wasn't all that sure that she wanted to read that book. What if it altered her opinion about the man thing. Living like she'd lived was like living in a swamp. Not a good place to be, but she knew the swamp really well. To get out on dry land would be so frightening. She didn't know her way around in normal society. She just couldn't burst her bubble and lose her Carousel at this point. She was too weak. So she put the book on hold.

Chapter 10
A Brown Haired Stranger

As the days passed quickly Liz improved tremendously. They say laughter is the best medicine and with her new companions it was always the order of the day. A new patient, Tobias, who had been a school teacher, had come into the pavilion, and in spite of his sad state he had the girls in stitches.

The fun began after group while the girls were having coffee in the huge kitchen. Tobias had a habit of walking in squares until he would run into a wall, then he would turn at a ninety degree angle and continue, making perfect squares in his travels. As he shuffled in the kitchen, he stopped abruptly and crooked his finger at Joan. Because she was such a kind person, she got up and went over to him. He bent over and whispered in her ear.

They could all tell by Joan's puffed, red face she was about to burst with laughter, but she very politely held on until Tobias had continued on his journey and was out of sight. Then she let it all out and bent over with laughter.

"So tell us," they chanted. "What did he say."

"It was profound," she giggled hardly able to speak right away.

"Come on, get a grip," Karen said.

"He said," and then she started to laugh again. "Okay, okay, I'm okay now. He said that he wished he would fart in the bath tub and go down the drain in the bubble."

The women just roared until tears were running down their cheeks. It wasn't all that funny, but the camaraderie they shared was fantastic.

After they settled down Liz questioned, "Whatever happened to him? I mean he has to be a smart man to be a teacher."

Greta answered, tongue in cheek because of Liz's addiction, "Alcoholism. He has wet brain. That's what they call it when a person crosses over the line with alcoholism. There is no turning back. Too many damaged brain cells. Wet brain is irreversible."

Liz shuddered. How close had she come? "Oh, God, that is so sad. Thank God I sobered up when I did. I never knew all these things about alcoholism before. I didn't even know I had a problem," she lamented.

Just then Karen said, "Uh, oh, trouble. Here come the guards. Someone's going to the rubber room again."

Liz was terrified of the rubber room. If a patient got out of control and the nurses couldn't handle him or her, they would send for security and the guards would swarm and surround the person, jump him or her and then the whole entourage would struggle toward the room they called the rubber room. It was called the rubber room because all the walls were padded as well as the floor. There was nothing in there and the patient would be stripped completely before being tossed in. The screaming that would go on afterward haunted Liz no end. She constantly lived in fear of getting out of control herself.

At night time she and Greta pushed a dresser against the door in their room so no one could come in because a lot of the really sick patients had a habit of wandering in the night.

Liz had been in for two weeks and was still a little shaky so Bart felt a couple more weeks were in order, and then he would implement his plan to help her. In the meantime Liz got to know a lot of different patients in the pavilion. One woman patient would always stick out in Liz's mind. Her name was Katherine and she went regularly for shock treatments. Liz hadn't particularly befriended her because she was quite sick and wasn't really capable of a friendship, but she had empathy for Katherine nonetheless and would listen to her tales of woe. One of her tales was about how much she hated the shock treatments. Liz felt so sorry for her. Katherine said it wasn't so much the treatments themselves, because they were given a sedative. It was that she couldn't remember anything afterward and that felt really strange.

Liz suggested that she talk to her own doctor and see about getting them stopped, but the woman was too far gone to take that initiative. In the end Liz was distressed to learn that after a weekend pass the woman didn't return. Later she was devastated to learn the woman had hung herself in her home over that weekend.

But there was another woman, Bess, that Liz felt she might have saved from grief. She was a middle aged kind of frumpy woman, but kind nonetheless. Her boyfriend, also middle aged and frumpy would visit her faithfully. It wasn't hard to tell that he doted on her. One evening he brought her a beautiful heart shaped box of chocolates. Liz thought Bess would be thrilled, but on the contrary, she was upset.

"What's wrong?" Liz asked. "Don't you like chocolates?"

"Sure I love chocolates. It's not that. It's Frank. He is so boring, so predictable. For once I'd like to try dating an exciting guy."

"Hmph! I've dated lots of exciting guys. It's really exciting alright when they've got their hands around your throat or when their fist is coming full in your face." Liz retorted, grabbing herself around the throat and sticking her tongue out sideways, and rolling her eyes.

Bess laughed at Liz's antics and never said another word about the chocolates, or Frank, and for many years later Liz would see Frank and Bess still together and wonder if she might have had a hand in it.

Liz was working very hard at trying to get well. She worked on her self esteem. And there were all kinds of lessons on assertiveness, which were good for Liz because she had always been afraid to say no to people. Plus there was lots of role-playing about dealing with other people's anger. Other people's anger had always immobilized Liz.

Then one afternoon Liz felt she needed a little alone time so she sought out a little nook around the corner from the common room. She was sitting peacefully reading when along came the penis man. He always frightened Liz. She heard that he had schizophrenia and she didn't exactly know what that meant, but he was certainly strange.

He came up to Liz and started talking a lot of gibberish. She couldn't understand him, and she was nervous. He continued as though he was really frustrated. Finally, her empathetic side kicked in and she thought she'd try something. She took him by the hand and asked, "What you're trying to say isn't what's coming out of your mouth, is it?" Tears started to roll down his cheeks as he shook his head up and down frantically. She had made a breakthrough and was very pleased with herself. After that she was no longer afraid of John, and even though she couldn't understand him they had made a bond. He would smile and nod every time he saw her after that.

The feelings that came up in Liz after she had reached John made her do some serious thinking, and she realized she was in the wrong profession. She hadn't always cared that much for office work. She was good at it, but it wasn't very satisfying. She knew what she wanted to do and she was excited. On her next weekend pass she would talk to her sponsor, Susan about it. She wanted to be a psychologist. Susan would know if that was a possibility for her.

****

Liz was busy making a chess set in ceramics for Johnny when a man around her age sauntered into the room. She hadn't seen him before and knew he must be a new inmate. He was good looking with brown hair, a pouty bottom lip and beautiful sea blue eyes. Liz had no idea when she first surveyed him that he was to have a major effect on the rest of her life.

"What are you making," he asked.

"A chess set for my husband. He loves to play chess. The only problem is I keep crumbling them and having to start over."

"A lot of anger, eh?"

"What are you talking about?" Liz asked indignantly. Who was he to tell her what her problem was. He'd just arrived himself.

"Anger. It makes you crush things. Hey what's your name? Mine's Don. It means brown haired stranger. That's me. I got brown hair and I'm always a stranger cause I roam from town to town. Never stay too long in one place."

"I'm Liz," she said reluctantly she didn't really care too much for his attitude.

"Oh, yeah, I think we're in the same group together."

"Oh?"

"Yeah, and that Joan is in our group too. She sure is hot. I wouldn't mind taking her out."

What's the matter with this guy? Liz thought to herself. *This isn't a dating service.*

Don was indeed in their group Liz found out later that afternoon. She also found out he too was an alkie. He had been in Creston, drifting through when he was robbed. All he had was the clothes on his back. His back pack with everything he owned in the world was gone. He wore a powder blue shirt, a jean jacket and blue jeans which he laundered daily while he wore a hospital robe.

At least he's clean about himself. Liz thought. She began to feel sorry for him because of his plight. He was good natured all the time even though he had nothing. So her heart softened toward him to some degree.

Liz continued to work on the chess set. She had so wanted to give it to Johnny on her release from the hospital. She was sure he'd be pleased, but every time she would try to scrape the excess off, the piece would crumble in her hand.

"Still mad, eh?" Don asked as he passed her table. "Why don't you make a picnic table."

"That's what the men do," she said exasperated.

"Ask Alice, the occupational therapist, I'm sure she'll let you and I'll help you. It'll get rid of that pent up anger you're carrying around."

Maybe he was right. Maybe she was angry. She was certainly frustrated with her situation with Johnny. She didn't know what he wanted. She felt she couldn't live without him and she was scared.

So began the manual labor on the picnic table. Liz opted to make a kid's table because she felt a large one would be beyond what she could accomplish. She wasn't even sure that she could make a small one. But with Don's help she totally amazed herself. The picnic table was a total success. And it did indeed help to get rid of some anger, with all the hammering and heavy lifting to put the table together. He was right.

Weeks had gone by and it was getting close to the time when all the ones in their group would be released. Liz had been there for four weeks. She now knew Don quite well and decided she certainly did like him. She even did the favor of telling Joan that he liked her, which backfired because Joan simply stated that no way would she ever have anything to do with a bar kinda guy.

Liz nursed his wounds for him by being there and listening. They became quite close as friends. Liz was not attracted to him in any way nor he to her. He could only see Joan and that wasn't working so he became somewhat despondent.

Because the members of their group were leaving the pavillion soon they hurried to finish the 5000 piece picture puzzle they had all been working on. It was a beautiful country scene with mountains and a river and fields full of wild flowers. It was an arresting piece of art and they had planned to glue it all together, frame it, and hang it in the library of the pavilion. Leave their stamp on the place.

Don had offered to frame it when it was all glued together and Liz had opted to help him. The puzzle was lying on the floor in the Occupational Therapy room face down so the glue could dry. First they had the monumental task of turning it over. They each took a side and slowly started to turn it. Liz never did know exactly what happened, but somehow they slipped and the puzzle went into pieces. Don's face was unbelievable. So was Liz's. And as they stared at each other's gaping mouths and bulging eyes they started to laugh uproariously. How would they explain it to all the others. Weeks had gone into putting it together. The more they thought about it the more they laughed. Liz felt closer to Don at that moment than she had felt to another human being for a long time. They shared a common ground, guilt, that linked them together. Fortunately, they worked hard every day to put the broken pieces back together and the rest of the gang was grateful, to say the least.

Liz and her friends would be leaving in a week so Bart was ready to disclose his plan. He had called Johnny to come for what he called a con joint. With himself to mediate between Johnny and Liz he had hoped that something could be worked out for Liz.

"Hi," Liz said shyly as Johnny entered Bart's office.

Johnny hung his head as he returned the salutation. He was nervous because of what he wanted to say.

Bart talked to them both for awhile, explaining to Johnny how Liz felt. Johnny just kept sitting there with his head hanging. Finally Bart asked, "So, Johnny exactly what is it you'd like to do. Liz needs an answer so she can carry on with her life one way or the other."

Johnny with head still hanging muttered the words, "I want a divorce."

Liz couldn't bear it! She bounded from her seat and ran out of the room sobbing. Don tried to grab her as she ran past, but she twisted out of his arms and ran to her room. Everyone left her alone for the day to sob her heart out because they knew she needed to cry out the pain or it would lodge inside her for years to come.

Liz suffered a huge set back, but by the end of the week Bart felt she was okay to try to make it at home. She had been in the hospital for five weeks and she had learned a lot of living skills. But if it hadn't been for Don she probably never would have made it. After being released Don applied for welfare and rented a small apartment up the gulch just above her place, so they could continue their friendship. He was with her on a daily basis.

He made her get out. He took her to the Town Frier where they served the best English Style fish and chips Liz had ever eaten. He walked her to all their meetings and on one occasion he insisted on walking her to Rose's apartment on Laburnum Drive which was approximately three miles away.

"You gotta be crazy. We'll never make it," Liz cried.

"Sure we will. Look at this beautiful day." It was spring and the day was indeed beautiful. They set out from the Gulch and headed downtown where they crossed over the huge suspension bridge. The sun was sparkling on the fast moving Columbia River like diamonds flashing rainbows. There was white water where the waves hit the pilings of the bridge. Birds flew all around chirping in the warm sunshine. The trees were budding with yellow green shoots. The sun warmed Liz's body. Don's company and the beauty of nature were the beginning of a healing for her that was soon to be ripped open again leaving her soul to bleed for many years to come.

They arrived at Rose's within a short period of time and Liz was pleased that Don had made her go. Rose was so happy to see her. She was still struggling with her own demons over Mary's death. The trio decided right then and there that the upcoming Sunday night they would take off for the White Bird in the states and go dancing to celebrate Liz's healing.

Spring, when a young man's or woman's fancy turns to thoughts of love. That's exactly what was happening for Liz and Don, only not for each other. They were good friends, but the man/woman attraction that should be there wasn't there for them. So they frequented the White Bird often with Rose, each one looking for a mate. Liz's Carousel was screaming inside of her.

After weeks of looking Liz unlocked her front door to let Don in for a coffee before he went home. They were both frustrated and disappointed and lonely. Once again their search for a mate had been unfruitful. The house was quiet and seemed so empty. No kid noises. The kids and grandkids were all in bed sleeping. Don, seeing the sadness in Liz's eyes, put his arms around her to comfort her. He really did like her. It was too bad there was no chemistry. She looked up into his kind eyes and smiled a warm smile. He returned the warmth in his smile and slowly they gravitated toward one another ending in a desperate, clinging kiss. They started to rip each others clothes off as they rushed down the hall toward her bedroom.

"Well that was weird, like sleeping with my sister," Don sighed as he turned and threw his legs over the edge of the bed to pull on his trousers.

"You said it!" Liz agreed. "Like sleeping with my brother."

"Oh, well, no harm done. I don't have any diseases and as long as you don't we're good to go. You're taking birth control, of course?" He looked at a silent Liz.

"Well, no, but I can't get pregnant. I haven't used birth control in fifteen years."

"That's good cause we sure don't want to have a kid when we don't even love each other, I mean, other than as friends."

"Don't worry. It'll be fine," Liz reassured him. "You might as well stay. It's after three. No sense walking up the road at this hour. Never know what you'll run into."

"Sure the damage is done already anyway. Make me breakfast in the morning?"

"Sure."

Don pulled his pants back off and they rolled over away from each other and went sound asleep.

True to her word, Liz made her friend a hearty breakfast, and just as they were finishing up the phone rang. The kids had all gone out to enjoy the beautiful sunshine at the park with the grandkids so they weren't even aware that Don had stayed.

Liz ran to grab the phone as Don teased her about her cooking. She was laughing and happy as she picked up the cold black receiver.

"Hi, Liz. How are you doing? I've really missed you," the voice crooned on the other end of the line.

"Johnny!" Liz stated, surprised. She wasn't sure how she felt. It took the wind out of the pleasant banter she had been having with Don. Her defenses went up immediately. Johnny meant pain! And then there was Don. They weren't an item, but he was there. Liz raised her eyebrows at Don and he just smiled warmly back at her reassuring her that he was okay with it.

"I'd really like to see you," Johnny said.

"I don't know. I've got company right now."

"I could call you back."

"Yeah, okay. Give me fifteen minutes." Liz's heart had started to pound. He could still do it to her, but Don was her friend and he was there first and had been with her through all the worst.

"What'd he want?" Don asked as Liz hung up the phone.

"I don't know. He wants to see me, to talk to me."

"Well, I think you better go cause if you don't you'll always wonder. I gotta get home anyway and feed the cat. You know I'll be around if you need me. Just come and knock on my door."

Liz threw her arms around Don's neck and hugged him soundly. He *was* a good friend.

"Get outa here, seester," He said jokingly.

After Don left Liz flew around primping. She had to look good for this one. She didn't want him to know how much she had been suffering. She still had her pride. She showered really well trying to wash away her little tryst with Don. She certainly had no intentions of sleeping with Johnny, but she needed to feel clean to face him.

Johnny called back fifteen minutes later and made arrangements to meet with her at the Terra Nova restaurant. That would be a safe place. She couldn't take a chance on going to his apartment and she didn't want him at her place in case the kids came back.

"I'm so glad you came," Johnny whispered into her ear as he held the door open for her. She passed through under his extended arm and felt the magic that was always there for him as their bodies came into close proximity. They got settled in their seats and ordered coffee.

"So what did you want?" Liz asked.

"Just to see you. I've missed you terribly."

"So, where's Leah?"

"Leah got hooked up with Billy. They make quite a pair."

So Leah was out of the picture and now he was missing her. She wasn't about to fall for that old line. But she did! She was like putty in his hands. He sweet talked her right into a room upstairs and they flew to the moon and back on gossamer wings. It was as though no time had passed and Liz was ecstatic. Johnny promised to go with her for some marriage counseling at Bart's office. So once more they were an item.

Liz felt really bad that she had slept with two different men within a twenty four hour period. Her damn Carousel had her dancing at the end of a string like a puppet. Now, what had she done? Was she a slut or what? She reassured herself by the thought that at least no one was hurt by it. Don didn't seem to mind if she saw Johnny, and Johnny would never know. She'd make sure of that. Besides he'd said he wanted a divorce. How was she to know that he'd change his mind. Little did she know, though, that that twenty-four hour session would have more consequences than she could have ever believed possible.

Liz - The Lost Child

Chapter 11
Shattered Dreams

"So, Susan, what do you think? Could I do it?" Liz asked.

"I know you can do it. You're smart. You're compassionate, kind and patient. I know the dean at the college. I'll talk to her and see about getting you in. You would make a great psychologist."

"Six years, though! I'll be forty-four when I'm finished."

"Well, you'll be forty-four in six years whether you're a psychologist or not. Better to be a psychologist than what you are now, eh?" Susan said as she patted Liz on the back.

Susan, true to her word set it all up for Liz, and Liz went to the college and filled out an application. She was accepted right away and was to begin with the next semester in September taking Psych I and English I. She needed those two courses in order to get into University. She was so excited. No one in her family had ever gone to University. She had been a drunk, but she would be the first.

Well one thing that's going to have to happen is a weeding out at home. I can't possibly do another school term with all the hub bub in the apartment that I went through the last time. Liz thought to herself. It was a great idea, but the best laid plans of mice and men often go awry, and Liz found she just couldn't kick anyone out.

That is until all hell broke loose between Liz's girls and Lotus. Lotus had the idea from her cultural background that when Liz was out, Jimmy was next in line to be the authority in the house and as Jimmy's wife she came next. For months she had been trying to boss the girls around and they were having none of it. Things had worked themselves to a fever pitch and when Lotus purposely broke the big, purple balloon that Janie and Bonnie had been playfully tossing around, the girls went nuts on her. Lotus smacked Janie and of course Janie smacked her right back. In a total huff Lotus started slamming cupboard doors making a hell of a racket. Liz came running out of her room and yelled, "Okay, okay, that's it! Everyone over the age of twenty has to move out! I've had it!"

That was it. She'd done it. The only problem was Stacy took it that it meant her too. So she found herself a little apartment two doors over from Liz's for herself and Jason. Liz had never meant Stacy at all. She just wanted Lotus out of the house. So she ended up losing both her grandchildren in one foul swoop. That left Liz, Janie, and Bonnie at home. The girls were excited. They would each have a room of their own. But Liz wasn't exactly ecstatic. She was sad to see the babies go. But in the end the apartment was sure peaceful and she'd need it that way for her schooling. It would be a strenuous course.

Stacy landed a job up the gulch, also, which would make it easier than trekking over town to Boston Pizza. And she had other plans as well. She took several correspondence courses to upgrade and be in a position to take the Registered Nurse's course at Selkirk. So mother and daughter were going in the same direction.

Jimmy had secured a job cleaning offices. So he and Lotus found a cute little apartment in downtown Trail over a convenience store. They were happier being on their own, as was Stacy, so Liz was pleased that she had caused no grief between herself and her children. Anyway, it was time for them to leave the nest.

In the meantime, Johnny and Liz were once more an item. They dated, dined together, slept together, and loved each other once again. Liz was a little miffed, though, that Johnny hadn't kept his word about going to Bart for marriage counseling. But she was happy, so she didn't want to rock the boat.

Two months went by, and Liz had missed her period. "I can't be menopausal, can I?" She asked Val over the phone. Val had finished her schooling, and she had more time for Liz now, so the girls were in the habit of calling each other on a regular basis again.

"Stranger things have happened. You're not pregnant, are you?"

Liz laughed, "No! Of course not. I haven't used birth control in fifteen years and nothing's ever happened. I can't get pregnant, *I don't think*," Liz muttered. *Oh, God, I couldn't be. Not now!* she thought to herself.

The next day she went right to the drug store to get a pregnancy test. But to her dismay one of the women from A.A. was in the store.

She tried twice more to get the test from Shoppers and each time there was someone she knew in the store. She was embarrassed at her age, thirty-eight, to be buying a pregnancy test. Finally, on the fourth try she was able to purchase it without anyone that she knew seeing her.

Early the next morning she did the test and lo and behold there in the bottom of the tube was a little round black donut indicative of the fact that she was, indeed, pregnant.

"Oh, my God! What am I going to do now?" she muttered aloud. She estimated from the amount of time she'd missed that she had conceived in the very twenty-four hours she had been with Don and Johnny. She was devastated to say the least. *How could this happen? Fifteen years! I can't believe it."*

She quickly dressed and headed for the club without even putting on her makeup. She needed someone to talk to.

When she arrived at the club, Erica, the nurse, was washing coffee cups at the kitchen sink. "I'll tell you, the guys around here sure try my patience. I'm sick of all these cups hanging around dirty. Everyone is supposed to wash their own," she moaned. Then she looked up and noticed Liz's face. "What's the matter with you? I've never seen such a long face before and *no makeup?"*

Liz started to cry. "I-I-m pregnant," she wailed.

Erica grabbed the edge of the sink and sunk to her knees on the floor with laughter. "I'm sorry, I'm sorry," she said between titters. "I know it's not funny, but I just can't believe it. Are you sure?"

"Yes," Liz moaned. "I took the test this morning."

"Well that's too bad but, of course you'll have an abortion. I mean, you're mental if you don't. Single, trying to stay sober, not to mention your age. Everything's against you"

"I'm not single," Liz wailed.

"Well you might as well be. You're certainly on your own. I would give it some serious thought."

Liz felt totally deflated. Maybe Erica was right. After all she was a nurse and she had been sober a lot longer than Liz. It seemed the sensible thing to do. She wanted to go to University and a baby could stop all that. But abortion was such a serious decision. She had always been pro-life. What a pickle her Carousel had gotten her into this time. Of course, she never mentioned the rest of the problem. Like, would the real father please stand up.

She'd had a lot of things go wrong in her life, but she'd never been in such a conundrum. She had to see Bart and right now. She made an appointment with him, and it really didn't help. He confessed that his stand on the matter was that he was definitely anti-abortion. But it wasn't his place to advise her either way. He did help her in one way though. He said to talk to someone who'd had an abortion and ask them how they felt about it now.

Liz knew the perfect one to ask. She was of the same makeup as Liz and Liz knew she would get a good answer from Dar, her childhood friend from Ontario, who was now living in Edmonton. Liz called Dar immediately.

She hadn't talked to Dar in a long time. She had been to Edmonton only once to see Dar and her sister, Carol, after she sobered up. It was like no time had passed between them. And the same was true when she started to talk to Dar on the phone: it was like no time had passed. Liz told Dar her dilemma and Dar said to her, "Don't you do it Liz! I mean, it's up to you what you do, but you and I are so much alike I'm sure you'll be the same as me. I have nightmares all the time. I dream about looking for that baby and I can never find it, and I am devastated in my dream. I've never been able to rest ever since. I feel like a baby killer. Please don't do it!"

That was it. Liz's mind was made up. She would go through with it. She had contemplated adoption, but she knew she could never bring herself to give up her own child. She thought about Jason and how happy Stacy was that she had kept him in spite of all the hardship. So the only thing left for it was to tell Don *and* Johnny. She had to be totally honest for this to work.

First, she told Don. He agreed that after the child was born he would undergo a blood test. And then he proceeded to get totally drunk after three months of sobriety. Liz cared so much for him, but she couldn't tolerate his drinking. He was not a violent drunk like Lenny or Johnny. He would just cry in his beer and feel sorry for himself. He was not a mean man. Eventually, Liz talked him into going into treatment which he agreed to do. So he left immediately for six months in Maple Ridge.

And then there was Johnny. Liz told him she was pregnant, and then before she could say anymore he asked, "Are you sure it's mine? I mean, we were apart for quite awhile. How do I know you haven't seen someone else in the meantime."

Liz was so hurt. It was true there had been someone else. But there had been extenuating circumstances. He made it sound like she was some kind of slut or something. After that comment she just couldn't bring herself to tell him about Don. "Of course, it's yours!" she stated, angrily.

She wished with all her heart that the baby was Johnny's anyway. She liked Don very much, but she didn't love him, and she couldn't imagine having a child that wasn't conceived in love. So she set out in her own mind to fully believe the fetus growing inside her was her husband's.

Liz went to see Dr. Trent. She told her the whole story. She was more comfortable with Dr. Trent than she was with her own mother. She was not afraid of being judged. Of course, Dr. Trent didn't let her down. Whatever Liz wanted, Dr. Trent was willing to go along with, but the one thing she insisted on was that Liz go to Vancouver to have an amniocentesis because of her age. Women pregnant at her age were at high risk to have Down Syndrome babies.

Of course, Liz agreed that she should go, but she was terrified. One of the areas where she got major anxiety was traveling alone. She had no vehicle. She had never been to Vancouver. It was a huge city. She was terrified of the amniocentesis itself. Going alone was out of the question. Welfare would pay for her trip because it was for medical reasons, but they wouldn't pay for someone to go with her. Johnny just had to come, that was all there was to it. He'd have to find a way to get the money.

Liz approached him. She wouldn't be going for another couple of months. She would have to wait until she was four months pregnant because there was too much of a risk for the baby to have it done before then. Johnny very reluctantly agreed to go.

Then a week before it was time to go, he backed out. "I've applied to go to Selkirk to be a social worker. I've been accepted and I start Psych I and English I this September. I'm sorry, Liz. I know I said I'd see you through this, but I just can't. It's so important to me to get somewhere. I never thought I'd ever be able to go to college. Doors are opening for me, and I don't want to be tied down."

Liz was crushed! Once again he had broken her heart. How many times could he do it? She was to find out soon enough. She called Susan, in tears, as soon as she got home. And Susan and Val showed up on her doorstep with specialty coffees, Kleenex, and lots of sympathy.

"I can't live without him! How am I going to have a baby all by myself. I don't even know if I can still look after a baby. It's been so many years and I'm getting older. I definitely can't go to Vancouver by myself. I'll freak right out. And to top it all off, he's going to be in the same courses as me at Selkirk. Oh, I just won't be able to go. My dream is shattered. I couldn't possibly sit in the same class with him, pregnant, and him maybe flirting with other women. I would really crack up. Now I'm not even going to be able to go to University. I was so proud and I hoped my parents would be too. They won't even come to visit me." Liz rattled. She went on and on, and Susan and Val let her until she was finished. She had pouted and carried on like a distraught teenager. And that was exactly where she was at. When a person sobers up they are, emotionally, the age they were when they started to drink. There is no emotional growth as long as a person is drinking or drugging. NO PAIN, NO GAIN!

"There's always a solution to every problem. You've learned a lot about problem solving. If Plan A doesn't work you have to get a Plan B," Susan offered. "Don't think about school yet. That's in the future. Don't be in a big hurry to give it up and even if you decide to, there's always next year. As far as Johnny goes maybe you're better off without him. I know, I know, it doesn't seem that way right now, but if he isn't going to be responsible then what good is he? And as far as the baby goes, we'll all be there to help. It'll be like having one of our own. It'll be our A.A. baby."

"Hey and about the trip to Vancouver, I need a break from Jake. A vacation would go good right about now. Schooling's over and I haven't got a job yet so this could be quite an adventure," Dar chanted.

And an adventure, indeed, it turned out to be.

Chapter 12
Heather House

Liz and Val climbed aboard the 6:00 p.m. bus. The trip would be twelve hours long so they would arrive in Vancouver at 6:00 a.m. They would have to sleep on the bus *sitting up*. The bus was crowded so they couldn't each grab a seat by themselves to stretch out a little. But that didn't deter the girls from having a good time.

"Are you comfortable?" Liz asked.

"Jes!" Val answered. "That's Mexican. I can speak Mexican, you know," she said giggling.

"Arriva, arriva, undulay. Me too," Liz bantered back. Nothing could have spoiled their trip -- Val because she had a chance to get away from Jake for awhile, and Liz because she had someone to come with her. Val had taken the money out of her savings and was paying her own way. Liz was so grateful to her dear friend.

During the night they tossed and turned and barely slept at all. Never having rode a bus at night, they were unprepared to say the least and so by the time they reached Vancouver they were completely punch drunk. Plus they had no idea where they were going or how to get there. There wasn't much thought put into preparations for the trip. Nonetheless the girls were still in good spirits.

They fumbled around the bus depot for awhile until they decided the best plan of action would be to call a cab. Surely the cab driver would know where they were to go. They had been given instructions by Liz's social worker to go to the Heather Pavilion which was a form of hostel for people on low income. The cost was only $1.00 a night for a room and people with relatives in the Vancouver General Hospital on a long term basis could find shelter at a very low cost.

First of all the cab driver had no idea where Heather House was and so he drove them round and round, or perhaps he knew all along and wanted to run up their clock, because eventually he seemed to find his way there. The country bumpkins were none the wiser. They just giggled the whole time they were climbing out of the cab and getting their luggage out of the trunk. They were so tired that they couldn't stop laughing. Liz almost felt like she had when she used to smoke marijuana in her Lenny days. Not even the drizzling rain could dampen their spirits.

First of all, they had a problem finding a doorway into the building. The only door had no outside handle. They went round and round lugging their suitcases, until finally, Liz said, "Let's go to the main doors of the hospital and see if anyone knows how we get in."

"Okay," Val agreed, eager to find their room and lie down.

They walked all the way around the huge building and up the paved drive where the main doors were. Liz was astounded. It was pouring rain and yet the maintenance men were busy mowing the lawns, in yellow rain suits no less. She had never known anyone to cut the grass in the rain. She made a comment to Val about it and Val muttered, "I guess it rains here all the time, so they have to cut it sometime rain or not." That made sense to Liz.

"You're so smart," she muttered to Val and then the girls broke out in fits of laughter again.

"I saw a show one time where these scientists deliberately deprived these men of sleep to see what the effect would be. And after a certain number of hours without sleep they would become almost hysterical with laughter. Do you suppose that's what's happening to us?"

"I don't know," Val rolled her eyes and laughed. And the two just roared again.

Inside the hospital, a pert little nurse in a white uniform told them to go to the third floor and inquire about the tunnel that ran between the two buildings. Eureka, finally, some direction.

They got to the third floor, asked directions, and found the tunnel opening. Obviously work was in progress in this part of the building. Long sheets of clear plastic hung from the ceiling. They passed through the tunnel and walked onto the third floor of the adjacent building, carrying their heavy suitcases the whole way. They had to pack enough for at least five days, because Liz had to remain in Vancouver for three days to make sure that no bleeding or miscarriage occurred after the amniocentesis.

They skulked through the hallway looking into room after room of eerie emptiness. There was dust, spider webs and peeling paint everywhere. Old fashioned beds with striped mattresses, old prostheses and antiquated hospital equipment were strewn everywhere.

"I think we're in the wrong place. I am s-o-o-o tired," Val lamented.

"Look there's a door leading to a stairwell. Maybe we're just on the wrong floor. I'm sure the nurses wouldn't send us to the wrong building. Let's go down a floor and see what happens.

So they did. But when they went through the door that was it! They were fire doors and there was no way of getting back in through them once they closed. The two women were locked in a stairwell at 6:30 a.m. with heavy luggage, no sleep the night before, and no help in sight. Val went right to her knees and began to laugh hysterically. And Liz did the same.

When they finally got a grip on themselves Liz said, "Come on there has to be a way out of here. We'll just keep going down. And so they did until they reached the bottom floor where they were able to go out the door that had no outside door handle, exactly where they had started out from the cab. Then they started to laugh all over again. Liz thought she was going to pee her pants when finally a nice young man came along who showed them precisely where they needed to go.

They found their room number and were dismayed to find that there were two single hospital beds pushed tightly together and pushed tightly to the walls on either side. There was no way to walk between the beds so they had to climb up from the bottom which Liz did with great difficulty. There were, however, nice patio doors with a little balcony with plants growing in large pots which gave the place a little touch of class. Plus, there was a tiny fridge on the side of the room opposite to the beds and a small table and two chairs.

Shortly after climbing into the beds the two girls fell fast asleep for hours. On awakening they felt more refreshed and more sensible than they had when they arrived. After asking directions they found their way to the large cafeteria in the hospital building and had an excellent supper of mashed potatoes, gravy, delicious meatloaf and green beans in a butter sauce topped off with apple pie and ice cream. They were definitely revived.

They also found their way to a hospital meeting after they saw a notice hanging in the front lobby. Everyone in the room greeted them with warmth and kindness which was so appealing being as they felt so alone and so far from home. They discovered that, indeed, the warm A.A. spirit had the same intensity here as it did in their home group, and they were grateful.

They met an older lady with sandy brown hair, bright red lipstick and a bright green dress that covered her slightly rounded body. Liz knew instantly that there was something not quite right with the woman, perhaps too many brain cells destroyed, but she was kind, nonetheless. She insisted that the two young women come on a tour of Vancouver with her, come to her house for supper, and then come to a meeting at the huge city Alano Club the day after Liz's amniocentesis, if she was feeling well enough. The girls agreed, feeling a little apprehensive.

That night the girls retired in their tiny cramped room after showering and brushing their teeth in the large common bathroom. Liz fell asleep instantly even though she had slept most of the day. The trip, the pregnancy and the early morning antics had exhausted her. But Val was unable to sleep, fortunately, because she was awake when the fire alarm went off. Liz was so exhausted she slept through the whole thing and Val had a frightful time trying to wake her up. "Come on, Liz. You've got to get up. Don't you hear that alarm clanging? What's the matter with you. I can see smoke coming up all around the windows," Val cried with frustration.

Liz just couldn't wake up. "Can't you go ahead and come back for me later? Jus let me sleep a little longer," she slurred. "Maybe it's jus a practice. Can you go and find out?

Pl-e-e-e-a-se," Liz moaned.

"No, get up, get up." Val pulled on her friend until she almost pulled her right onto the floor. Finally Liz stirred and she could hear the clanging loud and clear.

"Oh, my God. Oh, my God. There really is a fire." Liz cried and jumped up and ran to the hallway where everyone had congregated in their pyjamas and nightgowns waiting for further instructions.

"Just stay put until we find out what's going on! Leave your luggage," A maintenance man in a forest green uniform hollered.

"We don't want to start a panic. I am in contact with the floors below where all the smoke is coming from."

After standing in the hallway chatting to other guests for a half hour or so, they were told that they could return to their rooms. The fire department had come and everything was under control. A large steam pipe had burst on the floor below and the smoke they had seen was actually very thick steam, but because of the heat it had set off the alarm and the sprinkler systems.

Liz didn't have too much trouble getting back to sleep, but Val was awake for hours. She found her way to the lounge where several people who also had difficulty getting back to sleep were visiting with each other. Val, always very congenial, made some good friends that night.

The next morning Liz was totally rested and Val wasn't too bad herself. She had finally been able to sleep after talking things over with her new found friends. Liz was rested, but she was terrified. She was scheduled for her amniocentesis at 10:00 a.m. They got dressed and found their way to the new wing where the test was to be conducted.

Liz was getting more skittish by the moment. First she was interviewed by a kindly nurse who asked all kinds of embarrassing questions and Liz had to disclose the fact that she wasn't sure who the father was. So they took information on both Don and Johnny just in case. She was also asked if she'd like to know the sex of her unborn child. She hesitated for only a second and then answered quickly, "Yes! Yes, I would." She would have liked to have another boy. She only had one and three girls. But in the end she didn't really care as long as the baby was healthy.

Then she was directed to change into a skimpy hospital gown for the test. She waited around getting more anxious by the moment. She didn't know much about the test except that the needle was huge, maybe eight inches long, and that it was going to be stuck through her stomach into her womb in order to suction out some of the amniotic fluid so they could test to see if the baby had all the right chromosomes and was normal and healthy. She also knew there would be no anesthetic, local or otherwise, and she was scared. But Val stayed with her through the whole procedure, holding her hand.

And it wasn't so bad after all. The only discomfort Liz felt was when they drew the fluid out. It felt as though they were pulling a thick string out through her stomach. A very strange sensation, but not painful in the least. But the best was to follow. The nurses did a sound scan immediately afterward to make sure the baby was okay. Liz and Val watched with amazement as a little tiny baby stretched her arms up over her head and flexed her whole body pushing her stomach out like a contented kitten. Liz's eyes filled with tears. How could she possibly have considered an abortion. Thank God she hadn't listened to Erica. There were going to be tough times ahead, but God had given her another chance. A chance to do what was right with this child. Her sober baby!

Later Val called Jake to let him know how things were going. Liz stood in the hallway by the phone booth watching Val with excitement. "Tell him about the sound scan, tell him about the sound scan, oh, and the stretch," Liz mouthed to Val while stretching her hands over her head in mimic of what her baby had done. She was so excited she couldn't keep the grin off her face. She was amazed at the new technology. There had never been such a thing when she'd had her other kids.

Liz rested in the common room with Val and her new friends after a good lunch. They bantered back and forth with patients and visitors and Liz felt warm and contented. The worst was over and she'd had a look at her new off spring making the situation more real to her. She could hardly wait to hold the baby in her arms.

She was jarred out of her pleasant thoughts by Val laughing uproariously. A young man, Jerry, who was nicely healing from the loss of his left leg had just asked Val if she knew anyone who had lost a right leg so they could share the cost of footwear. And so went the afternoon with pleasant kibitzing around. Val had an excellent sense of humor and Liz was amazed at how easily Val made friends. She was also amazed at how these people rallied round each other when they were suffering so much. There was a definite camaraderie amidst their pain.

The next day Liz was feeling fit as a fiddle so when the older lady, Marge, that they had met at the hospital A.A. meeting came to pick them up they were more than willing to see the big city sights.

First they made a brief stop at the Queen Elizabeth Park. Liz was thrilled with the beautiful multi-colored gardens with many different varieties of flowers, the lush emerald green lawns, the fountains, the conservatory and the huge, bright multi-colored parrots that people were having their pictures taken with. The birds were royal blue, scarlet red and mustard yellow and captivatingly beautiful. Marge talked Liz and Val into getting their picture taken by the young Mexican man who owned the parrots, and insisted on paying.

Then they traveled through the city past Science World with the world's largest OMNIMAX dome theater situated on top of the building looking for all its worth like a space satellite. and then they passed by B.C. Place with its huge, white dome which looked like a giant mushroom. Liz was agog with all the sights. Next they drove past the Imax theater on the water front. Liz thought it looked like a giant ship with ten huge white sails.

Of course it wouldn't be right to tour Vancouver without visiting Stanley Park with its hordes of bright pink flamingos, pretty faced otters, killer whales and white whales. Liz watched in wonder as the artists, lined all along the foot paths, sketched picture perfect images of their subjects within minutes. Marge insisted on buying their lunch and then they continued to tour.

The girls felt so indebted to Marge for all she had done, and yet they couldn't help but feel embarrassed when, in a large London Drug Store, Marge grabbed a ball cap off the shelf and a baseball. She put the cap on sideways, crossed her eyes, and yelled batter up at the top of her lungs drawing the attention of all the other patrons. Liz and Val both wanted to crawl in a hole.

And for the rest of the day wherever they browsed, Marge insisted on buying and paying for whatever the girls mentioned that they liked. They tried to stop Marge, but she would only insist all the harder. The girls were beginning to feel a little uncomfortable. When out of earshot Val whispered to Liz, "We can't let her keep doing this. I feel cheap."

"I know," Liz whispered back, "But how do we stop her. She is so persistent."

"I don't know let's tell her we've had enough and head back."

"Sounds like a plan."

So they did, but Marge insisted that they come to her house for supper. She wouldn't take no for an answer. Liz was getting tired and really wanted to head back to Heather House, but there was just no stopping this woman. She was driven.

When they arrived at Marge's house they were appalled at the disarray. There was junk piled everywhere. Then Marge reached into the fridge and brought out a large precooked ham. She cut open the plastic package and instantly the room was filled with the most putrid odor. Liz looked at Val and rolled her eyes. Then she went over to the counter where Marge stood looking at the ham.

"What's the date on the label of that ham?" Liz inquired.

"Oh, I don't know," Marge answered, "but I'm sure it's fine."

Liz screwed up her nose. She knew it *wasn't* fine without even looking at the label, but she didn't want to offend Marge. If Liz could just get her to look at the date herself, Liz wouldn't feel so bad. But Marge wouldn't take the bait so Liz did some mouth-breathing and grabbed the package herself. The expiration date on the package read May 15, 1983 and it was July already. Liz pointed that fact out to Marge and finally convinced her to throw it out.

"I'll just have to find something else then. Oh, I know, I've got the perfect thing. It's a surprise. I can't tell you what it is."

Marge took some strange looking meat out of the fridge and proceeded to make sandwiches out of it. When she was finished she placed them on the table for the girls to eat and proceeded to leave the room.

"Where are you going? Aren't you going to eat? Exactly what's in those sandwiches?" Val asked.

"I'm going to the bathroom to wash up and change for the meeting. I'm not really hungry. Just eat the sandwiches and tell me if you can guess what's in them," Marge answered grinning and promptly left the room.

"Oh, my God! Here we go again. Remember the lady with the soup? I'm not eating any of these sandwiches. Are you?"

"Are you kidding," Liz laughed, "But what are we going to do with them?"

"I don't know, but I'm not eating them. Quick grab some of that Saran Wrap and I'll shove them all in my bag."

Liz could hardly contain herself as Val pulled a face and stuck all the sandwiches in her over-sized red bag.

"Did you enjoy the sandwiches?" Marge asked as she came out of the bathroom all prepared to go.

"Oh, yes," the girls answered simultaneously.

After the meeting Marge dropped the girls off at the Heather House and the girls just rolled around their beds laughing uncontrollably.

"I'm so hungry," Liz moaned. "I'm weak."

"Me too. There's always the sandwiches," Val roared.

"Not on your life. I wonder what's in them."

"Probably rattle snake," Val laughed.

"What are we going to do with them? There isn't even a garbage can in here and we have to leave tomorrow morning," Liz asked.

"I don't know, but I'm sure not carrying them back to Trail with us. I know I'll bury them in the flower pots on the balcony. Probably be good for the plants."

Liz gut roared as Val went out on the balcony with her big red bag and a large spoon.

The trip home was a little easier as they took the day bus. But the next few weeks were not easy for Liz as she waited anxiously to hear from the hospital. Finally after two weeks she got the good news. The baby's fine, and it's a Girl! Liz sobbed her heart out with relief. Now all she had to do was get through the next five months. Easier said than done!

Chapter 13
Baby Blue

Pink is for girls and blue is for boys. Liz was having a girl and she should have been in the pink, but instead she was very blue. She was missing Johnny something terrible. The old emptiness had wrapped itself around her like a cloak and she was feeling hollow again. The Carousel couldn't even make its turn with her in a pregnant state so, after fighting her feelings with all her might, she finally caved in and phoned Johnny.

"Hi," she said, shyly.

"Hi," he answered sounding disappointed.

"Were you expecting someone else?" Liz asked.

"No, no, no one," he stuttered.

"Well, I know you don't want to get into anything again, but the club is having a family picnic tomorrow and, seeing as *we* are pregnant I thought maybe you might like to go with me. I mean, that is, if you planned to go." Liz still wasn't sure whose baby she was having, but she hoped with all her heart it was Johnny's because she still loved him and after all they were married. She made herself believe he was the father.

"Uh, yeah, I'm going, but there's a problem," he faltered.

"Oh, what's that?"

"Well, Billy dumped Leah and she is feeling like drinking, and I promised I would go to the picnic with her cause she doesn't want to be alone."

"What about me? What about my feelings? I don't want to be alone either," Liz cried.

"Liz you know I can't get involved right now. I'm just friends with Leah. There's no pressure there."

"Oh, sure I'll believe you where thousands wouldn't," Liz wailed and slammed down the phone. Her heart was broken, not to mention the humiliation of actually calling him, and then being so cruelly turned down.

She thought she was going to lose her mind with the anger she felt. Talk about wanting a drink! There was only one thing to do, call Susan. So she did.

"I can't go," Liz wailed in Susan's ear.

"You have to go," Susan replied. "Don't give him the satisfaction. Besides you need to be there with all your friends. You need all the support you can get right now."

"Oh, Susan, I don't know. It will be so hard to watch him with Leah. She is so pretty and so nicely built and I am a big fat pig right now."

"Don't talk like that. You are every bit as pretty as Leah. Besides there's something special about a pregnant woman, kinda like a beautiful ship in full sail. You put on all your makeup, do that gorgeous chestnut hair in a nice do, wear your best maternity top and pants, and stick your nose up in the air at the two of them. I'll be there to pick you up at nine o'clock in the morning, so be ready!"

Liz bathed and washed her hair that night and laid out a blue gingham maternity top that made her look fresh and young. She also laid out a nice pair of maternity jeans along with a cute straw hat that made her look so feminine. Then she went to bed.

Two hours later she was still tossing and turning. Then two more hours. She glanced at the digital alarm clock -- 3:00 a.m. She was so tired, but no way could she sleep. She kept picturing Johnny and Leah together. Then she'd start to cry. She sobbed and sobbed and looked at the clock again -- 4:30 a.m. *I've got to stop thinking about them. I've got to get some sleep if I'm going to look good tomorrow. Oh, I think Susan is wrong. I can't go and face them. I'm not strong enough.* She tried desperately to change her thoughts and finally settled on thinking about how many times she'd moved over the years.

In Scarborough until 13, then Bradford. Then Toronto with Brian. Then back to Bradford when Brian went to prison. Several moves there, then to Beeton. On and on and on she went until, to her dismay, she discovered that she had actually moved twenty-two times in twenty-one years and that certainly didn't make her feel any better. How unsettled her life had been. But the thoughts did finally lull her off to sleep at 6:30 a.m.

Then an hour later the alarm went off screeching through her system like finger nails down a black board.

"Come on, Mom," Janie chanted. "Stacy and Jimmy will soon be here with Jason and Jasmine for the picnic. Bonnie and I have had breakfast already. So let's get moving."

Liz moaned, "I don't think I can go. I only got an hour's sleep."

"Come on, Mom, you gotta go. Susan is taking her gang out and then coming back to pick us all up. It'll be so much fun with Jason and Jasmine. There'll be kid's races and horseshoes for the guys and lots and lots of food. You gotta come."

Liz knew she had to go, Janie was right. She sure didn't feel very pretty, though. But by the time she had breakfast, put on her makeup, did her hair and got dressed, she realized Susan was right. She was as beautiful as a ship in full sail. She looked so healthy. Her cheeks were rosy. The pregnancy had actually done her the world of good. And a really easy pregnancy it turned out to be, for which she thanked her lucky stars because her life sure wasn't.

Liz was grateful that they all arrived at the picnic before Johnny and Leah. She needed to compose herself. When they finally did arrive Liz noticed that Johnny was dressed to the nines in a new cream colored silk shirt with pleats down the front and new black strides. He looked wonderful and Liz's heart did a flip. But the women all hustled to surround Liz and keep her busy fixing food. Johnny and Leah didn't stay very long because most of the women were very cool to her. Liz was relieved when they left. Now she could enjoy the day with her family. She tried. She really tried, but her heart was breaking once again.

The dry, hot month of July quickly turned into August, and Liz was suffering terribly with the heat. Trail was like an inferno. The blazing sun hit the rocky mountains all around and held the torrid heat in making Trail, in the bottom of the valley seem like a bake oven. Not only that she had to undergo yet another heartbreak. Lotus took off with little Jasmine and left Jimmy lock, stock, and barrel. They had no idea where she had gone. It seemed that once she got permission to legally stay in the country, she was through with all of them and made no bones about it.

Jimmy, heartbroken with the loss, took right off as well and hitchhiked to Ontario. Liz was devastated. And then to top it all off Bonnie came home with the news that she was pregnant with Darren's baby.

When Liz first came to Trail, she had walked the streets browsing all the nicely decorated shop windows. She had stopped in front of a bridal shop where several stunning white gowns were displayed. She dreamed of seeing her beautiful daughters walk down the aisle in one of those dresses. And a dream it was! How could she afford gowns or weddings like that. She didn't even have a job and now she was pregnant, had two grandchildren and another one on the way. Her life was a joke!

When she was young she'd had two encounters with palm readers who had both absolutely refused to read her palm. Now she knew why. Her life was going to be too ugly and painful for anyone to foretell.

And then to top it all off her best friend, Val, called with more bad news.

"That son of a bitch, Jake, cheated on me. With my sister-in-law no less. My *own* brother's wife. All the years I fought my desires to stay faithful to him and he up and cheats on me. If I'd known that I woulda went after that George Clark in Castlegar. I sure had the hots for him, but oh, no, I had to be Mrs. Faithful. Well, I sure fixed them. I beat the crap out of her and I'm moving out."

"Oh, wow, that's too bad. Where are you moving to, Trail, I hope?" Liz asked.

"No, I finally landed a job as a geriatric care aide worker in Nelson. I was going to travel back and forth, but now I might as well move there. No way I'm staying with Jake."

"Oh, man, I'm gonna miss you!" Liz lamented.

"I know, I'm gonna miss you too, but I'll keep in touch. Of course we won't be able to be on the phone for five hours any more. It's long distance," Val laughed, "But I'll definitely keep in touch, cause I love you, my friend. I don't know how I would have stayed sober without you."

"Yeah, me too," Liz said.

Liz was upset that Val was leaving, but nothing is ever all bad and on the upside at least she still had Rose. Rose had promised faithfully to stand by her and be her coach through the birthing, and Liz was relieved she had. She couldn't imagine having another baby alone, especially under the circumstances.

Also on the upside, Stacy applied at Selkirk College for the Registered Nurse's course and was accepted without a problem. She had always been a Grade A excellent student. She would be starting in September. Liz was very proud of her. At least one of the family was going to have a professional career.

Then in October Liz decided to take pre-natal classes to help keep her mind occupied. There was nothing like that available when she'd had her other children, and she wanted to take advantage of all she could. She was older now and a little more in control and she was going to use every device available to make this a pleasant birthing.

At first she felt a little uncomfortable because Rose was unable to accompany her to the classes, and she was the only single parent amongst so many happy couples. Liz was lonely to start with, that horrible emptiness was plaguing her again, and there was absolutely no way for her Carousel to turn now. When the class was shown a film of happy couples giving birth, crystal streams poured down Liz's cheeks as she wept silently in the darkened room. On the bright side, though, she met a lot of really nice people who she would meet again and again over the years to happily discuss the progress of their offspring. And there was one woman that she especially liked who would turn out to be a very good friend in years to come.

Liz's life was never without surprises, though, so she wasn't too dumbfounded to hear from Brian O'Shea, her first husband, the father of her first three children. She figured his guilt must have caught up with him because, after all these years, he wanted to meet his children. Bonnie and Stacy refused the offer of plane tickets to fly to Texas to see him. After all, Stacy was one year old and Bonnie was just a new born when he left Liz so many years ago. And they didn't want to fly that far away from home to visit someone they didn't know. Disappointed the girls didn't want to go, he asked about Jimmy, and Liz told him Jimmy had gone back to Ontario and that he could get in touch with her sister, Jane, in Bradford. Perhaps she might know where he was. Little did Liz know Jimmy was on skid row in Toronto, and that Brian's phone call would end up hauling him out of that mess. Finally, he would be good for something.

And another high spot in Liz's life at that time was her introduction to two new A.A. members, Roy and Earl -- The Movers.

Brian & Liz

Chapter 14
The Movers

Roy was the most jolly person Liz had ever met. He had the bluest, kindest eyes she'd ever seen. He wasn't much taller than Liz, and he had a stomach just like hers, at seven months pregnant. He would rub her stomach and then rub his and say, "So when are *you* due?"

And Earl was the opposite of Roy. He was tall and thin with red hair. But he also had kind blue eyes. Liz was reminded of Laurel and Hardy, but these two guys were not dumb by any means. They had created a moving team with their two trucks to keep themselves busy while they were trying to stay sober. Their motivation was to help any women in A.A. who had no money and needed to move in a hurry. There was always lots of that going on.

Because of the sadness in Liz's life and because the apartment reminded her so much of Johnny, she decided before she got any bigger that she'd like to engage Roy and Earl's services and move right out of the gulch -- her twenty-third move!

She rented a house on Topping Street in West Trail in the shadow of the mountain. The backyard was a stone wall covered in moss, it was actually the side of the mountain, but the large windowed porch in the front had a view that was stupendous. She could see all of Trail. She was half way up the side of a mountain! The road in front of the house was carved out of the mountain and standing on the road she was level with the roof tops of the houses on the mountain side below. She could see all of East Trail as well as downtown and the Columbia River snaked its way from one side of the city to the other with dark green, white capped water. And to her left she could see all of the smelter, appearing like a huge ship with masts, overlooking the city.

The house itself was a beauty. A little different than the large apartment, but with only she and Janie left at home the two bedrooms were enough. Bonnie and Darren had found an apartment in West

Trail as well. Liz wasn't exactly happy about that move, but Bonnie was as head strong and determined as Liz herself was.

Liz's newfound house was an older model, but it had brilliant hardwood floors throughout that you could see your face in. Plus, there was a huge stone fireplace in the living room, its best feature. Not to mention the huge windowed porch off the living room which Liz would be able to sit out in the nicer weather and enjoy the view. She was happy. This would be a new beginning.

The day they moved in Liz couldn't have been in a better mood. Roy and Earl were always goofing around and while hauling the couch up the back stairs they placed all the legs on top of it. One of the legs slowly spiraled and rolled off. It bounced from step to step as Roy hollered, "Oh, no!" And then it bounced from the bottom step to the road where it rotated until it dropped right down a huge drain. Roy ran as fast as he could, belly flopping in the wind, trying to catch it and when he looked down the drain, he slapped himself on the forehead and hollered, "Sorry, the drain runs right down underground to the river.

Well, Liz couldn't help but laugh at the looks on the faces of the two movers. How could she be mad at them? They were so lovable. They were the brothers she had always wanted to have. She would just have to prop the corner of the couch up with books. She'd done that before in her lifetime.

After she got all moved in Janie and she took advantage of the windowed porch by filling it with plants so that it looked like a jungle. Janie definitely had a green thumb and so the plants thrived. For the most part Liz was satisfied with the move. There were only two drawbacks. The first being there was no washer and dryer so back to using the Laundromat or washing clothes in the bath tub. She ended up doing just that rather than trucking down the big hill and back up with bags of laundry. Twenty years had gone by and she was still pregnant and still washing clothes in the bathtub. Would anything ever change? The second drawback was that she could see all over Trail, which in itself wasn't bad, but she discovered that she was living right above Riverside Avenue and Johnny's apartment. She could see all the comings and goings at his place as plain as day. And a lot of comings and goings there proved to be -- young students, both male and female, from the college gathering at Johnny's with tons of books to study. It seemed he was very popular. Liz was furious that he was going to the college where she was supposed to be going while she was getting larger and larger and more out of shape by the day.

All was not lost, though, because Roy and Earl were as faithful as any brothers could be and were constantly taking her out to dinner or to Nelson on shopping sprees. They tried to cheer her up. Like two expectant fathers they fussed over her constantly. She was so grateful for their attention. She loved them both dearly.

Life went on in this pleasant way. Then Liz was surprised one day when Janie came to her wanting some answers about her father. Liz supposed that because Brian had gotten in touch with the other girls it had started Janie thinking. Where was Norm? Liz didn't even know. Then she remembered that Carol, her childhood friend in Edmonton still kept in touch with Mandy, Norm's sister. She hoped that she could get Mandy's phone number from Carol and that Mandy would know where Norm was. She had never berated her children's fathers in front of them. After all, even though they had not treated Liz fairly the men were still the kid's dads. And Liz was always fair, if nothing else. She did get the number from Carol and contacted Mandy. She got Norm's number and called him for Janie. Janie was thrilled. Finally, a father she could get to know. Norm hadn't treated Liz very well, but he had always been good to the kids so Liz knew, instinctively, he would be good to Janie, and he was. It was a new beginning for Janie and Norm that was to continue for the rest of Norm's life. Norm had remarried and his new wife had left him as well and he was now living in camper in a camp ground by himself and he was very lonely. So he was thrilled to hear from Janie as well.

Not only was Janie happier, but Liz's heart soared when Bonnie approached her and asked if she would stand up for her at her wedding. It wasn't so much the standing up for Bonnie that had made Liz's heart soar, it was Bonnie's words. "After all", she'd stated, "you're not my mom, you're my best friend and it's your best friend that should be your bride's maid." Some things were finally looking up for Liz's little family.

After the marriage license was procured off they all went to the court house in Rossland. Mother and daughter, both pregnant, at the wedding! Bonnie wore a beautiful, turquoise linen suit with a turquoise, grey, and white silk blouse. With her copper hair gleaming she was a beauty. And of course Darren with his dark skin and black hair was handsome in a black suit and white shirt with a cherry red tie. When the vows were said, and the papers were signed they all drove down the Rossland hill in Darren's brand new, black Trans Am with the golden eagle spread across the hood. Darren had done very well for himself as a logger so Liz was not worried about Bonnie being taken care of.

After the wedding Liz was feeling melancholy so she tried once again to invite her parents , John and Alicia, to come and see her new home. To her delight they finally said yes! She was two years sober and it appeared as though they were going to trust her again. Liz was pleased.

They came the next week and Liz stood with her papa in the windowed porch showing him the sky as the sun set over the city. The sky was deep violet as darkness crept towards the west and the lights of the city were already twinkling like diamonds against the purple hue.

"I guess it's true what they say," John stated, "Every place has it's own beauty. This is enchanting."

Liz was more than pleased, she was ecstatic. She had shown her papa something that he was pleased with. That hadn't happened in years. Maybe there was hope to mend the fences and once again find her papa's love that she had lost so many years ago, the loss that had started the crazy Carousel on its wild turning that never seemed to stop. But her pleasure was soon brought to an abrupt halt.

"So here you are pregnant again and no father to be seen," Alicia lamented. "I told you not to get mixed up with A.A. men. They,re all alcoholics."

"Oh, mama, what do you think *I* am?" Liz answered, exasperated. "If all the men felt that way, who would want *me?*"

"That's true, Alicia. Leave the girl alone," John spoke up.

Liz's ears perked right up. She had never heard her papa talk to her mama that way. And what he said next really took her by surprise.

"So how do you do your laundry?"

"Oh, I wash the clothes in the bathtub."

"That's not good in your condition. Mother, I think we better order this girl a new washer."

"Well, I-I-I don't know. Oh, go ahead do what you want."

Liz was flabbergasted. Papa was coming around. She wanted to hug him, but as she approached he put his hand up. There was still a wall that couldn't be climbed, yet, but she was grateful nonetheless.

Within two weeks a brand new, bright-white, spin dry washer was delivered to her door from Sears. It was the first new appliance she'd ever had!

Then on December 13th, 1983 Earl phoned to ask her if she would go to the mall with him and help him pick out two gifts for his nieces, eight and seven years old. She told Earl she'd be honored to and they bantered back and forth over the phone in their usual manner until Liz let out a shriek.

"Oh, my God! I'm not going anywhere with you Earl! My water just broke!"

Norm

Chapter 15
A Second Miracle

"Oh, my God! And you're all by yourself?" Earl asked.

"Yes, but don't worry. I'll call the club, surely someone will be there to help me. By the time you get here from Castlegar, it might be all over."

"Yeah, that's true. Well, I'll let you go so you can call somebody. Make sure you call right away."

"I will, and remember don't worry. It's not like it's my first." Liz answered. She hung up the phone and looked down at her burgundy, velvet robe. It was just soaked right through. Nothing she could do about that, so she dialed the club and right away Beulah answered. Beulah was a fairly new member who was dating Francis, the club janitor.

"Hi, Beulah. This is Liz. Who all is at the club?"

"I'm here by myself. Francis went to the store and no one else is here right now," Beulah answered. "Why what do you need? Oh my God, you're not going to have the baby are you?"

"Yeah, my water just broke. Ew, what am I going to do?"

"Hold on, the door's opening. Hey, Shelly, can you take me up to Liz's? Her water just broke."

"Sure," Shelly answered. "We're outa here."

"Hang in there, Liz. We're on the way." Beulah yelled into the phone, and then threw the black receiver in the cradle, grabbed her coat and took off on the fly.

Shelly, a fairly new and hard-nosed member who Liz didn't much care for and Beulah were at Liz's in minutes. It wasn't so much that Liz didn't care about Shelly, she was terrified of the anger that just oozed out of Shelly's pores. Nonetheless, Liz was ever grateful to the angry woman's quick response. Beulah wandered behind with a string mop while Liz went from room to room gathering up things she'd need for the trip to the hospital. Then Liz disappeared into the bathroom to get dressed.

Finally, after what seemed like an eternity to Beulah, all three took right off for the hospital in Shelly's old beater. Liz had tried to call Rose, but she wasn't home. The baby wasn't due until December 31st. She was to be a New Year's baby so Rose wasn't expecting a hospital trip that quick.

They drove down Topping to Oak and then down Oak to Riverside to cross the old bridge instead of going across the new bridge, which led directly to the hospital. They hoped to find Rose who was now living on Second Avenue in East Trail. But the detour proved to be a big mistake. As they were passing by the house where Johnny lived, Liz spotted him across the road in the Elks parking lot talking to a pretty blonde girl, not Leah, a girl Liz had never seen before, and they were doing a lot more than talking. They were making goo goo eyes at each other, and then Johnny leaned over and kissed the girl soundly on the lips. Then the girl got into a small white sports car.

"Hey, there's Johnny," Beulah cried. "Do you want to stop and tell him about the baby?" she asked and then realized her mistake as she watched the kiss.

"Screw the bastard, ouch!" Liz wailed as a pain gripped her mid section. She was too angry and too caught up in the pain to cry.

They arrived at noon at the hospital. Liz was given a hospital gown to don, an inspection afterwards, and the usual enema, all in that order. Shortly after, Rose arrived apologizing profusely.

"Sorry, sorry, Harry and I were out getting a Christmas tree for my place." Rose had a new beau. Harry was in the army and Rose was totally enthralled with him. Liz was happy for her, but more happy that she was finally there. So far not too much had happened. She'd had some light labour, but shortly after Rose arrived the labour started in ernest.

Liz was so glad she'd had the pre-natal classes. She was more than prepared. She practiced the breathing techniques and also found a focus point. She watched the big round black clock with the white face on the wall across from her bed. She focused on the second hand and realized the pains only lasted about a minute, so that wasn't so bad. She knew that once the second hand reached the top again they would start to subside. She was very proud of herself for not panicking and for taking control of the pain. Also she had read the book The Experience of Childbirth by Sheila Kitzinger which had a section about childbirth without fear. It said that if a woman could relax there would be far less pain. She was trying her best to do that and focusing on the clock was helping her. Plus Rose kept her in stitches in between pains so the time went quite quickly.

The nurse came in for another check. "Four centimeters," she cried. It won't be long now.

Liz was pleased. This birthing was going to be a piece of cake. -- It was supposed to be a piece of cake, but by supper time and another inspection nothing more had happened.

Rose begged off for supper, and Liz was sorry to see her go, but she knew Rose needed to keep up her strength in order to help her. The labour continued with much more intensity and still nothing was happening. Something was wrong! The nurse called for Dr. Trent, who came right away. She ordered an ultra sound.

"Liz, there seems to be a problem. The baby is facing the wrong way."

"Oh, no, you mean she's breech?"

"No, thank goodness. It's just that her face is down coming into the birth canal instead of facing up. She can't be born that way. Her neck would be bent up backwards."

"What can we do."

"I'd like to wait and see if she'll turn herself. She seems to be trying to. But in the meantime I'm going to give you some Demerol for the pain. It could be a long drawn out procedure and you need some rest."

"I didn't want to have any drugs. I wanted to go au naturel, but I don't think I can carry on much longer."

A long drawn out procedure it turned out to be. Liz was in severe labour all night with no rest and by the next day she was totally exhausted, and out of control. She could no longer focus or think straight. She got very cranky with Rose and felt just awful, but she couldn't seem to help herself.

"Okay," Rose stated firmly. "Hold onto my hands tightly and focus on my eyes. Liz put both of her hands into Rose's and totally focused on her deep brown doe eyes. It was like a miracle. She could actually feel energy going from Rose's eyes into hers and filling her whole body. Her strength was renewed and she was able to go on a little longer. Rose kept passing energy to her all through the day and then by about 4:00 p.m. Dr. Trent said the baby had turned and they could go to the delivery room.

Rose, in a green hospital gown, and a nurse in a turquoise silk pant suit helped Liz to stand and they walked her to the delivery room in the hopes that the walk would speed the delivery.

Once in the delivery room she climbed up onto the table in a semi-sitting position with her legs in stirrups, no leather straps to bind her this time.

After about an hour of intense labour and pushing, the baby was finally delivered. Liz looked down and was totally dismayed. The baby was BLACK! How could that be? She had never been with a black man in her life. Then she shook her head and tried to clear her eyes that were foggy from lack of sleep. It was 4:50 p.m. She had been in labour for 28 hours. As she focused better she realized the baby wasn't black she was the deepest shade of purple so close to black and it frightened her near to death.

"What's wrong? What's wrong?" Liz cried.

"She's not breathing! She's not breathing!" Dr. Trent yelled. "Give her here to me, quick!"

Dr. Trent worked on the little purple bundle for ten full minutes with no results. First she tried a plastic apparatus for mouth to mouth and then she threw it and tried plain old mouth to mouth. Finally she hollered, "Breathe, damn it! Breathe!"

Still nothing happened, so she gathered the wee bundle in her arms and ran. "Sorry, Liz you can't see your baby. We're going to put her in an incubator."

One of the nurses and Dr. Trent ran out of the room leaving Liz alone with Rose and one other nurse. The afterbirth had been delivered with the help of one of the nurses and Liz was sitting up straight. Crystal streams left silver tracks down her face as she prayed out loud. "Please, God, I know I've been bad. I've never gone to church or anything, but please, please let my little girl live. I know I thought about abortion and I'm sorry. I'll do everything in my power to stay sober and take really good care of her, if you'll just give me a chance. Oh, please God, please." Then she wailed like a banshee.

Rose was holding Liz and rocking her back and forth when Dr. Trent burst through the door. "I think we've got her! She's breathing with the respirator and her colour is looking much better. We'll have to leave her in the incubator and watch her closely, but I think she's going to be okay. Dr. Trent looked frazzled as she came to inspect Liz to make sure everything was alright.

Liz was cleaned up and moved to a room with four other women. She was sleeping soundly when her arm was gently patted. She opened her eyes and couldn't focus. She couldn't figure out who was there. She was seeing double. She shook her head and finally her eyes cleared and there was Janie with a grin like a Cheshire cat. She's beautiful, mom. I just saw her through the nursery window. Liz was so pleased with Janie. She would share this child with her. Never mind the stupid men. *Who needs them.* She thought drowsily.

Later a nurse brought Liz a big plate of the best stew she had ever tasted, along with home made bread. She ate like she had never eaten before. Actually, she hadn't eaten a bite in three days.

The next day a precious little bundle wrapped in a pink blanket and wearing a bright pink wool toque was plopped into her arms. Joy catapulted from Liz's arms straight to her heart. The baby would have to be watched closely by a pediatrician for a few months to make sure she had no brain damage, but to Liz she looked just perfect. She was the second miracle in Liz's life. The first one being that she didn't have to have a hysterectomy when her pap smear was pre-cancerous.

The ususal hospital stay in 1983 was approximately three to four days, but Dr. Trent allowed Liz to stay for seven because of her age and because of the fact that she would be going home alone. Janie had asked if she could go to Oliver in the Okanagan with her friends for two weeks and Liz had let her go because she didn't want her staying alone in the house. Liz enjoyed her seven day stay. It gave her plenty of time to rest and enjoy her beautiful new offspring. She tried desperately to figure out who the baby belonged to, but all she could see in her was her own side of the family. The baby looked very much like Stacy when she was born. Liz was disappointed.

She'd hoped the mystery would be cleared up at the birthing. But the disappointment that it hadn't, in no way took away the joy she felt when she held little Baillee in her arms.

Too soon the day of release came. Rose drove Liz home in the morning in her big black Lincoln and then left because she and Harry had made plans for the weekend. Liz didn't really mind because Rose had been such a faithful coach and had visited her every day at the hospital. Now she needed a little time to herself.

The only problem was that Liz was so weak that she found by supper time she couldn't even make herself anything to eat. She was beside herself as to what to do. Thank goodness the baby had breast fed to satisfaction and was sleeping soundly on Liz's big double bed in what she called the blue room. She called it the blue room because she had decorated it with all kinds of blue accessories blue glass vases, royal blue rug, powder blue sheers and a powder blue spread. She surveyed the room one more time as she lingered in the doorway feeling proud of her accomplishment, but her ability to accomplish certainly wasn't helping her now. She couldn't even put a meal together.

She retreated to the kitchen and sat at the chrome set feeling as weak as a kitten and totally despondent when suddenly the back kitchen door flew open wide and there stood Earl with his arms encircling the biggest paper package she had ever seen. She knew what was inside before she even saw. A delicious odor permeated the room and Liz knew instantly he'd been to the Town Fryer. The package was filled to overflowing with the best french fries in the world and huge pieces of battered fish and crab meat, tons of crab meat. Liz had never eaten crab meat before, and she was delighted with the flavor. She would remember Earl and this meal for the rest of her life. She would also remember her promise to God.

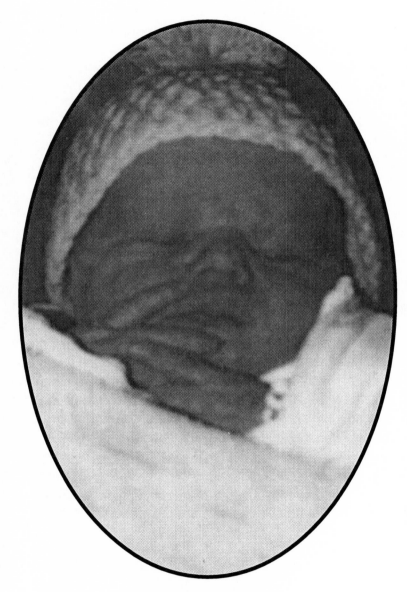

Baby Baillee

Chapter 16
Happy New Year?

Liz continued to be weak, but before long Janie came back from Oliver and was a big help to her. Then in just seven short days Christmas was upon them. Liz was still too feeble to cook a big dinner, but she wanted the whole family home so the girls agreed to take care of the whole day's events. Liz was content. Stacy was there with Jason, Darren and Bonnie came too and the three girls concocted a scrumptious turkey dinner while Liz sat around enjoying the pleasant banter in the warm kitchen atmosphere. Her heart swelled. She missed Jimmy, but there was nothing she could do about that so she opted to enjoy the day in spite of his absence.

After Christmas day had passed, she began to think about New Year's Eve. Christmas had always been for the kids, but New Year's was her night to howl, and now that she was slim and trim again she began to make plans. New Year's had always meant a new gown and a new hair do. She couldn't afford a new gown, but she booked a hair appointment and dragged out the black Grecian gown she had worn to the A.A. banquet in Coeur d'Alene where the young man had mistaken her for a movie star. It fit like a glove! She was ecstatic. A pair of fish net stockings and she would be all set. But she needed a date.

Now that the baby was born, and she was back to her normal self she was convinced that Johnny might just be interested again. She would knock his socks off with her new figure and the black dress. She swirled around in front of the mirror in dainty waltzing steps. Even though she was almost forty and she'd had five kids she still maintained a perfect figure. How, she didn't know, but there it was reflecting back at her through the looking glass. Once again she was Cinderella getting ready for the ball. She kept the dress on to give her confidence and she dialed Johnny's number.

"Hi," she said, shyly. She had never so blatantly chased after a man in her life before, but she was still so in love with Johnny that she couldn't help herself, besides she definitely had to keep the Carousel under control. She had a new baby to care for and she had a promise to keep.

"Hi," he answered sounding defeated.

"Uh, I was wondering what you're doing New Year's Eve. There's a dinner and dance at the club. Are you going?" Liz asked.

"Yeah, I'm going," he answered quickly.

"Well do you want to go with me? I mean, I'm available. I know we've had some rough times, but things can be good between us again. I just know they can. It's a new year. Let's make a new start, okay?"

"Uh, Liz don't make this any harder than it is, will you?"

"What do you mean?"

"I-I-ve met a girl at the college. We're dating. I didn't mean for it to happen. It just did. She's in my class and well we were studying a lot together and things just happened. I didn't mean for them to."

Liz's mind flashed back to her trip to the hospital. The girl in the parking lot! In her need to be loved again she had forgotten about that. Now there she was with egg on her face again and she was *mad*.

"I thought you couldn't be in a relationship. I hope you're not bringing *her* to the dance at the club." Liz spit out.

"Well, yeah, I-I-I," he stuttered until Liz cut him off.

"You bastard! Why don't you take your floozy somewhere else. This is the club where I have to go. I don't have a way to get out of town. You could go anywhere in her fancy little white sports car."

"How did you know she has a sports car?"

"Oh, never mind!" Liz didn't want to admit she had seen them kissing. She was furious with him. They say love is akin to hate and she was loving and hating him with a fervor.

"I don't want to go any where else. This is the club where I go too. All my friends are there too," Johnny grumbled.

Liz slammed the phone down in his ear. She knew how stubborn he could be. Well, she could be just as stubborn. She remembered Susan's words, *Don't let him push you out of the club. You need to be there for your sobriety. He's the one doing the wrong. If you hang in there eventually you'll be the winner. Just wait, you'll see.*

Well this wasn't going to be easy, but she would be there with bells on in her sexy black gown and her fish net stockings. She had to be strong. Susan was right. She couldn't back down now.

The days went by as they always had since the beginning of time, and so came the big night. A lot of the wind had been taken out of Liz's sails with her knowing that Johnny was bringing another woman, but nevertheless, she did her very best primping. Her chestnut hair was gleaming and piled high on her head in a beautiful up do that was sprinkled with silver sparkles. The fish net stockings were sexy on her curvy calves that showed through the slit up the side of the dress every time she took a step. Her figure was perfect. She strutted in front of the full-length mirror in her blue bedroom admiring the results. She was ready!

But it was a different story when she walked into the room and saw Johnny with his date. She also was dressed to the nines in a silver gown with blonde hair flowing down around her shoulders shimmering in the colored lights.

The members had done a stunning job of decorating the hall. The hardwood floors were gleaming and the colored lanterns strung just below the ceiling reflected off the floor. A huge punch bowl graced the center of a table and was surrounded with chips, cheesies, chocolates and other goodies for the guests to nibble on. Not that Liz noticed any of it. She was in another world. A world she didn't want to be in. A world full of fear and hatred for Johnny and his date.

The disc jockey was playing "The Wind Beneath My Wings" as Liz stood in the doorway not knowing which way to turn. Karl let out a wolf whistle in her direction. Billy looked up and spotted what the whistle was all about and confidently strolled over to Liz and whisked her onto the dance floor and *she* let him!

"Pretty rough, eh?" Billy soothed.

"Yeah," Liz mumbled with tears in her eyes.

"Well if it's any consolation the girl is so much like you it's uncanny, even down to the way she holds her hands when she's talking."

Liz looked over at the girl and realized Billy was right. It made her feel a little better that Johnny had picked a girl like her. Maybe it meant that he was still tied in to her. Maybe he still loved her somewhere deep down. Maybe he just couldn't deal with what was happening in her life, the baby and all. Maybe it *wasn't* her personally! She'd always had low self-esteem and being rejected so blatantly had triggered the doubt in herself once again and left her feeling crippled. She felt so ugly, but then again, on the other hand the fact that he'd chosen a girl like her might mean he still found her type attractive and maybe she wasn't being tossed aside like garbage that was no good any more. She looked up into Billy's eyes and smiled a warm smile grateful for his comment and looking to him for further admiration. She needed it more than breath and blood.

Billy swooped her around the dance floor, Liz felt warm and protected in his arms, and she blossomed under his attentive spell. The Carousel tugged ever so slightly. She began to think maybe Billy wasn't so bad after all, which was a dangerous position to be in considering his reputation. But, nonetheless, he certainly helped her get through the night. He kept her busy all evening, and she noticed, as well, that the women at the club were being none too kind to Sarah, Johnny's date.

Liz made it through the evening and at midnight when Johnny and Sarah kissed she wasn't immune to Billy grabbing her and planting a hot lingering kiss on her lips. Johnny and Sarah left shortly after midnight and that's when Liz fell apart. As long as she had to keep up a brave front she was fine, but once they were gone, she was crushed.

When she arrived home, she went into the windowed porch and looked down at the Elk's parking lot. Sarah's white sports car! She watched and watched and Sarah never came out. It got later and later. Sarah was spending the night. Liz's heart was ripped out. She imagined the two of them together entangled in ecstacy just like she and Johnny used to be in that very apartment, in that very bed. A sob ripped from her throat and she ran to her bedroom away from the view from the windowed porch.

She lay awake until four in the morning. She felt like she was losing her mind. Her thoughts spun around in her head at top speed and then she did something that she swore she would never ever do. She phoned Johnny and begged. She pleaded for over an hour sobbing her heart out to no avail. He wouldn't change his mind.

Finally she had to give up and she put the phone receiver in it's cradle and stumbled to the windowed porch again to torture herself a little longer.

She looked down just in time to see Sarah running to her car with Johnny in hot pursuit. Unbeknown to Liz, Sarah had quietly picked up the receiver on the extension in Johnny's apartment. She had heard the whole conversation. Johnny had lied to her and told her that he and Liz were through and that Liz wouldn't care if they dated. Also unbeknownst to Liz, Sarah was actually a very nice person and had been taken in by Johnny. Now she was furious too. Justice was done and finally, totally exhausted, Liz fell into bed somewhat gratified. At least, Sarah had left.

****

Weeks had gone by since Baillee's birth. Baillee was her name as far as Liz was concerned, but not so for the rest of the world. Liz hadn't registered her birth yet because she wasn't quite sure how to go about it. Should she be a Smith after Don or a Moore after Johnny?

Early one morning Liz sat staring into her coffee cup and swirled the liquid around as she contemplated the situation. She was going to have to register Baillee's birth sooner or later, but she felt embarrassed to inquire about the proper way to go about it. She didn't want Baillee to be illegally registered so she gulped down the last bit of coffee and bit the bullet, threw caution to the wind and said, "Well here goes."

"Hello, could I please speak to the Court Registrar?"

"And who should I say is calling?"

"My name is Liz Moore."

"Thank you. Just one moment please."

Liz almost hung up the phone, but she knew she had to be brave and find out the best way to go. With a red face and an unsteady voice she explained her situation to the Registrar.

"Well, I don't know Mrs. Moore. I don't believe we've ever had this situation come up before. Tell you what, I think that being as you are married and your last name is Moore that it would be safe to say that the baby should be registered under the name of Moore. That's the course that I would take."

Liz was relieved. She actually wanted her to be registered under Johnny's name because she still hoped that Johnny was Baillee's father. She still loved him in spite of everything that had happened and maybe now that Sarah had taken off ...? The Carousel tugged relentlessly. Would it never give up?

After the call to the Registry was made, and Liz was feeling a little more light hearted she made another cup of coffee and enjoyed the quiet. Janie was out with her friends and Baillee was sleeping peacefully. Then a loud, urgent banging came at the back door. She nearly jumped out of her skin before she leapt up to answer the door, wondering who would be calling at that time of the morning.

She cautiously opened the door and was immediately grasped and surrounded by a pair of strong male arms. Don! He was back and laughing like a fool as he swung her around in the air.

"Wow, when did you get back?" Liz asked as she hugged her dear friend.

"Hey girl, just now. I just blew in on the bus. Well where is the little critter?"

"She's sleeping, but come on you can have a look at her if you're quiet. I don't want her awake right now. I just got her down."

They walked stealthily together over the creaking hardwood floor and Liz quietly opened the bedroom door with her finger to her lips and formed a silent sshh.

Don's eyes lit up as he beamed down at the sleeping little bundle. He saw big, round, pink cheeks, rose bud lips, slightly parted, with soft baby's breath puffing out, and a tuft of silken, chestnut hair gracing the top of her perfectly rounded head.

"Oh, she's mine," he whispered. "She looks just like my boys when they were born." Don had been married, but because of his drinking his wife had left him and taken off with the boys years ago.

Liz didn't like what he was saying in the least. She slipped into total denial. This baby was Johnny's. That was the way it was. Simple. She would hear none of what Don had to say. They left the bedroom as stealthily as they'd come.

"How can you tell?" Liz argued. "She looks just like me when I was a baby."

"Oh, no, I can tell. Get a divorce and marry me, Liz. We get along fabulously and I'm sober now. I've got the program and I know I'm going to make it."

"Oh, Don, don't ask me that. I don't love you, and you don't love me. It wouldn't be fair to either one of us."

"Come on maybe we could learn to love each other. She's ours I'm sure of it and we could raise her together. I really miss not having my boys. It's like I'm getting a second chance."

"NO!" Liz blurted out more forcefully than she meant to. She was angry that he was trying to burst her bubble. She wanted to fully believe that Baillee was Johnny's.

"It's him isn't it? You're still in love with him. How can you be after all he's done to you? Well, what about the blood testing? I told you I would consent to a blood test."

Liz felt helpless. She hadn't told Johnny that she'd slept with Don. She didn't want to tell him in case there was a chance to re-unite their relationship. Liz didn't realize it, but she was headed for disaster. She was playing a dangerous game and she could come out the loser. But she did consent to see the doctor about getting blood testing set up for Don's sake. She owed him that much at least. She knew Johnny's blood type was AB positive. So he would never have to know. Don stayed for a while for coffee and then took off with his head hanging after again unsuccessfully trying to convince Liz to marry him.

The very next day Liz called Dr. Trent and booked an appointment for that afternoon.

"Well, Liz, You are O positive. We'll have to see what Baillee is. It takes two O positive parents to have an O positive baby, so if Baillee is O positive then we're looking for a man with O positive blood.

That was easy enough. Johnny was AB so she hoped that Baillee wasn't O. Then after a grueling week of waiting the tests came back. Baillee was O positive and Don was A positive. Liz was agog. There wasn't anyone else! How could that be? So back to Dr. Trent.

"The only other thing it can be is that one of Don's or Johnny's parents are O positive and it skipped a generation," said Dr. Trent.

"Well, that's the end of it then. I'm not going any further. But I sure wish I knew who her father was. This means I could go through my whole life not knowing," Liz lamented.

"There's genetic testing, but that's expensive," Dr. Trent answered her.

"How expensive?"

"Probably in the neighborhood of twelve hundred dollars."

"Might as well be a million. I *will* go through my whole life not knowing."

Liz left the doctor's office feeling totally exasperated. She got a hold of Don and told him the bad news. He still insisted that Baillee was his, and Liz still insisted she wasn't. It was a stalemate. So after a short stay Don up and left town again. Not only was her friend, Don gone, but Rose had opted to move to Edmonton where her kids had moved to look for work, and Susan, Liz's special sponsor, had landed a better job in Kelowna and was leaving town too. And with Val already in Nelson, Liz felt totally abandoned.

She became obsessed with trying to discover who Baillee's father was until she almost drove herself crazy. She purchased a Polaroid camera and took hundreds of pictures which she studied in depth, checking every feature of her baby's tiny face. And she was constantly watching expressions and gestures and checking her little body for any kind of sign that might reveal her paternity. She was worried about medical history and such things not to mention her own satisfaction. Besides what would she tell Baillee when she was older?

So with Johnny still dating Sarah, who had succumbed once again to Johnny's charm, with Don, Rose, Val and Susan, her most intimate friends, all gone from town, and with the mystery of Baillee's genetics, Liz was left totally alone, frustrated, and heart broken.

During that time she found it very difficult to keep Baillee content. It was as though the upsets Liz was experiencing were somehow being transferred in her breast milk to the baby. The end result being that one dark and lonely evening she lapsed into a complete and brutal anxiety attack. She couldn't breathe, she couldn't think, she was in a thorough state of panic and terror.

Janie was terrified so she immediately called an ambulance. Liz was taken away as Janie looked on. Liz would remember Janie's panic stricken face until the day she died, but there was just nothing she could do about it at the time. At the hospital she was prescribed Valium once again and sent home right away. Janie had called an Alanon lady in Liz's absence who was tending to Baillee.

The next morning Janie pleaded with Liz to let her go to Oliver with her friends again. Liz didn't blame her for wanting to get away so she let her go. Over the next few months Janie spent more time in Oliver than she did at home It seemed as though there was something of great interest to Janie there. *Perhaps a boy?* Liz thought.

As a result, Liz was totally isolated caring for the baby. She began to feel very strange. Her head felt like it was full of pins and needles. She couldn't concentrate and she kept having minor anxiety attacks. Not as severe as the one when she was taken in the ambulance, but nonetheless she was very antsy and afraid of another big attack, so she made a phone call home.

"Hi, mama. I haven't been feeling so good. I don't know what's happening to me and I'm kinda scared being alone so much with the baby. Do you think I could come home for a week or so at least until Janie comes back?"

"Sure, we would love to see the new baby. Your papa will come right over and pick you up."

It wasn't that Janie could do any great wonders for Liz. After all she was only fifteen, but just having someone in the house made Liz feel a little more at ease. That is the way of it with panic attacks. They are eased by another's presence.

So Liz packed a few things and a few hours later John and Alicia were there to pick her up. Liz was taken aback and her heart ached at the way her parents looked. When had they aged so much? When had her papa gotten so thin? They had started to look like two little potato people with drawn and wrinkled skin.

Liz spent a week with her parents and felt a hundred percent better so she returned home a day before Janie was to come back. But Janie phoned shortly after Liz got home and pleaded with her to let her stay another week. There *was* a boy. Janie wasn't about to take no for an answer and Liz was just too weak to fight her.

By the middle of the next week Liz was in a state again. It was the middle of the morning. Baillee was crying and there was no placating her. Liz took her and put her in the middle of her big bed and closed the bedroom door to shut out her cries. She sat in the easy chair in the living room rocking back and forth and crying herself. She was very afraid! Then she started to slip into that yellow fog again.

"Oh, my gawd! I've gotta do something fast before I completely slip away. Baillee!" Her main interest was Baillee. What would happen to her? Who would look after her? She needed to call Dr. Trent. But Dr. Trent would want to put her in hospital again. She couldn't go and leave Baillee. She was incapable of making a decision. She was at a loss as to what to do.

Finally, in desperation, she grabbed the phone and dialed Dr. Trent's number.

"Dr. Trent, I think I'm losing my mind," she wailed into the cold black receiver. "I can't look after Baillee properly. She keeps crying and I don't know what to do to stop her. Janie is away. I have no one to help. I feel like I did the last time I had a nervous breakdown, but I can't go to the hospital because I have no one to watch Baillee," Liz moaned, crying and blubbering.

"Where is Baillee right now?" Dr. Trent asked.

"I put her in the middle of my bed and shut the door because I was afraid."

"Are you afraid of hurting her?"

"No, no, I would never do that."

"Good, okay, we've got to get you into the hospital. There isn't anyone who can take Baillee for you?"

"No all my friends are gone and Stacy is working, going to school and looking after Jason all by herself. And, of course you know, Bonnie is pregnant. And Janie is only fifteen, besides she's not even here."

"Well, Baillee will just have to go into the Daly with you." Dr. Trent stated.

"NO!!!" Liz shouted, "I won't have her in there with all those really sick people. What if someone hurts her?" Liz was beyond reason and totally freaked out. She began to shake uncontrollably.

"Okay, okay, Liz. Tell you what I'll call pediatrics on the second floor and see if they will keep Baillee upstairs while you are downstairs in the Daly. What I want you to do is call the A.A. club right away and get somebody up there as soon as possible so you're not alone. I'll call you right back with instructions."

Chapter 17
April Fool's Day

As soon as Liz hung up, she immediately called the club. The only ones there were the regulars, Beulah, Francis and Shelly, the tough girl Liz was afraid of. Beulah and Shelly were the ones who had driven Liz to the hospital when she was in labor with Baillee. It was like deja vu. When Liz told them her state, they dropped everything and headed up to Topping Street.

In the meantime, Dr. Trent called back and told Liz the pediatrics idea was a go and she should pack some clothes for herself and the baby if she was able and get there as quickly as possible. Liz informed her that Beulah and Shelly were on their way.

The two women arrived and Liz was all packed, if you could call it that. She had no idea what she had with her. She had just thrown clothes for her and Baillee into a satchel.

As they were going out the door, Beulah announced, "Hey, it's April first. It's April Fool's Day."

Some joke! Liz thought.

Beulah and Shelly chatted incessantly on the way to the hospital, but much of what they were saying went right over Liz's head. At least she wasn't afraid this time. She knew what the protocol would be. But she was worried about Baillee. What would she do about breast feeding?

Liz couldn't remember much about being admitted. She only knew that just like the last time, she couldn't stop crying. Baillee was taken right away by a nurse to pediatrics on the second floor. Liz was relieved that she was being taken care of, but at the same time was feeling guilty for abandoning her.

Liz was soon to find out that this trip into the Daly was not going to be any picnic like the last time. First of all, there were no jolly, pleasant women to ease her anxiety and to laugh with. And secondly, this time she was really going to have to work at her problems in order to get well.

On the bright side though, Dr. Trent brought Liz a finely decorated baby carriage that had been her own. Liz was pleased as she hadn't been able to afford a carriage and it meant that she could bring Baillee downstairs on occasion for visits. Liz visited Baillee four or five times a day to breast feed her, and Baillee was thriving with all the attention from the nurses in peds. They were ecstatic to have a beautiful, healthy, happy baby to play with in between tending to sick kids. Liz wasn't worried about Baillee getting sick because she knew as long as she was nursing her baby, she would be immune.

Just as she did the last time, Liz was enrolled in occupational therapy. Only this time instead of having Don to help her, perhaps, she had his child. The whole business of Don claiming the baby was his, and wanting to marry her; Johnny running around with Sarah; not knowing her baby's father; and trying to stay sober through it all was driving Liz over the brink of sanity. But unlike the last time she was not filled with anger. It was more like an all consuming guilt that would not allow her to rest. Instead of making ceramics, which didn't in the least interest her, she opted to knit cute little baby booties for Baillee. They were designed like a pair of little girls shoes with a strap across the instep. Liz embroidered pink flowers with green leaves on each toe and sewed a tiny pearl button on the side for each strap. She was pleased with her effort, but nonetheless still totally despondent.

She joined the group, as before, but because there were no happy positive women, she sat like a bump on a log not saying much of anything. There were two young men who seemed very disturbed and totally lacking in self confidence, a young woman who seemed extremely angry, and a university professor who had lost his job and ended up under psychiatric care because he was worried beyond control about his finances.

Liz vaguely heard him reply to Bart, the therapist, that he only had $10,000.00 in the bank. She thought to herself, *huh I wonder what that would feel like. I haven't had any money to speak of since I spent all the kid's college funds years ago. Oh, well, I've got three bucks and I get another welfare cheque in a week.*

As though reading her mind, Bart immediately turned his full attention on Liz and said, "Liz, tell Mr. Bowen how much money you have."

Liz responded proudly, "Three dollars and eighty nine cents."

Mr. Bowen crooked an eyebrow and said, "But how much do you have in the bank?"

"Nothing. I don't have a bank account. No sense in it. I never have enough to put in it anyway. But I'm not worried. I get another cheque in a week," Liz answered.

Mr. Bowen was astounded. He could not believe his ears.

"So, you see, Mr. Bowen, not having money doesn't have to be so devastating."

"I can't believe this young woman. She has children to look after. She has no money and she's not worried. Amazing. She's one in a million."

"Maybe so, but you see the point you can survive. She is."

"Well I take my hat off to you young woman. I certainly admire your stamina."

Liz felt encouraged by the professor's words and so after that she began to loosen up a little and she started to talk about some of her background.

Over the weeks, Bart gently and subtly prodded her and drew her out of her shell. By the time four weeks had gone by Liz was ready to crack and spill all the contents of her troubled mind. It was time!

Bart, the attending psychiatric nurse, and the group members watched and listened intently as Liz sat with her head down and began.

"I have a terrible secret. This is so ugly and so hard to tell," she stammered.

"Years ago my common-law husband, Lenny, used to beat me to a pulp," she continued trying to avoid the crucial matter. "He was cruel, I mean, when I first met him he was nice to me," she kind of chuckled nervously, "He used to call me Princess at one time." She lifted her head to see the response with a slight smile on her face.

"Go on," Bart gently urged.

"Well, I don't know what happened, but he got mean after a few years. He was mean to my kids even. He, uh, he verbally abused

134

them all the time. I mean I wasn't all that aware of it," she gulped down a big lump in her throat. "I guess I was in denial. I remember one time the kids were watching T.V. and there was this show about this step father who was really mean to the kids. He would yell at them and wack them unmercifully. One of my kids said, 'Hey, he's just like Lenny.' And I can remember thinking, *Not my Lenny who calls me Princess.* My kids needed me so bad then and I wasn't there for them and then, and then," Liz started to sob.

The nurse passed a Kleenex under Liz's nose. Liz grabbed it without even looking up as she continued to tell about Lenny beating her and the kids and molesting Stacy, then threatening to kill her, then killing himself, all the while sobbing convulsively.

"I'm a terrible mother. I *should* have been shot," she wailed. She rocked back and forth as years of abuse and shame and horror bubbled up from the depths of her soul. After about a half an hour of this rocking, sobbing and bubbling forth, she gradually, slowly raised her head and looked from under her eyebrows from one to another in the group. She was astonished to see silver streaks down Bart's face. Then she turned to the nurse, same thing, crystal tears streaming down her face. Mr. Bowen looked sad and yet proud of her. The two young men even looked understanding, but as she focused on the angry young woman in the group black eyes shot daggers at her and she spat out, "I hate your guts!"

Liz was devastated. She was in a very vulnerable position. She had just bared her soul believing that she was the most foul person in the world and yet hoping for some verification that she wasn't. Her well-being depended on it. But Bart, being the great counselor that he was quickly broke in.

"Laura, what's going on with you right now? What's this hate and anger all about?"

Then just as Liz had broken down. The young woman began to break down and bared *her* soul about how she had been sexually abused by her father and her brothers ever since she was six years old. She told of how they would hurt her and bite her and how her mother never ever did anything about it.

Then a strange thing began to happen for Liz as the girl continued to hurl filthy accusations in her direction. Liz started to feel a great deal of empathy for the girl, but at the same time she began to defend herself. She needed to, to survive. It was exactly what she needed to get her bearings and forgive herself. She began to realize even though her part in her children's abuse was bad enough there were extenuating circumstances. She hadn't known the kind of man Lenny was. She had nowhere to go to get away from him. The doctor had even told her to sit tight until she called family services and hadn't gotten back to her, and she *had* gotten out when an opportunity arose. Slowly, gently she began to feel human again. She continued to reassure the young woman that she was sorry for what happened and was sure her mother must be too. So a dual healing was taking place at the hands of Bart. Even Mr. Bowen was feeling that his troubles were not the worst in the world and he began healing as well.

Liz and the young woman became friends as the weeks went on. And Mr. Bowen's deep respect for Liz helped her heal even more. He was in awe of her.

And at one group meeting after all the discussions on low self-esteem, the concept of it all illuminated in Liz's mind as though a beacon shone through her dark world.

"So, you mean the bottom line, the secret to my addictions is learning to like myself, and being comfortable in my own skin?"

"Exactly," Bart beamed. "If you're in a room with someone you don't like, what's the first thing you want to do?"

"Get out," Liz instantly replied.

"Aha! But what if it's you? Where do you go?"

"I don't know."

"Escape into the bottle? Men? Different people have different escape routes or find different ways to kid themselves into feeling better about themselves like gambling, power trips over other people, putting other people down to feel good about themselves, and in your case, the more interest from the opposite sex, the better."

"Okay, so how do I stop? How do I learn to like myself?"

"By stopping the negative self-talk that goes on in your head. You know, like, 'I'm so stupid; I'm ugly; nobody would ever want *me*,' that kind of stuff. Things that have been etched there since childhood. And by accomplishing things you like to do. Feeling proud of your accomplisments; learning what your skills are; getting to know your good stuff. Helping others. Respecting yourself. Being kind to yourself, as kind as you are to others. There's all kinds of ways."

"Like Dr. Ward getting me to write forty-three things I like about myself?"

"Yeah," Bart exclaimed, excited he was finally getting through.

"I did kinda feel good after reading what I wrote. But it soon wore off."

"That's why you gotta keep doing it, daily."

"But I'm so used to the man thing. It's my way of life. If I quit I'll be lost, I'll have nothing to hang onto. It'll be so hard."

"Like quitting drinking?" Bart queried with a furled forehead.

"Yeah, it was really, really hard."

"But hasn't it been worth it."

Liz stared off into space, thinking, thinking. "Yeah, but if I don't drink and don't do men, what will I have left?"

"Yourself."

"Is it enough?"

"Yes! You're a beautiful person. You have a great potential to love. The world needs your love." Bart said, smiling warmly.

****

As the weeks went by the tiny group covered all kinds of subjects from parenting, to childhood, even to death and dying. Two things that Bart passed on to the group would remain with Liz forever. *It is inevitable, children love their parents and parents love their children no matter what, except in severe cases of dysfunction,* which helped Liz a little with her anger towards Alicia. She came to realize that Alicia wasn't a bad person and didn't really hate her. She was just an imperfect woman who actually wanted the very best for her children. She just didn't know how to execute her ideas properly. She merely followed what she had been taught. And the other thing Bart told them was *When someone is dying you are not there for you, you are there for them.* The latter being very good information that Liz was going to need in the not too distant future.

Also Bart suggested two books to the group, The Magic Bottle for alcoholics and Women's Reality, especially for the women. One important thing that Liz learned from the Magic Bottle, written by a female recovering alcoholic who had become an alcohol counsellor in the slums of Chicago, was that alcoholics have a low tolerance to emotional pain. That stuck in her mind for years to come. It was true. She was strong as far as emergencies or physical pain went, but whenever she suffered emotional pain she became a basket case. She knew everyone's tolerance to physical pain was different, but she never realized that about emotional pain. It was a real breakthrough for her.

And the other book Women's Reality was a gem. A woman psychologist who was asked to help with the trouble between the black's and the whites in the Southern States discovered, through her research and attempts at helping that it was, indeed, a white man's world and that everyone else followed behind with women somewhere near the bottom. She pointed out that all their lives women had to put up with derogatory comments that they didn't even realize were put downs which etched away at their self esteem. Comments like, *Oh, you didn't get your boy, oh well better luck with your next pregnancy; Oh, of course, it'a a woman driver; Oh, that's just silly women's talk.* Liz had heard these kind of comments over and over again all through her life and didn't realize they were debilitating her. She would watch from now on and not let them affect her.

****

After having been under Bart's care and in the Pavilion before, Liz had relaxed enough to work with Dr. Ward. He'd had Liz make a list of forty-three things she liked about herself to help her with her self-esteem and set her on the road to a good recovery. At first, she hadn't been able to think of a thing, then, he'd prompted her with some suggestions. She'd gone to her room and was able to come up with only sixteen, but eventually he'd helped her to find twenty-seven more to complete the forty-three.

Indeed, his therapy had worked, along with Bart's sessions, and she was feeling much better about herself. It was needed not only to combat her feelings about herself as a mother, but to ward off the devastation of being rejected by Johnny.

Dr. Ward also discussed the matter of the panic attacks with her. He was an expert on medications for panic disorder. He explained that since she had done some damage to her brain with her drinking she was suffering a chemical imbalance and would perhaps suffer from panic disorder for the rest of her life, but the good news was that there were medications on the market to help alleviate the worst of it and so he prescribed a medication called Parnate.

Liz was excited to start the medication, but there was one drawback that she didn't give much consideration to. She had to avoid certain foods, like wine, (which was no problem anymore), pineapple, bananas, raisins, and chocolate. As a matter of fact it was easier to say what she could eat rather than what she couldn't. But the worst of it was she couldn't take any cold medications or anesthetics of any kind while she was on it. This was to prove almost fatal to her before the year was out. Nonetheless, she was so anxious to be rid of the panic attacks she was ready to try anything.

Shortly before Liz was discharged, Stacy visited her with exciting news. The little house next to her apartment in the Gulch was empty and her landlord owned it as well. She hoped Liz would consider moving next door so they could help each other out with their children and their lives. After some consideration, Liz decided it would do her the world of good to get off the mountain where she was constantly seeing Johnny with Sarah, and then perhaps she could forget about him completely and get on with her life. After all she was a new woman now. She no longer needed to drink and she no longer needed to feel so bad about herself. Little did she know, though that the Carousel that had plagued her since childhood wasn't going to be that easy to dispose of.

Chapter 18
Return to the Gulch

Roy and Earl were on the move again with all of Liz's earthly belongings. Fortunately, they didn't lose anything this time and Liz was ever grateful.

Her new home was a flat-roofed building with two bedrooms, a small kitchen, a large living room, and a bathroom which were all nicely decorated, but *la piece de resistance* was the huge tiered yard. After the mountainous backdrop at the Topping Street house it was a delight even though it was overgrown with weeds and foot long dead grass.

But not to worry, a strange thing was happening to Liz. She had more energy than she had ever had in her life before. As a matter of fact, she undertook to totally transplant the whole yard. She would get up at 6 a.m. and work until dark and even then some, even though she was hardly able to see. The only other task she undertook was to care for Baillee, but once the babe's needs were taken care of, Liz was out in the yard again. She was driven by some unknown force until she fell into bed every night exhausted. After a nice hot bubble bath, of course.

Jason, now three years old, would often come over and *help* Liz. She wasn't sure if help was the right word. He *tried* to help and all went well until she was bent over pulling weeds on the third tier level. Jason came running towards her shouting, "I'n a football player, Gramma." Before she could get up or deke out of his way he tackled her, true to football form, knocking her over onto the second tier level. Shocked out of her wits, she got up and dusted herself off. She didn't know whether to spank him or hug him when she looked down into his proud grinning football face.

But the work continued in spite of Jason's frequent visits. She built rock walls, seeded each tier in fresh grass after digging up all the weeds, put in flower gardens and even installed a pond with a little waterfall. The end result was a delightful English garden with stepping stones leading down to the house.

The only thing Liz could think to attribute her energy to was the Parnate medication. She had never been able to work like that in her life before. She felt like she was on speed. She wasn't able to sit for a moment and relax. As a result she was losing weight rapidly and becoming very gaunt looking. Not only that the anxiety attacks continued to get worse and then one night at three in the morning Liz could stand it no longer. She found herself in the throes of a severe anxiety attack. She was alone with Baillee and scared out of her wits. Finally she broke down and called Roy.

Roy, as a good friend, was more than happy to come to her rescue. He showed up in his big yellow truck rubbing the sleep from his eyes. He drove Liz and Baillee up the hospital hill and waited in the truck rocking a crying Baillee back and forth while Liz went in to emergency where the nurse talked her through her attack.

The next night was like an instant replay. Liz didn't have the heart to call Roy and get him out of bed again so she just called emergency and explained her situation to the nurse on duty. The nurse stayed on the phone with her until 4 a.m. when the attack started to subside and then advised Liz to see her family doctor the next day.

Dr. Trent took one look at Liz and said, "Oh, my gawd, you look terrible. That bloody stuff is killing you." Little did Dr. Trent know how close she was to the truth.

In the meantime Dr. Trent set up an appointment for Liz with Dr. Ward to have the dosage of her medication adjusted. When she saw him, Dr. Ward explained to Liz that it would take time for the Parnate to start working properly. Appeased for the moment Liz continued her daily routine of caring for Baillee and tending to her home and yard. Then when Baillee turned six months old Liz was saddled with a further worry. The Ministry of Human Resources felt that in order to get young mother's back in the work force it was necessary to cut the amount of their cheques by $100.00 a month. The cut back was to take effect when their babies turned six months old. "To give them incentive," the worker had said.

"This is ridiculous. I can hardly live on what they give me now let alone getting $100.00 less," Liz moaned as she gazed at her cheque.

And she was absolutely right. Because Baillee had developed an allergy to milk after being weaned from her mother's milk, Liz had had to put her on Prosobee, a special milk made from soy. And *very* expensive. Inevitably, Liz would run out of money for the last week of the month. So she developed the habit of writing a cheque at the drug store for Baillee's milk and hoped against all odds that her welfare cheque would be deposited into her account before the druggist's cheque went through. It worked like a charm for a few months until finally it caught up to her. *A cheque bounced!* Her bounced cheque was displayed under the glass on the counter top for all to see. She was totally humiliated, but she would have done anything to keep her baby in milk. Now she was at a loss as to how to do it. In desperation she made Baillee a bottle of water with sugar in it to try to keep her going. She had no idea who to go to for help. If she borrowed the money for the milk, she would only have to pay it back again, and then she would be short again the next month. It was a vicious circle that there was no way out of. Human Resources was right. It certainly did give her incentive to start looking for work even though she hated the thought of leaving her precious Baillee with a sitter.

On the bright side, though, at least her Parnate finally started to kick in and the panic attacks were subsiding. Also on the bright side, John and Alicia called saying they were coming to visit. When Liz got her cheque, she squeezed out $2.98 to buy a little plaster statue of a man with the words *I love you Dad* sculpted into the base. She was learning in A.A. to make amends to the people she might have hurt with her drinking, and she hoped that she could heal the rift between herself and her papa. She had always loved him and never understood exactly why he'd abandoned her when she was so young. Perhaps if she could mend fences with him she could finally put the Carousel to rest. Johnny had moved in with Sarah and so there was no longer any hope there and she was destitute.

When John and Alicia arrived, Liz presented her papa with the little statue. Tears filled his eyes as he said proudly, "Mother, would you look at this!" The ice was broken and Liz and her papa spoke to each other more in the next hour than they had in all her life time. Liz was happy, but she was also scared. John had become terribly thin. She knew he was dying. It was imperative that she reconnect with him before it was too late.

Yes, Liz was happy reuniting her relationship with her papa, but not so Alicia. She became very quiet and seemed to be upset. Finally, she interrupted them saying brusquely, "Well, come on, let's go to the store and see if we can help you out a little bit here with some diapers and some milk for that poor wee babe."

Liz was certainly grateful for the help, but she could have died with shame when they were going through the check out at Kresge's. She had discovered a large package of Pampers under a shelf that was on sale for a ridiculously low price, but the box was all covered in dust. At the till the clerk said, "Here let me dust that off for you."

Alicia quickly replied, "Oh don't worry about it. It will fit right in at *her* house."

Liz couldn't believe her ears. She couldn't understand why her mother had been so cruel. Was she jealous, perhaps? Was she upset at John's attention to Liz? Was that the reason why John had stayed away from Liz? To keep Alicia happy. Nonetheless, in spite of Alicia's cruelty Liz *was* relieved that her parents undertook to keep her supplied in baby milk.

But even though Liz was making some headway with her papa, in the weeks to follow her Carousel started to drive her crazy again. The need for a man to hold her and love her became overwhelming. It started to show on the outside until finally at a meeting one night Gene approached her and said, "You've gotta get out of yourself. Look at that young woman over there. She's two weeks sober and shaking like a leaf. It's time you started thinking about sponsorship yourself. You've been sober almost four years and it's time to give some back. Besides it'll help you to forget your own problems."

Gene was right. Liz introduced herself to Cora, who was five years younger than Liz, and they hit it off right away. Liz's heart went out to her and she gave Cora her phone number and said, "Call me anytime." Weeks went by. Cora asked Liz to be her sponsor and Liz readily agreed. She helped Cora to do her fifth step. The fifth step being, to confess the harm that had been done during her drunk days, so as to ease her conscience.

As Cora related her shortcomings, Liz related her own back to Cora bonding their relationship into a friendship that would last a life time. The two women discovered that they had led a parallel life -- same kind of parenting, same abusive relationships, same debauchery, same great need for men. Their lives were cemented together with similarity.

Cora would haunt Liz's place at all hours of the day and night as Liz had suggested she do to help her not take that first drink. Liz was ecstatic. She was feeling very useful and not as lonely.

Then one night while Liz was attending her usual Saturday night meeting, a figure moved quietly into the main meeting room. Liz caught sight of the person out of the corner of her eye without really focusing. Gene caught her attention and nodded toward the new comer. Liz glanced up and was totally elated. There standing large as life was Jimmy! But what was he doing at a closed A.A. meeting? And what happened to him? His arm was bent at the elbow and held up by a white sling and the fingers of his left hand looked like sausages sticking out of the white cast. Liz observed him with a questioning look in her eyes, but neither spoke as the meeting was still in progress.

Immediately after the meeting was over, Liz raced to his side. "What happened to your arm?" she cried. "And what are you doing here? I don't mean what are you doing in Trail, I mean what are you doing *here* at a closed meeting?"

"I *need* to be. It's a long story, mom," Jimmy said. "Can I come to your place? I need a place to stay."

"Of course you can!" Liz replied immediately. She was overjoyed that he was finally home.

"I'll tell you all about what happened when we get home. But first let's go over to Cedar Avenue. They've got a good rock and roll band playing at a street dance. I wouldn't mind listening to the music for awhile."

"Sure," Liz said. "It's Silver City Days and I had planned to go over and listen to the music myself. I don't know where Cora is. She and I were supposed to go there together after the meeting."

"Who's Cora?" Jimmy asked.

"Oh, she's a new member that I've been sponsoring. I guess it's okay for me to tell you that being as you're here at A.A. and will meet her anyway."

Jimmy shrugged and headed for the door and held it open for Liz. She looked back at Gene, grinning like a Cheshire cat. She was so proud of her only son. He had filled out really nicely and was a handsome young man. He was the image of Brian O'Shea, his father, who had been the most handsome Black Irish man Liz had ever seen. She was proud to be seen with Jimmy.

They walked quickly down Cedar Avenue to where a large flat bed truck was backed across Cedar Avenue at Farwell Street closing off the traffic. The band was blasting out the CCR song "Hey tonight" as Jimmy and Liz arrived and made their way through the crowd to the front of the flat bed stage. The music reached right into Liz's inner being and she started to move with the rhythm, but no one was dancing. There were hundreds of people there, but not one single person was brave enough to break the ice and start the street dance.

Jimmy watched Liz as she moved to the music and said, "Come on, mom. Let's show this crowd how to dance." Liz responded immediately and Jimmy and she began to rock the place. Then slowly one by one couples began to join them until the whole street was rocking. Jimmy grinned at Liz, she grinned back at him with a little feeling of power. They had set the whole place a rockin'.

Later that evening, in the confines of Liz's home, Jimmy related to Liz how he'd been on skid row in Toronto and had nearly starved to death. Then he told her of the car accident with his cousin, her brother, Jack's boy. Both of them had been drinking and Bruce was driving too fast and when he hit a sharp curve, he lost control and rolled the car over and over again.

"I was up and then I was down and then upside down again. I thought it was never going to stop. Scared the crap out of me. I'm lucky all I got was a broken arm and some scrapes and bruises. Not to mention the damage we might have done to someone else on the road. I guess I've got your blood running in my veins. Anyway that was enough for me. I hope you don't mind me coming to the club."

"Mind? Never! I didn't know you had a problem. They say it *is* in the genes, though."

"One good thing happened while I was in the city though. Aunt Jane found me and relayed a message from my dad that he wanted to see me and would mail an airline ticket for me to travel to Texas to see him. So I went. He bought me a bunch of new clothes and a suitcase. He is filthy rich, mom. You shoulda seen the jewelry on him. He has this mansion of a home with a games room and a huge swimming pool."

"I'm not surprised. He always was smart. Sounds like he finally did something with it."

"Well maybe he's rich, but he'll never be you, mom. Actually he's a jerk!" Jimmy said as he picked Liz up and swung her around. "Well I think I'll put my stuff away. Where can I bunk in?"

"You can go in Janie's room for now. She's in Oliver *again.* She's got a boyfriend over there and I hardly see her anymore."

"Thanks, mom."

Jimmy disappeared into Janie's room and shut the door just as the back door flew open.

"So sorry I missed the meeting. Duane was giving me a really bad time and I couldn't get away from him," Cora lamented as she came through the door. Duane was Cora's husband who also had a drinking problem, but refused to quit. He could get violent when he drank so Cora left him.

Just as Cora was explaining what had happened to Liz, Jimmy stepped out of Janie's room with just his jeans on and a towel slung over his casted arm. Cora caught sight of his handsome face and broad chest and her eyes started to bug out. Jimmy was not immune to her attention. He drank in her petite figure, her blonde curls, her beautiful greenish, brown eyes and he was smitten. The sparks began to fly around the room and Liz was *afraid.* Very much afraid.

****

"You can't do this!" Liz cried.

"Why not?" Cora answered, as they sat in the front seat of her old chevy. Cora was just dropping Liz off after the Monday night meeting. Jimmy and Cora had been calling each other on the phone and Liz figured she needed to nip it in the bud. She'd had her own experience with a relationship before being a year sober and knew what that was all about and she was worried about Cora as well as her son. Cora was being stubborn. She'd been bitten by the love bug and even though Jimmy was fourteen years her junior, she was not about to be deterred. Liz was desperate. She was trying all avenues to convince Cora it couldn't work.

"He watches Dr. Who for crying out loud," Liz lamented.

"I like Dr. Who!" Cora shot back.

"Oh, my, gawd. You watch that show too? It's crazy."

Liz talked until she was blue in the face, to no avail. And a few days later, Jimmy laid down the law with her explaining that it was his life and if Cora was willing to go out with him he was going to take her out and that was that and would she please not interfere? What could she do? She threw her hands up in the air. Now she knew how Susan had felt with her and Johnny, but this was even worse This was her son!

After a month or so Jimmy moved in with Cora and her two daughters, lock, stock and barrel. Liz was worried sick. One of them was bound to get hurt and she didn't know which would be the worst, her son or her sponsee. She took her sponsoring very seriously, but she loved Jimmy dearly. In the end the two did seem to hit it off really well, though. Liz continued to sponsor Cora in spite of the situation, and Cora, except for her relationship with Jimmy was an exemplary sponsee.

After Jimmy left there was even more excitement in the Gulch. The sound of gas escaping from a burst pipe whistled eerily throughout the neighbourhood. Liz was freaked right out. The neighbours rushed over to Liz's and cried, "Come on, we better get out of here!"

Liz grabbed Baillee and climbed frantically into the neighbour's car. Fortunately, Janie was away. Then she remembered Stacy and Jason. "Oh, my gawd! My daughter and grandson! Can they come too?"

"Of course," the neighbour cried.

"I'll run and get them." Liz just flew. Stacy had a friend from Creston who'd stayed overnight and the girls were still in their flimsy nylon night gowns. The friend also had two pug nosed Boxers who could hardly breathe. "Come on, Come on. There's a gas leak the whole street could go up at any second," Liz gasped.

"Can I bring my dogs? I can't possibly leave them behind," Layla yelled.

"Uh, I don't know. It's the neighbours' new car. Oh what the heck, bring them."

Liz, the girls, Jason and the dogs ran as quickly as they could up the stairs to the road and all tried to cram into the neighbours' car. His eyes bugged out at the sight of the fat, snorting, drooling dogs, and the girls in their flimsy nightgowns and gorgeous figures, but nonetheless he hollered, "Hurry up, get in." They did. And the whole entourage raced up the hill to Warfield. Stacy and Liz laughed about that incident for years after.

Even though Stacy was right next door, she was always busy. And with Jimmy gone and Janie never around, loneliness began to wrap itself around Liz again. She had Baillee and Baillee was a blessing, but she still slept a great deal of the day and evenings and wasn't much company. So when the Fruitvale A.A. banquet and dance came along, Liz was primed to go. The only problem was what to wear? Not only that, her hair was a mess. It seemed that the medication she was on didn't do her long chestnut hair any justice. Besides she felt she was getting a little old for long hair. But she certainly couldn't afford a trip to the hair dressers. Nor could she afford a new dress. Vern, always to the rescue, offered to pay for her ticket, but with the dance only two days away she would have to do some scrambling to get in shape. Johnny and Sarah would probably be there. She no longer wanted Johnny back, but neither did she want to be humiliated in front of them.

So her adventure began. First of all she dragged out an old burgundy velvet dress that she and Alicia had sewed together at one time. It was a good colour on her, but it was a full-length dress and totally out of style. She mused over it for awhile, then grabbed her scissors. She cut a large vee in the neck to show just enough cleavage, then stitched it with an interfacing. She hacked at the length and hemmed it up to show off her still shapely calves. She decked it out at the cuffs of the long sleeves and at the neckline with some white ostrich feathers she found in the back of her closet. Then she tried it on. It was perfect -- very sexy and yet very classy. Next her hair. She grabbed the scissors as she sat at her dressing table with the big mirror. Then with her tongue in her cheek, she began to hack. The results were stunning. With a little gel and a little hair spray she made the short bob spiky here and there and shaped it to flatter her face. It was perfect. And it made her look much younger!

Finally the night arrived. She walked into the Fruitvale hall and heads turned. She was pleased until her eyes fell on the couple at the table in the middle of the room. Johnny and Sarah. She tilted her head up and walked across the room with all the confidence she could muster. She wasn't about to let them spoil her evening.

Cora and Jimmy were sitting at the next table over so Liz went to talk to them. She stood behind them with her back to Johnny and Sarah. And as she talked a good looking guy dressed in a white shirt, black tie and black leather jacket sidled up to her and started to flirt with her. It was exactly what she needed. She didn't know him, but she'd heard all about him. He was from Nelson and quite the ladies man. Liz was flattered. Just as he was kabitizing with her, Billy sidled up to her other side and said, "Hey, Pat, get out of the harem, eh!" Liz giggled. She was in her glory. She hadn't much cared for Billy, but since he had kind of rescued her on New Year's Eve, she was grateful to him. Now he was making her day. The end result being that Johnny and Sarah began to argue and left. Liz never knew for sure if they were arguing about her or not, but it sure seemed strange that after several men had gathered around her and she seemed to be the belle of the ball, the argument broke out. Susan was right. Liz hung in there and now they were the ones leaving. She had a wonderful evening and danced every dance til the wee hours of the morning.

But after the dance was over and Cinderella was back home again in her secluded little house she began to spiral down into the depths of loneliness. One evening just when she thought she would go mad, a knock came at the back door. She was alone and Baillee was sleeping. *Who can that be?* She said to herself. She certainly wasn't expecting anyone. She flung the door open and there standing large as life was the invincible Billy.

"Well are you going to invite me in?"

Liz knew she shouldn't, but she unwittingly, thought, *what the heck. I'm so lonely. He's been chasing me for four years. How long can I fight him off. I'll just let him in for an hour or so just for company. I won't do anything wrong.*

That was her biggest mistake, letting him in the door. One thing led to another and Liz found herself in Billy's arms and then in her bed with him. She had done the one thing she'd said she would never do! She had slept with a *married* man. The one last shred of moral fiber she had left had been destroyed. She was sick to death with herself. That cursed Carousel! Would it never leave her alone? Would it not leave her one thread of decency? She seemed to have licked the alcohol problem, but would she ever beat the Carousel?

She was devastated and let Billy know it. But having finally achieved his goal he was unsympathetic. "Don't worry about it," he said, "It won't kill you." Famous last words. It almost did.

Chapter 19
A Near Death Experience

Shortly after the episode with Billy Liz received a phone call that would light up her life for years to come.

"Hello, Liz?" Darren muttered into the phone. His voice was a little shaky.

"Yeah, Darren, what's happening? Oh, my God! Is Bonnie having the baby?"

"Yeah, yeah! I'm at the hospital. She wants to see you right now!" he shouted into the phone.

"I'll be right there. I'll call Stacy to pick me up. Janie can watch Jason and Baillee."

Stacy had acquired a bright yellow beater of a car. It reminded Liz of a giant yellow beetle. It was rusted and the doors never shut properly, but it ran and got her from point A to point B so she was thrilled with her very first vehicle.

Stacy came on the fly and the two women rushed as fast as the yellow beetle would take them up the hospital hill. Stacy dropped Liz off at the door and Liz bolted through and rushed for the elevator. The elevator zoomed to the 4th floor, but it didn't seem to go fast enough to suit Liz.

She catapulted out of the steel doors and came face to face with Darren who looked like he was about to catapult through the doors the other way.

"Oh, I'm so glad you're here. I need a break," he said as he wiped the sweat off his brow with the back of his hand. "Come on, she's in here." Liz followed his lead reluctantly. She knew the pain of having a first baby and she wasn't sure she could stand to see her own daughter in such pain. She swallowed hard, bit the bullet, and careened through the labour room door.

She couldn't believe her eyes. It looked like Grand Central Station. The room was full of people. There was Doctor Trent, three student nurses, two regular nurses and the secretary from the

Clinic. And there was Bonnie in all her "glory", with her new little bundle just crowning. Liz looked at everyone with a questioning look. What were they all doing there? Her poor daughter! Liz wanted to rush over and cover her up. Bonnie didn't seem to care about the large audience though, and Liz reflected back and realized that she wouldn't have cared if the Queen of England had been in the room when she was giving birth. The only thing she had been aware of was the severe pain.

"Oh, hi, Liz," Dr. Trent beamed. "Everything's going along just fine. You're just in time. I hope you don't mind all the people. With Darren's pitch black hair and Bonnie's copper red, everyone was anxious to see what colour the babe's hair would be. Of course, we had permission from Bonnie. She has been the talk of the clinic with everyone taking wagers about who the baby is going to favor."

Liz smiled. and was about to rush over and take Bonnie's hand when Bonnie let out a loud guttural groan and swore, "F**k, that hurts," she yelled.

"Here it comes," Dr. Trent said, excitedly as she rushed to pull the baby's little black head out. Liz could feel the room spinning. It was as though there were angel wings fluttering all through the room. She almost lost touch with reality. She felt as though she had crossed over into another realm. It was her first experience watching the birthing of a child and she began to realize it was a most spiritual experience. Tears welled up and spilled over and flooded down her cheeks. She rushed to Bonnie and took her hand. She had been so brave. She hadn't screamed or cried out at all.

Dr. Trent bundled the little critter up and handed him to Liz. And Liz just beamed -- another grandson as dark as Jason had been fair.

****

After the excitement of the birthing things at the little gulch home slowed down tremendously. The yard was all done, Baillee was an exemplary baby, and the house was gleaming clean. It seemed there wasn't a lot for Liz to do so she took to parking herself on the front balcony to sun tan, once a very relaxing prospect. However, this venture had its drawbacks. On many occasions she would witness Johnny and Sarah driving by on their way to town. Melancholy began to set in again, and Liz spent a very sad summer in her Gulch home.

Finally, the fall came, a rainy, drizzly, cold fall which only added to Liz's melancholy. She sat huddled in her big easy chair, her mind mulling over her life. Her thoughts drifted to Edmund. She smiled fondly as she recalled riding on the cross bar of his bike his arms wrapped tenderly around her, looking up into his twinkling eyes. Then her pleasant thoughts were interrupted by a dull pain in her lower right anatomy. She shifted trying to ease the pain, but it wouldn't let up. *I'll just wait a bit. It'll go away, probably just gas.* But it didn't go away and gradually it became worse until she was wrought with sharp stabbing, burning pain. She grabbed her side and went to get up. She froze, she couldn't move. Moving made it seem as though her side was going to burst open and spill her guts all over the chair. She reached out slowly for the phone on the end table beside her. She called 368-5651. Vern's voice echoed in her ear as though it were a million miles away. "Good day, Alcoholics Anonymous, what can I do for ya?"

"Oh, Vern, help me, something's wrong, something's really wrong. I can't move." Liz squeaked into the phone.

"I'll be right there," Vern hollered as he took off forgetting to hang up the phone.

Minutes later Vern burst through the door and rushed to Liz who was doubled over in the chair. Teri, a new young red-headed member, followed close on his heels.

"We better get you to the emergency," Vern gasped, out of breath from being overweight and rushing up the stairs.

He grabbed Liz by her hands and gently tried to pull her up from the chair. She screamed, "Don't move me, don't move me! I can't stand the pain. He abruptly let her go and she settled back into the chair rocking back and forth.

"Call an ambulance," Teri yelled in a state of panic.

"Gimme the phone, gimme the phone," Vern pleaded, at a loss as to what else to do.

Liz handed him the phone and he quickly dialled 911. "Hurry, hurry, the girl is in terrible pain," he yelled after he had given directions to the dispatcher.

Within minutes ambulance attendants burst through the back door. One stood over Liz with a needle full of morphine ready to inject into Liz's arm as she moaned in pain.

Suddenly alert and terrified, Liz screamed, "No! Don't! I'm on parnate, you'll kill me."

"Oh, my gawd, what are we gonna do? We can't get the stretcher through your back door and moving you is going to send you over the edge." the attendant cried.

The other attendant with the gray beard answered, "Let's get a kitchen chair and transfer her as gently as we can and tilt it backwards and transport her to the stretcher."

As the attendants lifted Liz, she screamed and immediatley passed out. She came to lying on her back on a stretcher with flannelette sheets and a grey wool blanket over her. A cool, gentle rain was prickling her face as she slowly returned to consciousness. It was dark already and the warm glow of headlights whirred past intermittently lighting up her dark world. Then fully conscious again the pain hit with greater severity. But something more important hit her fuzzy mind. "Baillee!" She yelled. "What about Baillee, I can't leave her."

"Don't worry I'll stay with her." Teri said, kindly.

"Call my daughter, Stacy. She lives right next door. She'll be home from work soon," Liz moaned before she slipped into unconsciousness again as the stretcher slid into the back of the ambulance and the door slammed shut.

Liz buzzed in and out of consciousness as the siren screamed and the vehicle rocked around the corners.

Finally, in a warm hospital bed, she looked up with blurry eyes to see a young female doctor with long brown hair looking down at her. A pretty little thing, but where was Dr. Trent?

"Hi, I'm Dr. Jane Smith. I'm filling in for Dr. Trent. She's away. I suspect you have an ectopic pregnancy, so we'll need to do a urine test. Do you think you can pee in the bed pan?" the doctor said sympathetically.

Liz's mind whirred, *pregnancy, how can I be pregnant. I haven't missed a period. I haven't been with anybody. Oh, my gawd! Billy! What's an "ectopic" pregnancy. Oh, man I can't have Billy's baby.*

"Liz, are you awake?" the doctor asked.

"Yes, yes," Liz moaned as the nurses lifted her onto the bed pan. With great effort she was able to pee what seemed like a teaspoon full.

"It's enough." the doctor said, as she rushed away from the bedside.

Shortly after, the doctor returned to say the test was negative, and they would have to do a blood test and an internal. The doctor donned a rubber glove and proceeded to do the examination. Liz thought she was going to go through the ceiling. She screamed in pain. She dug her heels in trying to escape the doctor's probing fingers, but to no avail.

With the internal procedure done the doctor rushed away again, only to return and inform Liz that it was indeed a tubal pregnancy and that the baby had died. Her mind drifted, as tears rolled down her cheeks. She couldn't have Billy's baby, but the thought of a dead baby inside her before she even knew about being pregnant grieved her deeply. *Was it a boy? Was it a girl?* she pondered. What difference did it make? It was dead! Nonetheless, she wanted to know.

The doctor's next words brought her right back immediately. "I understand you've been taking parnate. We won't be able to operate for at least five days. You'll have to have the parnate completely out of your system or surgery might kill you. The alternative isn't great, either. The dead fetus is going to start to decompose and there's a danger of peritonitis setting in. We'll have to put you in isolation for five days. No moving, no getting out of bed, nothing by mouth, and the strongest antibiotics we can administer, and hope for the best.

Liz was in so much pain, she didn't care. There would be no pain killers for her either, for five days. Could she survive? Would she survive the poisons pulsing through her body? Was this her punishment for going with a married man? She could sure use a drink right about now! God damn that Carousel! She just had to quit it before it killed her. But could she?

Chapter 20
Isolation

Liz's head whirred as she heard the hospital room door fly open. She turned her head to the right to see who was coming in, and her blurry eyes slowly focussed on a plastic tube extending from a hanger, and ascending down to a needle buried deep into the back of her right hand. She had been in isolation for three days and had been in and out of consciousness. It was all a blur to her.

"Hey, girlfriend," a cheery voice cried out. "Oh, you look so sad. Is there anything I can do?"

"Val!" Liz croaked as tears of pent up loneliness started to stream down her face. She reached out her hands and Val took them warmly in hers. "It's so good to see you. It's been a long time."

"I know. Sorry I haven't been around I've been so busy working at Willow Haven. I just love my new job. Anyway, enough about me, what happened to you?"

Liz proceeded to tell Val all about her experiences from sleeping with Billy, to Vern coming over, to the ambulance ride. On and on, it all blurted out of her. She was so happy to have a friend to confide in.

Then after a half hour or so the door flew open again and a huge manly looking nurse in a white uniform came bolting through the door. Liz hadn't seen her before. She was the head nurse and she was on a mission, and Liz could tell by her demeanor it wasn't going to be too kindly. "You'll have to leave right now," she stated abruptly to Val.

"No!" Liz squeaked out. "She's my best friend and anything you have to say, you can say in front of her."

"I'm in charge here and I say NO VISITORS," the angry nurse blurted.

"I'll go," Val returned coolly to the nurse, not wanting to cause a scene. Then she turned empathetically to Liz, "But I'll be back." She waved and smiled a warm smile as she backed out the door.

"You young girls! Think you can fool around and not get caught! Where's your husband? Do you even know who the father is?" The ugly nurse hissed coldly. "I need you to sign some papers. "You kind of girls always get what you deserve," she continued as she started to go over the consent papers on the clipboard with Liz. That done, she left as abruptly as she'd come. Liz rolled over to put her face to the wall in shame and screamed in pain with the movement.

After some time, the door slowly opened again and Erica stuck her pretty face in the door. "Psst, Liz, are you awake?" she whispered. "Oh, my dear, you look terrible. Look at your hair! It's so oily and stringy looking. I'm just coming on duty. I'm going to go and talk to the head nurse and see if I can wash your hair for you right in the bed with a basin. Would you like that?" she asked sympathetically.

Liz nodded. She was dizzy with pain but having her hair washed would feel so good. She had always loved someone to fuss with her hair. It totally relaxed her. She had always been a little afraid of Erica's abrupt manner, but she found her to be so caring at her job.

Within a few minutes, Erica returned with her head hanging and said, "Sorry, Liz, she won't let me wash your hair. I don't know what her problem is. She said you're not to be moved, but I could do it easily, I know I could. I can't go against her word, though. Sorry," she muttered again, sadly. Liz turned her head away in defeat as Erica left the room.

The next day the surgeon came in to see Liz. She related the whole story of the nurse's abruptness and her insulting words. The doctor asked firmly, "Who treated you like that?"

"I think she's the head nurse," Liz cried.

"Well, we'll just see about that." he retorted. Then he began to tell Liz of the procedures for the surgery. She didn't really care. She just wanted it to be all over. She didn't know how much more she could take.

Just after the doctor left, the door creaked open again. Liz turned her head to the right and there standing large as life was a gorgeous young man in a blue hospital gown.

"Hey, I see the sign on your door NO VISITORS. You been in here alone for a long time. Thought you might like to see someone. What do you think of the bitch? The head nurse, I mean." Liz smiled weakly and nodded. "She don't scare me." he said. My name's Brian Symons. What's yours?"

"Liz." she answered.

Brian stayed for a while consoling Liz, and after he left her spirits felt lifted. She would never forget the handsome young man who had taken the time and the risk to sneak in and say hi to a lonely destitute woman. He restored her faith in human kindness.

Finally, Liz was wheeled into surgery. She was scared, but relieved.

"99, 98, 97" Liz whispered and then it was lights out.

"Hey, sleepy head. How you doin', " Henry blatted out smiling widely. Donald peered over his shoulder smiling sheepishly. Donald always smiled sheepishly because he was an A.A. member who was constantly falling off the wagon and coming back with his tail between his legs. He was Henry's project and Liz loved them both dearly because they were so kind to her after Baillee was born, but, today, something was wrong with Liz.

"Get the hell out of here," she screamed at them looking for something to throw.

"Hey, whatsa matter?" Henry cried as Donald backed out the door.

"Just get out!" she screamed.

They left immediately shrugging their shoulders. This was so unlike quiet, meek little Liz. Liz struggled to get out of bed and then started screaming at the nurses. She flopped back in the bed. She could hear herself, but couldn't seem to stop herself. *What's the matter with me?* she thought desperately. Then she screamed again at the nurses. Finally, she fell back into a deep sleep.

The next morning the young, pretty doctor was shaking her awake. "Liz, how are you doing?"

"Okay," she answered groggily as pain shot through her mid section. She cringed. Then she waited to see if she was okay. Was she going to scream at the doctor? No! She was okay.

"What did the nurses give me?" Liz asked. "I was so weird yesterday, totally out of character."

The doctor looked at Liz's chart and said, "Codeine."

"Don't ever give that to me again." Liz stated firmly. "It made me crazy".

"Oh, must have had an allergic reaction. I'll mark it on your chart." After examining Liz the doctor announced, "You'll be going home in a few days. Do you have any help? There'll be no lifting for you for at least six weeks and Christmas is coming."

"I'll have lots of help. My girls will rally round, I'm sure." Liz answered as the doctor headed for the door.

After the doctor left the surgeon popped in to check his handy work. "Did you see the fetus?" Liz asked shyly.

"Yes. It was the size of a large egg."

"Was it a boy or a girl?" Liz asked sadly. She hadn't even known she was pregnant, but still she felt a loss.

"You don't want to know that, do you?" the doctor stated.

She *did* want to know. But instead of pursuing it, in shame, she hung her head and slowly shook it from side to side.

****

"What a tree. It looks like it's going to topple over," Janie cried.

"I know," Liz replied sadly from her vantage point on the couch. It was ugly, but in the state she was in she hadn't been able to do any better. Johnny had stopped by to see her, having heard she'd had surgery. What for, he didn't know, and she didn't tell him, but he had kindly offered to get her a Christmas tree from the bush. A Scotch Pine, it was. Who puts up a Scotch Pine for a Christmas tree? It was ugly, but the girls had decorated it as well as they could and secured it to a hook in the ceiling.

Liz sat on the couch unable to do anything. She was still really sore. Stacy was saying, "You know my nursing instructor said that parnate is antiquated. Nobody ever uses it any more. I don't know why Dr. Ward ever gave it to you. You could have died, Mom."

"I know," Liz said as she hugged Baillee closer to her.

Then she was startled as Bonnie let out a high pitched scream. Liz looked up just in time to see the huge Scotch Pine toppling over with little Wesley in his walker right underneath it. In one giant leap Darren was across the room grabbing the tree and firing it. It landed on top of Bonnie and Janie who were conversing in the corner.

Darren didn't care as he rescued Wesley from his walker all covered in pine needles. The look on Wesley's face was priceless, not to mention the girls' heads sticking out through the Scotch Pine. Liz slowly started to giggle and then grabbed her stomach in pain as she roared with laughter. She was still tender from the surgery. What more could happen in her life? Little did she know there were more adventures yet to come.

Chapter 21
Biker Babe

A cold, soggy winter in the gulch passed slowly for Liz as it seemed to take forever for her to heal. But finally, the March sun beamed through beautifully and warmed the little town of Trail. It warmed Liz's spirits too. *Spring when a young man (or woman's) fancy turns to thoughts of love.* Even though Liz had learned a lot about her addictions from Bart and how to heal herself, knowing and doing were two different things. She had the ideas solidly set in her mind, but the heart is treacherous and the ideas Bart had taught seemed to fail to reach there. So by the time summer arrived the Carousel was tugging at Liz's heart strings unmercifully.

"Sit still, will ya. You're gonna knock us both over," Roy shouted, frantically as Liz giggled uproariously atop his shoulders.

"I gotta get this sign up and I can't quite reach. Hang tight. One more stretch...Oh, my gawd!" she screeched as they toppled to the ground.

Roy rolled over and got up onto his knees, "Are you okay?"

Liz laughed hilariously, lying on her back looking up at Roy on his hands and knees.

"Stop it," he cried. "We coulda been hurt."

"Well, we weren't," she laughed as she tickled his fat belly. "Now get me up there again so I can put this sign up properly. People won't know which fork to take and they'll never find the campground, it's so secluded," she insisted.

It was the annual Trail A.A. Campout and Liz was the secretary on the committee. Ivan was the chairperson. Ivan and she worked perfectly together to make the whole thing a success every year. It was an accomplishment that she was really proud of, and she was grateful to Ivan for trusting her to be his secretary. She kept a perfect record of the events, the money needed, and even the amount of pancake mix needed to feed a hundred people who showed up yearly from all over B.C. and Washington State. Of course, Roy was part of the committee and Liz just loved working with him. He had asked her out once, but it turned out to be a fiasco. She loved him dearly, but more like a brother and the dating thing just didn't work. Although they ended up at each other's throats during the date, they still remained friends. However, in spite of his friendship, and the closeness of the A.A. group, she was still feeling empty inside.

Putting Bart's ideas into effect had been a lot harder than she'd thought it would be, and the Carousel tugged relentlessly as she discussed the meal plans with Erica who was in charge of the kitchen. Not only did Liz secretary for Ivan, she worked very hard in the kitchen struggling with huge pots, the like of which she'd never seen before, and made humongous piles of mashed potatoes. She felt like she was in the army pealing all those spuds. Just then the kitchen door flew open and Cora came running through.

"Oh, my gawd, the bikers are here! We've never had bikers before. I hope they're friendly." Cora lamented.

Liz ran to the front door of the hall and sure enough several motorcycles were just pulling on to the grounds where Roy was wielding a huge fire hose to keep the dust down.

The head rider looked up to where Liz stood in the doorway, and touched his forefinger to his forehead in greeting. She smiled shyly, and retreated back into the hall, face all red and grinning profusely. She'd never had anything to do with bikers before. She was afraid of them, but at the same time she recalled the movie she had seen in her teens, *The Wild One* with Marlon Brando, and her blood ran hot. She would have to work really hard to keep the Carousel in check because the biker who had greeted her was extremely handsome in his tight, black leather pants and his brown suede vest, no shirt, his bronze coloured bi-ceps gleaming in the sun.

Liz, Cora and two other girls from the club had settled in nicely in their assigned cabin with two bunk beds. The first day was under their belt, all the meals had been served expertly by Liz, Cora and Erica with the help of several other women in the group, and now it was time for some fun.

Liz had purchased a second hand guitar during her sobriety and had taught herself to play with the help of some books. She had always loved to sing and always had a dream of singing on the stage. But for now she would just have to play and join the others in singing around the huge, yellow/orange blaze that flared up from the camp-fire. She was feeling wonderful with the smell of the wood burning and the sweet pine smell of the forest and the good friends surrounding her. She was singing her heart out, "I keep a close watch on this heart of mine." Billy sidled up close to her on the log she was sitting on, and joined in her singing. "I keep my eyes wide open all the time," he sang, and rolled his eyes flirtatiously at her. She stiffened, but finished the song, and then abruptly jumped up from the log leaving her guitar behind. She couldn't afford to get close to Billy again. She had sort of fallen for him during their little tryst, but his reaction to her pregancy and her hospital stay, had broken her heart. He had totally brushed her off and made light of her near death experience so as not to take any responsibility for his actions, and she wasn't about to let her heart rule her head this time.

She stomped away from the fire and was walking toward the woods down the long lane in the bright moonlight when she heard footfalls coming behind her. She picked up her speed thinking that Billy was in pursuit.

"Hey, hold up a minute!" The words broke through the silent night.

Liz turned then and in the moonlight she could make out the shiny leather pants and the gleaming bi-ceps. Her heart started to pound ferociously. She wasn't sure if it was the Carousel or fear. She stopped dead in her tracks at his command and waited for him to catch up.

"Hi," he said cocksure of himself.

"Hi," she returned, shyly.

They walked and talked for what seemed like miles. She told him how she'd worked as a clerk typist over the years and was proud of that fact. She also told him how uncomfortable she'd felt in that environment, though, being a drunk and all, and how it seemed to her that it was a plastic world where no one seemed to be real. She went on and on about her life and its trials and tribulations. He hung on every word and agreed with everything she said. He sympathized. At last, a soul mate! The Carousel whirred with delight. So when he slipped his arms around her waist she didn't object. Liz, retreating from Billy's spell, wrapped herself around this stranger in unmitigated passion. The silvery moonbeams smiled down on them, and her heart spun with delight as the Carousel carried her away. She'd thought she was getting better by rejecting Billy, but now she wasn't so sure.

****

"Hey, where did you guys all go last night," Cora moaned as she wiped the sleep from her eyes and grasped the warm styro-foam cup of coffee to take the early morning chill out of her fingers. Jimmy had to work for the weekend so he wasn't able to come to the campout and Cora had bunked in with Liz and two other women and had woken up to find herself alone in the bunk house.

Liz grinned widely as did the other two women. The bikers had gotten what they'd come for, a free toss in the hay. But it had backfired for Lance who had bedded Liz down. He actually liked her, so later that day, he took Liz for a bike ride around the loop through Castlegar, Nelson, and back to Fruitvale where Camp Tweedsmuir entertained the small A.A. group. Liz was ecstatic. The ride was wonderful. She hadn't been on a bike since her teens. She was a little nervous at first, but Lance totally reassured her with his capabilities with the bike, and when they pulled in to a rest stop Liz was totally swept off her feet -- beautiful white water cascaded down over wet, black rocks, the emerald green forest surrounded them, the sky was azure blue and an eagle soared gracefully above. Lance's handsome face leaned over her to kiss her. That finished her off. She was smitten. Badly smitten.

They returned to the camp and Liz spied Billy off in the distance. He was furious as his eyes, like lazers, pierced through her. She got off the bike, removed her helmet, shook her long chestnut hair loose and took Lance's arm as they headed into the hall for supper. She'd show Billy he couldn't play around with *her* heart.

Lance ended up staying for a week. He didn't want to leave Liz. Sadly, he finally had to go, and Liz was alone once more. He wrote to her often and she to him, but it wasn't enough so when he wrote and invited her to the A.A. Biker's campout in Wenatchee, Washington she was thrilled. Little did she know what lay in store for her.

The Bikers

Chapter 22
The Brass Bed

Liz boarded the big Greyhound bus in downtown Trail. She was excited she was going to see Lance, but on the other hand she was apprehensive. Her anxiety attacks had begun to bother her again, and she wasn't all too happy about leaving familiar territory. All the girls she'd shared the bunk house with, including Cora, had agreed to come for the excitement of a biker's bash, but at the last minute they'd all reneged. She waved nervously out the bus window to Ronnie, an A.A. member who'd walked to the bus depot with her. Liz loved Ronnie too, as she did all the A.A. members even though he marched to his own drummer. Ronnie had always wanted to be a biker and dreamed constantly of Harleys. As a matter of fact, he always said his Higher Power rode a Harley. He was an entertaining, dynamic member, and he so longed to accompany Liz to this rally, but lacked the funds. Now, as the bus pulled out, Liz wished desperately she'd had enough money to be able to bring him along.

She wriggled deeply into the plush seat to read her romance novel, and she was actually enjoying the ride until the bus stopped abruptly at the border to the United States. She started to sweat profusely, her heart raced, her mind screamed out, *Let me off! Let me off!* She was terror stricken. It had come over her like a wet blanket, instantly and all encompassing. She tried to take a deep breath and couldn't. A ball of air lodged in her chest and pumped right back out again. She couldn't breathe. It was happening again! She gasped for air. She grabbed at her chest. The woman across the aisle looked at her suspiciously.

"I suffer from panic disorder," Liz squeaked out.

The woman looked at her kindly. "I've heard of that. I have a nephew who suffers from it. They say it helps to breathe into a paper bag. I have one in my case if you'd like to try it."

Liz reluctantly took the bag from her, but she was too embarrassed to breathe into it.

"Thanks. I think I'm going to be okay now," Liz murmered. The onslaught of the attack seemed to be receding. Because her mind was occupied with something else, her muscles started to relax and she was able to breathe a little easier.

"Keep the bag just in case," the lady kindly replied.

For the rest of the ride to Spokane Liz buzzed in and out of anxiety, but because of the bag in her pocket she felt a little more secure. Then she started to think about the stop over in Spokane. She would arrive at 5 p.m. and the bus for Wenatchee didn't leave until two in the morning. What the hell was she going to do? She pictured herself running frantically through the depot, totally out of control and the men in the white coats coming with the paddy wagon to take her away.

She had to come up with a plan. Susan always said, *You've got to have a Plan B*. Susan's beautiful voice echoed in her mind and she felt a little more at ease. *Remember anywhere you go in the world A.A.'s will welcome you and take you in*. Now Ronnie's voice echoed in the confines of her mind. *That's it! That's it! I'll call A.A. as soon as I get there. I'll take in a meeting*. She started to relax a little more.

The big bus emitted noxious fumes as it pulled into the huge Spokane depot. It pulled to a stop and Liz stepped down. She was amazed to see how many little old ladies, pulling suitcases on little wheels, were travelling alone. Why was *she* so scared. These ladies seemed right at home smiling sweetly at her. She looked like a ghost with her pinched white face.

As soon as she was inside the depot she fumbled for a dime, looked up A.A. in the phone book and dialed. A friendly voice answered immediately and directed her to a meeting taking place at 5 p.m. at the YWCA. She followed the instructions they gave her and made her way a few blocks over to the big building. She was still somewhat anxious, but knew there was light at the end of the tunnel. She just hoped someone would have a suggestion as to what she should do for the rest of her time there.

Her fears were unfounded. When she spoke about her dilemma openly at the meeting she was overwhelmed with the response afterwards. Especially from a good looking, neatly clad, young woman, who looked for all the world like a school teacher.

Liz's deductions weren't far off, she was indeed, a kindergarten teacher, and a sober alcoholic. She invited Liz to her home, fed her a delicious supper, bedded her down in a comfortable frilly guest room especially made for girls, and waited up to wake Liz at 1:30 a.m. to drive her to the bus depot. She did all this because her husband's name was Lance, she had met him across country at an A.A. function, had travelled alone on a bus to see him again, had fallen in love with him, and married him. *And* still loved him deeply. Liz was amazed at the story. Small world, indeed. Would this be Liz's fate as well?

Carol, the teacher, dropped Liz off at the bus depot and rushed away so she could get some sleep before classes in the morning. Liz hugged her warmly and thanked her deeply before she left and now she looked around at the cold empty marble walls of the bus depot. A few people darted here and there, but mostly it was empty. She found her way to the bath room to breathe into the bag. She was gasping for air now that she was away from the dear, A.A. member and all alone again. She didn't seem to be able to be alone. Perhaps she didn't trust herself to look after herself? Had she ever taken good care of herself ? What wild venture was she off to now? A Biker's Bash. What was wrong with her?

She gazed out the bus window and tried to settle in. The moon glared back at her a huge, golden, harvest moon. It was beautiful, but it seemed to be mocking her, laughing at her. Where was she going? Was she crazy?

She arrived, after a sleepless night on the bus at 7:30 in the morning, to a strange town, a strange little restaurant, *but* a very welcome face looking over the top of a booth at the back. She had never seen such a beautiful, welcome face in all her life. He *was* handsome.

"Hey, beautiful. You made it all in one piece, eh?"

"Barely," she said, "I didn't sleep well and I'm really tired." She didn't tell him about the anxiety. After all he was a tough biker and she was trying to impress him.

"Well, I've got just the thing for you," he stated, grinning.

"What?" she asked.

"You'll see. It's a surprise," he said, beaming. At that moment he looked like *a very pleased with himself* little boy.

They drove in his truck to his apple orchard. The apple orchard that he owned and where he lived was vast. Rows on rows of apple trees, all picked clean. There were boxes and boxes of bright red apples, ready for shipping, piled all around what looked like a dug-out basement. Liz looked around and there was no house! *Where was his house?*

"Well, this is it!" he stated firmly. "Home Sweet Home."

Liz was taken aback as they went down concrete steps into the dug-out. There was one huge messy, messy room. And in the middle of all the squallor was a beautiful, brand new, gleaming, brass bed made up with new bedding and a white flowered comforter.

Liz started to laugh, partly because of his rushing out to buy the bed for her, partly because of the bed standing out like a sore thumb in the middle of the mess, and partly because of sheer nervous anxiety. She just roared.

"You don't like it?" he queried.

"I love it!" she exclaimed and threw her arms around him with delight. His place was a mess, but he had thought enough of her to go out and buy a bed fit for a princess.

Just then her bubble burst. A very sexy, attractive woman came sauntering through the door. "Like your bed?" she asked smiling warmly. "He bought it especially for you. I never got any of that kind of treatment," she stated continuing to smile warmly.

Who is she? Liz thought. She was astounded, but didn't totally dislike her. Her manner was warm.

"Oh, Liz this is Laurie. Laurie, Liz." The girls nodded to each other as Lance continued. "Laurie is between places right now. She's a hooker. She's been staying with me until she finds another place, but she'll sleep outside with Peter in his sleeping bag while you're here."

Oh, my gawd! What have I gotten myself into this time?

Liz's face must have looked flabbergasted, but Lance just continued as if nothing was at all out of place, "You get some sleep. I've got lots to do to get ready for the campout. The gang will be coming in soon. When you get up we'll all go for a ride."

After Laurie and Lance left. Liz crawled into the bed and after tossing and turning for awhile, the new bed carressed her into sleep.

****

"Hey sleepyhead," Lance playfully coaxed as he tossled Liz's hair. The gang's all here pretty much. I made you a coffee and whenever you're ready we're gonna ride. That's what it's all about. So hurry up and get up. I'll wait outside for you." He did care for her, she could tell by the bed and his manner, but was this life for her? She was even more convinced that it wasn't when she wandered outside half asleep and spotted a good looking girl with long blonde hair just whipping her top off. She stood totally naked from the waist up, then sauntered over to a large double laundry sink and proceeded to wash her hair under the one cold water tap.

Liz gulped as Laurie sidled up to her. "It's not all that bad," she said "You'll get used to it. At least they're all sober. And Lance really does love you. I never seen him like he is, the brass bed and all." Liz reflected on the cartoon movie, *Lady and the Tramp*. Not that Lance was a tramp by any means. But they sure were from two different worlds. Could it work?

Chapter 23
The Pumpkin Head

Liz watched as the blonde washed her hair so brazenly in front of all the men, and started to feel squeamish. Then Laurie's words broke through, "That's Monica," she said pointing at the blonde. She's on the make. She just broke up with Terry over there, and he's just devastated. Weird to see a tough biker turn to mush because of a chick. We women really do have the power." she prattled on.

Liz wasn't so sure. She'd never had much power over men. She turned to where Laurie's finger made an imaginary line to where Terry sat slumped over on a camp cot looking totally dejected as Monica strutted her stuff in front of all the bikers. Liz watched in awe as Monica wrapped a towel, turban style around her long, wet hair. She shook her head to clear the cobwebs out. *What was she doing here? This was no place for her.* She glanced again at Monica, then back to Terry as Lance sidled up to her, and said, "Well, are you ready for the ride?"

Liz's head whirred with confusion. It was all too much for her. She couldn't possibly ride with this gang. She felt totally out of place and besides she just couldn't chance having another anxiety attack, and stopping the whole pack on the road to breathe into a brown paper bag. It would be too humiliating. She started to rub her stomach.

"What's the matter?" Lance asked looking concerned. "Not feeling well? The ride in the fresh air will fix you right up!" he declared.

Liz knew it wouldn't. She had to stand her ground. Just then Laurie, sensing what was going on, came to Liz's rescue, "Aw, Lance, let her stay behind and keep me company. I got my period and I don't feel too good either. She can keep me company." Liz breathed a sigh of relief.

Lance looked disappointed, but finally conceded. "Come on, guys. Let's get going." he shouted with great authority in his voice. The gang all followed his direction and started to mount their bikes.

There was a terrific roar as over forty bikes revved up for the ride. A dust cloud followed them out of the yard.

Liz and Laurie settled in beside the fire pit on the logs that had been provided, for a long day and a long visit. Liz liked Laurie, in spite of the fact that she was a hooker. She had heart and she had come to Liz's rescue in the nick of time.

"A nice girl like you doesn't really belong here," Laurie remarked.

"No you don't!" Another deep voice startled them from behind. They simultaneously turned to see Terry slumped over on the camp cot looking for all the world like a beaten pup.

"Hey, Terry, come and join us. I thought you went with the others."

"Naw, I didn't feel like it today."

"Monica, eh?"

"Yeah, the bitch broke my heart," he said as he laughed a very unconvincing laugh, trying to hide his hurt feelings.

These really are people just like the rest of us. Liz thought to herself. They have the same feelings, they just hide them under a tough exterior. She started to feel a little better about where she was. Besides, the pressure was off with the whole gang gone. She liked Laurie. And Terry seemed more human with just her and Laurie for company. So she settled in for what turned out to be a most enjoyable day. Terry was extremely good looking and very sexy in his leathers and he was funny. He entertained the girls until Liz thought her sides were going to burst with laughter. She actually was endeared to him and felt for his plight.

She was roaring with laughter for the umpteenth time when the bikers pulled back into the yard in the late afternoon. Lance spotted her merriment and a black cloud quickly surrounded his countenance. He jumped off his bike, parked it and sauntered immediatly to where Liz sat on the log jealousy written all over his face, his big hands forming fists. He squatted slightly behind her with one knee on either side of her head.

Liz was laughing so hard and so taken in with Terry that she didn't see it coming. All of a sudden she felt pressure on both sides of her head. Then the pressure slowly increased. Her eyes seemed to be bugging out. She sat totally still, sweating profusely as she felt as though her head would burst like a pumpkin. Lance continued to apply pressure to each side of her head with his knees until she almost passed out. Then he jumped up suddenly, laughed, a bitter laugh and said, "I thought you were sick. You look fine to me." He looked at Terry with daggers.

"Come on, Lance, we were just having fun. She didn't feel so good and neither did I. The girls cheered me up. No harm done," Terry exclaimed.

"Yeah," said Laurie, "Lighten up a bit."

Liz shook with terror. She'd had a close call. He could have killed her. He started to remind her of Lenny. This *definitely* wasn't the place for her. The damn Carousel just had to be halted before she killed herself. It was almost worse than the booze.

****

Liz jumped out of bed. It was her last day here. She would be leaving the next morning and she couldn't wait. But in the meantime there was a breakfast meeting at a fancy restaurant in downtown Wenatchee. She looked forward to the meeting. She sure needed one. She dressed and fixed herself in readiness. Then they climbed aboard the bikes. Lance was on the lead bike, of course and Liz, arms grasped tightly around his waist, waited for the roar to start. Even though she knew she didn't fit with these people, there was something about the roar of forty bikes that stirred her blood, and she couldn't deny that she did, indeed, feel kind of proud to be on the back of the lead bike as they rolled through the streets of town. Heads turned everywhere they went, and when they pulled into the parking lot of the restaurant people backed away. There was certainly a power to be reckoned with here.

But then Liz reflected back on a twelve step call she'd made at the Daly Pavilion a while back and she shuddered. A biker babe was hiding out in the pavilion because she had, purposely, in a state of anger and drunkeness, scratched up her biker boyfriend's brand new Harley with a nail. The scene replayed in Liz's mind. "How will he know *you* did it?"

"Because I scratched my initials in it."

"Oh, my gawd. The only thing I can suggest for you is to get out off town and fast." The scene brought Liz back to reality and she quickly pushed the thrill of it all out of her mind.

After the meeting Liz packed all her stuff and spent the afternoon with the gang in the orchard exchanging tales of their expeditions. It was not an unpleasant afternoon because she was happier knowing that she was leaving the next day. The only thing that marred the day was the fear of her anxiety on the trip home. As sure as God made little green apples, she knew it would come. But it would be the lesser of two evils. She had sucked up to Lance the whole weekend after the pumpkin head incident and she didn't know how much longer she could keep up the act.

Finally the morning came and Liz waited anxiously as the big Greyhound bus pulled into the little restaurant where just three days ago she had stepped down all excited to meet Lance. She climbed aboard the bus with her gear so relieved to be leaving and turned and waved to Lance, knowing she would *never* see him again. Somehow he knew it too as he waved his goodbyes, shrugged his shoulders nonchalantly and swaggered away.

She plopped herself down in the seat almost wanting to bolt back out of the bus. She wasn't so sure of herself now that the bus doors had closed. Eighteen hours of sheer mind terror awaited her on the ride home. She almost wished she was back at the orchard, but not quite.

As it turned out the ride wasn't so bad after all. The middle aged woman beside her was very distracting. And distraction was what was needed to thwart off the onslaught of the anxiety. As long as Liz's mind was busy with other things and she wasn't locked inside herself with the terror, the anxiety seemed to recede.

Liz, always ready to listen to others problems, was in total awe of the woman's story. She was married to a man who was what she called "a skin head". Liz wasn't exactly sure what that meant, but the woman seemed to indicate that it was something to do with the Nazis and white supremacy. The woman, who called herself Wendy, related that she was in sheer terror of her husband, and was running away. She was petrified that he would find her. She told Liz all about how she just couldn't live in that kind of environment. Liz knew intuitively that was true because the woman was a real sweetheart, very kind. They chattered incessantly the whole way to Spokane. Liz had made a new friend who promised to drop her a line, telling her her whereabouts every now and again, so Liz wouldn't worry about her. The trip from Spokane to Trail seemed to fly by. Liz felt much better as she headed towards home and familiar territory. With each mile that flew by, another weight was lifted off until she felt as light as a feather. That was it for her. This Carousel ride was over. But would the Carousel be happy to stay dormant?

Chapter 24
My Friend Irma

The woman was screaming like a lunatic and slamming cupboard doors one after another all through her kitchen. Liz sat cowering in the corner, terrified. Val on the other side of the table, all nicely set for lunch, was grinning like a Cheshire cat. Val had known Irma for years and was used to her antics, but Liz had just recently met her.

"That son of a bitch," Irma screamed again, as the phone started ringing off the wall. "Yeah," she screeched as she picked up the phone.

"We must have got cut off," the voice on the other end stated. The girls could hear every word as Irma held the phone out away from her ear. She grinned at the girls knowing full well she had slammed the receiver down on him just minutes ago.

****

Liz had arrived home safely from her biker trip a week before and she had been welcomed with open arms by Janie, but Baillee was another matter. Liz had been gone for five days and three year old Baillee acted as though she didn't even know who she was. It nearly broke Liz's heart. How could she have left her baby with Janie to go off on a wild goose chase. Damn that Carousel. She just had to get it under control. She was working with it to some degree. She still succumbed to its call, but at least she had nipped it in the bud with Billy and Lance. She had dropped both of them within a short period of time. Even though she'd almost died from the tryst with Billy at least she had dumped him shortly after, and Lance was gone too, no question about it. Years ago she would have clung to them in desperation. So maybe she was getting better to some degree. She promised herself that she would gather all her strengths together and give an all out effort to get off the Carousel completely, after all she hadn't had a drink in almost five years. She had beat the alcohol, surely she could beat the Carousel too. Being determined to do so, she decided to throw herself into the A.A. program with intensity. She promised herself she would sponsor the very next woman who came along.

****

"Hey, Liz, I want you to meet Irma," Henry stated with a big grin on his face. Liz looked at the woman nervously. She was tiny. She was built like a young teenager, but anger oozed out of every pore, and Liz was frightened. But she had made a promise to herself and a promise was a promise. Gingerly she reached out and shook the woman's hand. Arrangements were made and Liz became Irma's sponsor. Liz then introduced Irma to Val who was over from Nelson, visiting and attending the A.A. meeting.

Val went to grab Irma in a bear hug, but Irma backed away hands bent up at the wrists in an effort to push her away. "Hey, you've known me long enough to know I don't do that kinda stuff," Irma grunted. Val grinned. She had, indeed, known Irma for years. She knew all about her background, how her parents had been alcoholics, and how they used to leave her alone in their apartment all the time. Irma had told her how she used to cower under her bed all alone at six years old during thunder storms. Over the years the cowering stopped and a giant wall of courage was built in this tiny little girl and now she was the toughest thing on earth, at least on the outside. Liz was reluctant to sponsor her, but decided to throw caution to the wind and give it a whirl.

"Hey I gotta go to the lake tomorrow, but I'll be back next week why don't you come to my house for lunch," Irma extended to Liz. Liz looked at Irma, feeling somewhat intimidated and quickly glanced at Val. "Yeah, she can come to, the old sot," Irma stated gruffly, sensing Liz's apprehension.

****

"Men!" Irma screamed as she slammed the phone down again on her ex-husband, Cole's ear." Years of drinking together led to bitter fighting, and, in the end, led to Cole stepping out on Irma, and then leaving her to fend for herself with three babies. At least Liz could relate to that experience, having been left by Brian with three babies in tow.

Irma remarried a very good man, Andy, who didn't have a drinking problem, and who cared for her children as if they were his own, and now she was afraid of losing him because of *her* drinking. Thus she had approached Henry, another A.A. member she had known for years, and asked him to take her to a meeting. Like Liz, Irma had been married several times, and proceeded to expound on her past experiences as they ate their lunch.

"You know, I didn't always drink like I do now. When I married my first husband, Dick, he was filthy rich, I didn't drink at all. I was little miss innocent," she rolled her eyes and laughed. "That son of a bitch would hold me upside down by my ankles out the window of our tenth story apartment in Vancouver. I never even let on that it bothered me. Would make him madder than a hatter."

Liz shuddered at the thought, but imagined Irma holding up under fire.

"I think the worst thing he ever did to me, though, was when I was having a shower, the son of a bitch opened the shower door, stepped in and proceeded to piss all over me. What a pig! After that I started to hit the sauce and voila." she chuckled as she extended her arms.

Liz was astounded at Irma's experiences. She thought her life had been bad. But it faded in comparison to Irma's.

"Hey enough about the men. Andy and I are going to Christina lake this weekend again. We've got a nice trailer out there with lots of room, and, sponsor, you're coming with us. And don't worry about bringing anything. It's on me. A lot of drinking goes on out there and I'm gonna need ya."

Liz gulped as Val remarked, "Wow, what a sponsee, free trips to the lake. Wish I had a sponsee like that."

"Yeah, you can use me, but don't abuse me," Irma came back with and Liz was sure she would never use Irma as she gulped again. There would be no way she could get out of this one. What had she done to herself? She could feel the anxiety creeping up through her body. What she didn't know at the time, though, was that Irma was going be her saviour in the future more times than enough.

****

The day was beautiful and sunny, and in spite of Liz's nerves she began to relax and actually enjoy herself as she watched the sunbeams bounce off the lake like twinkling diamonds. She breathed in deeply, let out a sigh, and stretched like a contented cat on the lounge chair on the beach. Janie had offered to watch Baillee again, she was a gem. Liz didn't know what she would have done without her to help with Baillee. Janie didn't mind. She loved Baillee, and as the other kids had all left home, Janie was happy with her company and spoiled her rotten. The two girls would grow to be inseparable. Liz was pondering all of this when Irma's sharp voice broke through.

"Hey, come on, lazy bones. Andy's gonna take us for a boat ride out on the lake."

Liz squirmed, reluctant to say what she had to say. How could she let Irma know about her anxiety attacks. The woman was so tough, she would never understand.

"Uh, I don't think I can go."

"What are you talkin' about. Of course, you can go. It's a blast. You'll really enjoy, come on." Irma stated, firmly.

Liz pried herself off the lounge chair and slowly followed behind Irma, head hanging. She couldn't possibly tell her. She prayed she'd be alright. She hadn't been on any medication for the anxiety since the parnate and was just winging it. She had learned what to avoid -- elevators, eating out alone, going to theatres, travelling by herself out of town, going to the mall alone, walking across Trail's big bridge across the Columbia River. As long as she avoided these types of things, she was okay. She hadn't been on a boat for years and didn't know what the results would be, but she could feel the anxiety prickling up her body and she was scared!

Irma was talking and Liz wasn't comprehending a word, Her words were all jumbled together with the roar of the motor and sounded like they were being funnelled down a long tunnel. Liz couldn't breathe. It was happening again. Her chest tightened. She gasped. The pain ran up her left arm and gripped her heart. *This is a heart attack, It's real this time. Oh, my gawd, oh, my gawd. What am I going to do. I don't feel safe with this tough woman. Her husband seems nice, but I don't even know him.* Liz's thoughts carried her away into a world of extreme terror as a tear started to trickle down her cheek.

"That's it, let it go," Irma murmured, kindly. "Once you cry it'll pass. That's how it works for me. I get 'em all the time, but once I cry it goes away."

Liz looked at her astounded. *This tough lady gets anxiety attacks?*

Irma's tough voice pentrated, the brief kind tone gone completely, "But if you ever tell anyone I cry, I'll kill ya." she laughed as she grabbed Liz by the hand.

Liz had made a new friend, and a very cherished one, indeed, as she would find out in the future.

Chapter 25
Girl Friday

"So, who are your friends?" The serious looking lawyer queried as he looked over his glasses at Liz.

"All the people in A.A." Liz gasped out without thinking. *Oh, my gawd. What have I done? That's it. It's over. He'll never hire me now.* she thought as she looked up into the eyes of the prominent lawyer on the other side of the big cherry wood desk.

It was September, 1985, and Liz had been pounding the streets, with no luck, looking for a job. Her social worker had been right. Cutting back her monthly welfare cheque had, indeed, given her incentive to get out and look for a job. She had given up looking for a husband to take care of her and the Carousel lay dormant inside her, at least for the time being. It was time to get serious, after all, she had a baby and a teenager to take care of. Janie was going to need lots of things for high school.

The lawyer looked at her and smiled warmly, trying desperately to keep the grin off his face. He was going to hire her anyway, he was just putting her through the traces and her honesty impressed him. "Well, Lisa wants to take Fridays off and I need a receptionist for that day. It's only one day a week, will that work for you?"

"Yes, oh, yes," Liz cried, relief written all over her face. The incentive program through welfare would pay her $100.00 a month to work one day a week. The one hundred they had taken away from her. She wasn't going to be rich, but it would help and besides, she would have her foot in the door in the field of law. She wanted to celebrate with supper out or something. But that would have to wait. She was always broke. So instead she rushed over to the A.A. club and shared her good news with everyone there, and they were elated.

After Liz had worked several Fridays, Candy, the other legal secretary, had taught Liz everything she needed to know. She'd even trained her to use the computer which Liz had never done before.

She put sticky notes all over the desk saying "now press this, then press this" She was very kind and a great deal of fun. Liz felt right at home with her. And on one occasion she told Liz all about her friend who was a palm reader. And Liz told her about palm readers she had encountered in the past who refused to read her palm, and she'd always wondered why.

"Here, stick your hands on the photocopier and we'll take a picture of your hands. I'll take it to my friend. She'll read you. I know she will" Candy said. Liz complied and left the strange looking black and white picture of her hands with Candy.

The next day Candy came back with the news. "My friend said that the reason the others wouldn't read your palm was because your hands are full of pain. But she did say she sees better things in your future."

Liz sure hoped so. Life certainly hadn't been a bowl of cherries for her in the past. She just had to get that Carousel under control. That seemed to be the problem. She started to think it was just like an addiction, like the alcohol. At first she would get high and feel really good when a man would pay attention to her, but the aftermath was deadly, just like the alcohol. Maybe throwing herself into her career would help. She was determined it would. It had to. She had to be really careful now that she was working in a law office. Her mind drifted back to when she got the job in the Creston Court House.

She and her kids had just moved to B.C. to be near John and Alicia in the hopes that she would quit drinking while living near them. Because she had no job and no income she'd had to go on welfare and they also had an incentive program that paid $100.00 a month to help get a person back into the work force. Fortunately, or unfortunately, for Liz the jobs were in government offices and she was placed in the Creston Court House. She tried. She really tried. But after five months of being sober, she slipped. She recalled how she had drunk doubles all day at the Owl's Nest pub in the Kootenay Hotel and then weaved her way up to the Laundromat beside the Dairy Queen where she had parked the car in the hopes that it would distance her from the bar and nobody would notice her driving while drunk.

When she got to the laudromat she was staggering so badly that a bunch of young teenagers came out of the laundromat to help her. They turned out to be her saving grace. They tried to stop her from getting into the car, and when she persisted they jumped in with her continuing to try to discourage her from driving. One of the girls remarked that she liked the brand new moccasins Liz had just purchased. Liz, always very generous, immediatley took the moccasins off her feet and gave them to the girl. The girl tried to refuse them, but Liz insisted and then slurred, "Well, everybody out. I gotta get home." The kids made one last attempt to stop her from driving, but then reluctantly got out. Liz drove the gear shift into reverse and whipped the car backwards onto the highway so fast that it rocked on two wheels. The kids ran directly to a phone booth to call the police.

Liz tried to drive so carefully while peering out of one eye, the other one squinted shut. Looking with both eyes made everything appear double, two yellow lines instead of one, to try to follow. She got as far as Erickson, just on the outskirts of Creston, when she heard the siren screaming. "Oh, I wonder what's going on," she slurred. "Can't be for me. I'm going real slow."

She was going real slow. Too slow, and weaving all over the road. But still she refused to pull over. Finally the officer yelled at her to pull over through a megaphone. When she did, they piled her into the back seat of the cruiser. She was so drunk that she blacked out totally and didn't remember a thing about the ride to the station. She came to full consciousness as the officers questioned her about her next of kin. John and Alica CAN'T know, she thought. They were good upstanding citizens, which was really important to them. They would be mortified to have their names connected with the police station and Liz's drunkeness. She refused flatly to give the names of her next of kin and as a result she was immediately dragged, literally, to a cell. After spending a few minutes in the cell, she started to totally freak out. She was clostrophobic. She was torn between humiliating her parents and saving her own skin. She started screaming at the top her lungs that she worked in the Court House and how dare they arrest her. It was all to no avail. So finally because of her clostrophobia, she agreed to their wishes. She very reluctantly came out of the cell and signed the papers in a very scrawly handwriting. She felt like a total traitor. Her parents had been good to her, helping her get a new start and she had let them down again. A mug shot was taken and then she was finger printed. Now she had a criminal record on top of everything else.

On Monday when she, very sheepishly, returned to work, the Clerk of the Court yelled at her, "What the hell are you doing? I hear you're a real bitch when you're drunk. Well I don't want you in my Court so you better pick a different Court to attend for this one." Liz was devastated. Little did she know that the Court Clerk had a hard time keeping the grin off his face. He knew Liz as being so quiet and shy. He was amazed at the Jekyll and Hyde transformation, and found it rather amusing. He had to rush out of the room before he burst into laughter at the look on her face as he scolded her. He didn't want to let her go because she worked so well. He hoped she would learn a good lesson. Actually, he liked her.

****

Yes, Liz would have to be especially careful not to blow this job. She continued to work in the law office and was really careful about her personal life. Lisa and Candy seemed to like her very much, and she just loved them. They had been so kind and considerate in helping her to learn everything perfectly. She was so proud to be clean and sober and working in a *law* office. Things started to look up for her, and she seemed to have the Carousel under control as well.

Without a man in her life taking up her full concentration, she had more time for the family which was great because during the summer Bonnie had blessed her with yet another grandchild, Liz's fourth. Her new granddaughter, Angelina, would never take Jasmine's place, but she certainly softened the blow of losing Jasmine.

Sitting at her kitchen table drinking tea Liz reflected on how she'd rushed to the hospital just in time to see Dr. Trent coming out of the delivery room, all excited and exclaiming, "We've got another little Baillee, she looks exactly like Baillee did when she was born!" She'd grabbed Liz and hugged her. Liz had raced into the delivery room where Bonnie was sitting up in the hospital birthing bed, looking pleased as punch. As Liz looked down into Angelina's face she was astounded, she did, indeed, look exactly like Baillee and Liz would find, throughout the years, that the girls would be mistaken for twins on numerous occasions. Liz was thrilled with the only granddaughter she would get to watch grow up. Then the phone jangled interrupting her thoughts.

"Mom, I'll be over in about ten minutes. Are you ready?" Bonnie's voice echoed in the phone.

"Yeah, I'm just putting the finishing touches on Baillee." Liz hung up the phone and turned and looked at Baillee, now almost three, and she started to roar. It was Halloween night and Bonnie and Liz were taking Baillee and Wesley out for the first time. She looked at Baillee and started to break out into fits of laughter again. She had dressed her up as Buckwheat from the Little Rascals. She had blacked her face with Halloween make up and twisted her curly hair into little rags all over the top of her head. She grinned to herself knowing that Bonnie was going to have a fit when she saw her.

But things backfired as Liz went to lift Baillee into the truck beside Wesley, who was dressed as Alfalfa. He looked all the world like him with the piece of black hair that stood up all by itself, just like Alfalfa's, and with the big round freckles Bonnie had drawn on his face. As soon as his eyes rested on Baillee he let out one piercing scream and started to wail like a banshee. Then Baillee started into wailing too. Because Wesley and she were so close, she was upset about him crying and couldn't figure out why he cried so hard at seeing her. It broke her wee heart. Bonnie and Liz roared again at the looks on the two kids' faces while they tried to comfort them.

Then came Christmas of 1985, and Liz was invited to a get together at her boss, Mr. Catalano's, place. She felt all the world like a celebrity as she fussed getting herself ready, donning the black and silver dress that hugged her figure nicely. She dressed Baillee in a little, wine-coloured, velvet dress with a white lace collar. Her tight blonde curls graced the top of her head, and Liz was pleased with the beauty of her little daughter, and the sophisticated look of herself that reflected back at her from the full-length mirror. Who would have ever guessed she had been a drunk and a sleezy run around.

Mr. Catalano's wife took Liz and Baillee's coat as they entered the beautiful home. Liz had never seen anything like it, let alone been invited into a home like that. She beamed with pride as she stepped down into the sunken living room with the huge picture window on the other side looking out onto a myriad of coloured lights decorating the trees in the back yard.

"Well, what do we have here, Shirley Temple?" Mr. Catalano quipped. "She looks all the world like Shirley Temple. I can't believe the likeness." Liz was, indeed, proud. And when she glanced at Baillee she thought, *Wow! He's right. I never saw it before, but she does look exactly like Shirley Temple.* They settled in for a few drinks (of course Liz's were virgin drinks) and appetizers before heading out for dinner at the Terra Nova. Things were finally getting good for Liz.

Then things got even better. The next summer Lisa got pregnant and wanted to take a maternity leave. Of course, Liz was in line for the job. She was nervous, though, because she had only been a receptionist, now she would be taking over Lisa's job of conveyancing. Not only was Lisa very beautiful, she was patient and kind and taught Liz everything. But Liz was *scared*. This was a big responsibility and no easy task. Just after Lisa took her maternity leave, Mr. Catalano, the lawyer who had hired her, was called up to be a judge so his business was bought out by Jeanine, a new, aspiring, young lawyer he had hired.

So Jeanine, a new young lawyer, Liz, a new member of the team, and Candy having all the grit necessary to carry them through, started out on a new adventure. Liz loved Candy she had the neatest sense of humour, besides being kind and very good looking.

Liz threw herself into the job with Candy's help. She began to enjoy the challenge of the conveyancing and on two occasions ended up feeling very proud of herself. Part of her job was to search the property to be sold to make sure there were no liens against it. On the one occasion she discovered a Restrictive Covenant on a property that was to be sold by the school district to a young couple who wanted to build a new home on it. The Covenant was made by two elderly sisters who had donated the land to the school district with the terms that only a school house could be built on it. The couple wouldn't be able to build their house! Liz ordered a copy of the covenant and immediately took it into Jeanine who said, "Good work!" Liz's chest swelled with pride. And on the other occasion she discovered that another property in the process of being sold had an easement issued to the hydro company right across the middle of it. Her finding saved the prospective new owners a lot of grief.

Yes she was enjoying the job tremendously and her confidence was beginning to grow. Maybe she wouldn't be needing men to make her feel better after all. Not only that she was able to purchase her very first car. It was a four in the floor Dodge, red in colour with white racing stripes down the side. Not exactly the ideal car for a legal secretary, but the price was right.

That was the best of it, but the worst of it was with the stress of the job and worrying about Janie having to babysit Baillee all the time, Liz's anxiety started to increase.

Then Candy asked for Fridays off! Liz was freaked because a lot of the times Jeanine had to go to court which left Liz alone in the office. The first Friday she was alone, the office was quiet. Of course, there were no clients. She tried to work. *Focus! Focus!* Her brain cried out to no avail. Her head started to swim. She was losing her breath. The walls seemed to be closing in, and her brain was playing tricks on her. *What are you doing here? You don't belong here in this high society. You're just a drunk. You don't know nuthin'. Stop it! Stop it!* She started to sweat profusely. *I gotta get a grip. What if the phone rings? What if someone comes in? I know. I know. I'll call Irma. I don't know what she can do, but I'll call her anyway.*

Liz dialed Irma's number. *Please be there, please be there. Oh, what's the matter with me. I am so smart to work for a lawyer, but I can't even control my own thoughts.*

"Helloo," Irma's cheery voice sounded on the other end. Silence. "Is anybody there?"

"Irma, thank God you're home."

"Where are you? I thought you were supposed to be at work?"

"I am. I am, but I'm having an attack. Oh, Irma, I feel just sick. I can't stay here by myself, and I certainly can't leave. I'll lose my job. I gotta keep the kids. Oh, my gawd! Oh, my gawd!"

"Calm down. Can you feel your feet?"

Feel my feet? What the hell's that all about? Liz wondered. But as she contemplated what Irma was saying she thought about her feet and yes, she could feel them! She moved them around, wiggled her toes and then a funny thing started to happen. The attack started to subside. Her mind had started to focus on something else besides her anxiety. Irma was a genius.

"Hang on, I'm coming down there."

"Oh, I don't know if you should. What if Jeanine comes back? I don't want her to know my problem. I am too embarrassed."

"Never mind. I'll leave as soon as she comes. What's wrong with a friend dropping in to see you at your new job."

"Okay." Liz said with her tongue in her cheek. "Oh, and can you bring me a small carton of milk? I'll pay you when you get here." Every time Liz got an anxiety attack her stomach seemed to be on fire. She thought it was the extra doses of adrenaline causing her stomach to burn. *Or maybe she was crazy.* Nonetheless. drinking a glass of milk seemed to cool it down. And she'd learned in A.A., *If it works don't fix it.*

After that experience, Irma would often come and bring Liz lunch and they would go down by the river and eat and share experiences, and laughter. Liz grew to love Irma and she wasn't quite sure who was sponsoring who. Irma would even drive with her if she had to go to the court house in Rossland to deliver papers for Jeanine. Liz discovered that driving out of town or familiar territory also caused her anxiety to rear its ugly head. It certainly was debilitating, but Liz was determined. Come hell or highwater she was keeping this job.

And keep it she did. Life was good. Liz had her very first car. A good job in a law office. She was clean and sober. She had Irma to help with her anxiety and the Carousel was still. What could go wrong?

Liz & Baillee

Chapter 26
David

Liz sauntered into the A.A. meeting room with a Pepsi in one hand and a cigarette in the other. She stopped dead in her tracks. There sitting along the wall beside Gene was Brad Pitt, himself. Well not really, but he easily could have been. He looked enough like him. The Carousel jump started and Liz was on her way again. She turned her eyes away not wanting to stare, but in that instant she noticed what seemed to be like a cast on his arm. She listened intently as *David* spoke and explained how he'd been in a motorcycle accident and ended up crippled down one side. It had devastated him, and he'd spent all his time since getting sloshed. He'd become so sick and tired of being sick and tired that he was willing to try A.A. even though it was a big blow to his ego.

He was new. She knew he was new, but she couldn't help herself, the Carousel spun with delight. He was *so* handsome, and before everybody had left the club that night, she had slipped an empty matchbook, with her name and phone number scrawled on it, into David's good hand.

She was actually surprised when a few days later he called. She didn't really expect such a handsome guy to bother with her. She was delighted.

"Hi, it's David."

"Hi, David," Liz said, shyly.

"Hey, I was wondering if you'd go out with me Friday night."

"Yeah, I'd love to, but there's a hospital meeting that I'm kinda committed to. Could we take that in first and then go out?" she asked. She didn't want to lose the opportunity to date him, but A.A. did have to come first, after all, if she wasn't sober what good would she be to him.

"Sure. I could handle that, probably do me good anyway," David replied.

Liz was ecstatic. How was she going to make it through until Friday? What would she wear? *Oh, my gawd, this is too much pressure,* she thought as she twirled around and hugged herself.

"Janie, can I borrow that new pink jacket you just bought?" she yelled from her bedroom.

"Sure, mom, but don't get it dirty and *don't* rip it."

"I won't, I won't, I'm not a drunk anymore, you know," Liz answered cheerfully. Well that was taken care of. Now what else would she wear. She rustled through her closet looking for her best top and pants. The white stretchy stirrup pants would hug her figure nicely. And that new, low cut, pink tank top with the lace across the bust would show just enough cleavage without being sleazy. The outfit would go nicely with Janie's pink jacket with the white piping down the sleeves. Satisfied she went to the kitchen to do up the dishes singing, "Pick me up on your way down, when you're blue and all alone." She'd sure like David to pick her up alright. Maybe this time it would work, after all, she'd been sober almost five years and she had a good job. Surely, she could handle a relationship by this time. She'd even make up for his lack of time in A.A. by being exceptionally patient with him. She could even help him. All these thoughts whirled around in her head as she tackled the big pile of dishes. She didn't even yell at Janie to help her this time.

Liz was watching out the front window, anxiously, when David's moss green Ford Pinto pulled up. She was nervous, but she wasn't going to back out now. She rushed out the door yelling over her shoulder, "See ya later, Janie. Make sure Baillee's in bed by eight."

"Sure, mom, have a gooood time," she teased as Liz flew out the door.

David reached across the front seat and had the door open for Liz by the time she reached the car. She climbed in and smiled shyly at him. He smiled back and said, "Well, I guess we better get up to that meeting."

"Yeah, we better," Liz answered. She couldn't wait for the meeting to be over so she could spend some time alone with him. They arrived at the hospital and as they walked up to the front doors, Liz couldn't help but notice that David had quite a limp. She hadn't noticed it at the last meeting because she hadn't seen him walk. He had remained sitting until she left. She noticed a grimace on his face as he limped to the door and opened it for her. She knew it was a real embarrassment for him. He was so handsome and she imagined he'd had his share of beautiful women in his time, and she wondered if that had all stopped because of his deformity. Well it didn't make any difference to her. She found out, on the short ride to the hospital that in spite of his huge ego, he was very pleasant, indeed. Then an unbidden thought struck her like a flash of lightning. *I wonder just how crippled he is?* She quickly dismissed the thought and chastised herself for thinking it.

When they entered the meeting room, Gene just glared at Liz. He took her aside and said, "My gawd, Liz, didn't you have enough with Johnny? What are you doing with a brand new member?"

"Gimme a break, Gene, I've been sober almost five years. Don't you think I know what I'm doing by now? I've got a lot of sobriety under my belt and I can help this guy. I'm not gonna do anything stupid to upset him like I did with Johnny. I think I'm a little more emotionally mature now."

Gene shrugged his shoulders as he walked away. There was nothing he could do to stop her and he knew it. He'd have to talk to David, though, for sure.

Liz, feeling a little squeamish about Gene's comments, decided to sit on the opposite side of the table from David. She could see his handsome face better from that vantage point. All through the meeting she couldn't concentrate. She couldn't wait for it to be over, and she wondered why she'd insisted on going. Oh, well it was better for David to go anyway. She glanced at him one more time. Her eyes scanned his handsome face and then dropped down to his good arm. She was amazed at the size of his muscular forearm. He had an arm like Hercules.

Finally, the meeting was over. Now, she would have time with David. It was too late to go to a show or the drive in so they just went for coffee and talked. Liz discovered that David lived in a trailer court in Rossland, that his parents lived in Patterson near the American border, and that he had one younger brother. She listened intently as he told her all about the motorcycle accident. How he'd been thrown from the bike and landed on his head causing the damage to the mobility part of the brain that operated his left side. Liz was reminded of Carol Simpson, who she loved like a sister. Carol's first love had been killed by the very same type of accident. Strange how life evolved. Fortunately David's accident hadn't killed him, but it had certainly taken it's toll. It left him shattered. He was always used to being Mr. Studley and now his ego was bruised almost beyond repair. Liz hoped she wasn't making a big mistake.

After coffee David drove Liz to her home up the Gulch. He parked out front and they talked a bit more. Then, David's beautiful, azure eyes gazed into Liz's eyes holding her captive. Her body started to heat up and melt as his eyes probed deeper into her soul, looking for acceptance. She moved, like iron filings to a magnet, to his side of the car. Her eyes locked to his. His head bent down ever so gently, his lips found hers, and the Carousel carried them away to another world of bliss. After several moments of being in a clinch, David pulled away and looked down into her eyes. He grinned a silly grin and said, "Yeah, it works." Liz blushed crimson. How did he know what she'd been thinking?

Weeks went by and they dated constantly. Liz worked all week at the law office so she was exhausted by the weekends and started to complain about it. David, being the kind man that he was invited her to spend a weekend at his house, so she could relax. He wouldn't allow her to do a thing. "You lie on that couch and take it easy. What do you want? Music? T.V.? A Movie? I have tons of movies and tapes," David chanted

"No, I can't just lay here and let you do everything. At least let me help with lunch."

David bent over and kissed her on the forehead, "No, no, no, You work hard all week. What do I do? Nuthin." He put on a Bruce Springsteen tape and as the words of Springsteen's song, "I'm on Fire" penetrated Liz's brain, she laid back on the couch and rested completely, thinking all the while about the ecstasy she'd enjoyed with David over the last few weeks. Everything did, indeed, work and very well at that. But it wasn't just the sex that she enjoyed. David was a decent person under the tough front that he put up to the world. She loved him. She even thought about marrying him.

Then her mind drifted to the Sundays they had spent at his parents' place in Patterson. Diane and Geoffrey were such nice people. When she was at their sprawling acreage she felt like she was home. The acreage had been cleared and there was a beautiful big house and a large barn where Geoffrey kept homing pigeons, about fifty of them, a cow, and some goats. Her heart warmed as she thought about the warm summer day that David had taken her up the Nancy Green summit to let the pigeons fly home, for exercise. The day was so clear that they could see for miles from the top of the mountain. Nestled in the bottom of the valley miles below was Trail. The city appeared as though it was in the bottom of a deep stone bowl. And all around were huge mountains all dressed with magnificent pine trees. The mountains in the distance were of a purple hue with bright white snow caps that reflected the sun like diamonds. The scene took Liz's breath away.

As David opened the cages, one by one, the pigeons flapped their wings and soared off into the azure blue sky. They were instantly caught up in their freedom flight. Liz's heart soared along with them. They were free! She was free! She was sober! She was no longer a slave to the alcohol, and good feelings were starting to emerge inside her since she'd dispensed with a lot of the pain that had sucked her life away. And David was a big part of that newfound freedom. Her thoughts returned to the present as she watched David setting the table and talking to Baillee who was playing on the floor at his feet.

She could hear the washer spinning. David was even doing her laundry. She had told him she couldn't stay for the weekend because it was the only time she had to do her laundry and it was really piling up. He insisted that she bring her laundry to his place. He insisted just so he could have her company. She was thrilled, and so she had complied. After this first weekend, Liz knew she would spend every weekend at David's, if he asked her.

"I guess tomorrow we'll be going to mom and dad's for Sunday dinner as usual," David called.

"Oh, good. I love going there. I just wish your mom would let me help with something though. She won't even let me do a dish."

"That's because you're a single mom working so hard. Just enjoy. You deserve it." he laughed.

****

"We're here, mom," David chanted as he opened the back door to his parent's kitchen. Liz always felt like she was at home at Diane and Geoffrey's. They were the same type of decent living people as her parents.

As she walked into the kitchen and saw Diane with an apron on and smelled the delicious odor of the roast beef wafting up from the oven she was reminded of her own parents. She reflected on how she'd come to realize that her parents weren't all that bad. They hadn't raised her exactly perfectly, but who could expect perfect parenting from imperfect people. Through her fifth step with Susan, Liz had complained terribly about John, Alicia and Alan, and her upbringing. Susan explained that they were, after all, just human beings with failings the same as her own, and the sooner she could forgive them all the happier she could be. She was made to see that Alan had been just as insecure in his rearing as she'd been and that he wasn't that bad after all. Liz had even made contact with Alan by phone where he lived in Quebec. He'd become a minister and was a much nicer adult than he had been a child, at least to her. She forgave him and immensely enjoyed reminiscing with him about all the kids from their past. "Carrying resentments is the last thing an alcoholic needs," Susan had said, and Liz began to realize that a person could never be happy inside if they were full of resentments. So she tried her best to forgive everyone. Her life was definitely coming together, and with David in it, it was more than wonderful.

"Come on in," Diane greeted warmly.

"Hey where's that little Jimmy?" Geoffrey called from the living room, knowing full well the reaction he was going to get. Baillee went running to him and stamped her foot and said very indignantly, "Me not Jimmy. Me Baillee, told you b'fore."

Geoffrey just howled as he always did. He loved Baillie as if she was his own grandchild and Diane loved her too. As a matter of fact Diane got the greatest kick out of Baillee calling her *Mother* with such dignity and respect.

After dinner Liz and David got into their bathing suits while *mother* and Geoffrey took Baillee for a walk in the surrounding woods. She loved to paddle in the little creek that meandered across the property. The swim in the pool was one of the highlights of the day for Liz. The pool was too deep for Baillee so it gave David and Liz some alone time. The turquoise water would sparkle with diamonds as they swam and wrapped themselves around each other. David was right at ease in the water. It seemed to buoy him up so that movement was easier for him. Liz gazed at him unable to believe how handsome he was and that hairy chest! She'd always liked a hairy chest on a man.

After their swim, David and Liz wandered into the woods themselves, David with an axe in his good hand. "Fall's comin and mom and dad will need some wood. The least I can do is split a few logs for 'em," he said as he walked beside Liz. She breathed deeply of the smell of pine, and breathed out complete satisfaction. She was happier than she'd been in a long time. She settled on a log beside the huge wood pile and watched as David raised the axe over his head with his one good arm. She was amazed at the size of that arm and she soon knew why it was so muscular. He cut as much wood as any man with two good arms, and in record time too. She was mesmerized as she watched the axe fall again and again. The sweat trickled down his chest between his muscular breasts. Life was good! And Liz was content. But could it last for her?

****

"Hello, Liz." the voice echoed in the phone. Liz still cringed every time she heard Alicia's stern voice.

"How's it goin', mama?" Liz answered.

"Well your father's not feeling very well these days." Liz reflected on how sad it made her feel the last time she saw her papa. He was so thin.

"What's wrong? Liz asked, warily.

"Just old age I guess, we're not young anymore, you know. Anway we wanted to come and see you before your papa gets too old to drive. If that's okay?"

"Of course, it's okay. I'd love to see you."

Alicia and John came to visit. Liz had to miss a weekend with David which was hard, but she was really worried about her papa. They arrived, and Liz was appalled at how John looked. He was even thinner than before and he looked so sad. Liz's heart went out to him. She wanted to do something for him so she asked, "Papa, if you could do anything you wanted, what would it be?" She had in mind maybe taking him to the Oregon Coast where there was a huge nursery which grew all kinds of different Iris. She knew that her papa loved Iris and it had always been his dream to grow different varieties and sell them. He loved Iris more than any other kind of flower, and he had ordered different varieties from this very nursery in Oregon. Liz remembered the lime green ones and the black ones he had grown. She knew he would be delighted if she took him there.

His sad voice startled her back to reality. After thinking about it for awhile, he simply said. "I'd like my youth back."

Liz could feel the tears welling up in her eyes. She quickly blinked and recomposed herself.

****

The following weekend, August of 1986, David and Liz took off for an A.A. campout in Idaho in the United States. Liz was thrilled and so looking forward to it after the sad weekend with her mama and papa. She was worried sick about her papa and she needed some distraction.

Janie and Baillee were waving goodbye from the front deck as Liz climbed into David's car. "Hey beautiful." David said as he leaned across the seat and planted a big kiss on her lips.

"Hey David," she replied, sadly.

"Come on, cheer up. We'll have a good time this weekend. Get your mind off everything."

"I hope so. I'm so worried about papa. He doesn't have long to live, I can just feel it in my bones. I left the name of the campground with Janie just in case."

Liz was quiet as they drove the final distance to the campground up a dirt road that left dust eddys swirling behind them.

David and Liz set up the tent after they registered, but her heart just wasn't in it. After the tent was set up David put a pot of weiners and beans on the campstove. Then they ate, but the food tasted like sawdust. After supper they gathered around the camp fire with all the other A.A. members. There was a lot of people Liz didn't know and in spite of them being A.A. she felt very out of place. She had never felt this way before with A.A. people. She kept waiting for someone to come with a message for her to call home. It never happened but she spent the whole weekend worried sick and crying when she and David were alone in the tent. As much as he tried to comfort her by cuddling her close to his hard body, she just couldn't be appeased.

They left early on the Sunday morning at Liz's request. The campout had turned out to be a fiasco. She couldn't enjoy herself and so David didn't either. He was worried about her. Then on the drive home just outside Colville, Washington Liz started to choke. "I can't breathe, I can't breathe," she gasped.

"What's the matter?" David squeaked, frightened out of his wits.

"Oh gawd, I'm having an anxiety attack and it's going to be a big one. Get me to a hospital," she cried.

"Hold on, hold on!" he cried. What's an anxiety attack?"

Liz was totally humiliated. She hadn't told David about her anxiety attacks because it had been a long time since she'd had one and things were going well. She thought she was over them.

She tried to explain to him, but not knowing anything about them he didn't understand. He sped up and rushed her to the hospital in Colville.

She was taken in on a stretcher because her legs were paralyzed. Too much oxygen from hyper ventilating with a severe attack can render a person paralyzed in the arms and legs. A breathing apparatus with a long tube was strapped on to Liz's face. David watched anxiously through the window of the emergency room. Liz could see the worried look on his face and longed to comfort him, but she was fighting her own battle at the moment. She breathed out into the apparatus filling the tube with carbon dioxide, and then breathed her own carbon dioxide back in. It was the same as breathing into a brown paper bag. Anxiety attacks are never life threatening, but at the time, it feels like a person is going to die. As the carbon dioxide flooded through her body, she began to calm down and after an hour or so she was released.

David hugged her close and smoothed her hair back from her face. She was sure she looked a wreck and she was embarrassed, but David was not concerned about how she looked. He was concerned about her well being. He loved her too.

****

A couple of weeks later as Liz was in the midst of a deep sleep, a voice penetrated her brain and her arm was being tugged on. She opened one eye and looked at the alarm clock beside her bed. The bright red numbers flashed 3:15.

"Mom, Mom, help me. Help me get David up the stairs. I tried to get him up, but I can't. I sure like him. He's the nicest guy you've ever gone with," Bonnie slurred.

Liz breathed in the pungent odor of Bonnie's alcohol breath. "What are you talking about? What's the matter?" Liz croaked, half asleep.

"It's David. I was drinking with him in the bar. Darren's night shift and I got so bored I hired a sitter to watch the kids and went out for awhile. I sure like David, but mom he's too drunk to drive home. I can't get him up the stairs. He's too drunk to walk properly with his leg the way it is."

"Oh, Bonnie, oh, my gawd!" Liz was devastated. David was drinking again. Was it her fault? Things were so good between them. She'd tried so hard.

She crawled out of bed and between Bonnie and her they got David up the front stairs. She couldn't possibly let him drive home in that condition. But she was a little nervous. She'd seen a lot of violent drunks in her day and had no idea how David would be. He was a pussy cat. He was so funny, she couldn't help but smile at him even though she was upset about him drinking again. He tried to grab her and hold her but she dodged out of his way.

"Come on, you better sleep this off. I gotta get up at six in the morning so I gotta get to bed too."

No sooner did Bonnie and Liz get David settled on the couch than he passed out cold.

"What are you going to do?" Liz asked Bonnie. "You can crawl in with Janie if you want. Look's like you're feeling no pain either."

"I'm fine, Mom, just feeling a little tipsy. Had a good time, though. I'll just call a cab. I'm not really drunk, but I'd probably blow over. I gotta get home and let the sitter go."

Liz woke up in the morning to a strange sound. *What's that noise?* Her tired mind queried as she tried to come back from the depths of unconsciousness. Then as she awoke more, realization dawned on her. David was on the couch and he was *puking*. She ran to where he lay. He wasn't even awake and he had thrown up all over her couch.

"Oh, my gawd!" She clasped her hand over her mouth and nose at the putrid smell.

"Come on, David! Get up! I've got to get this cleaned up before I go to work." She was upset to say the least. She loved him but this was too much.

After getting David a coffee and getting him straightened around she cleaned up the couch and then headed off to work. David apologized profusely and headed for home with a head the size of a pumpkin.

Liz fretted all day at work. What could she do? What *should* she do? If she was the cause of David drinking again, she knew she would have to leave him alone. After all, there was nothing more that she wanted in this world than for David to achieve sobriety. And if she was standing in the way, she'd have to bow out graciously. But could she? She loved him so much. She needed him. It wasn't even the Carousel this time. She really loved him, and so she had to give him up. Resigned to do just that she called him after work and told him the news. He was already half in his cups again with a bit of the hair of the hound that had bitten him the night before, and he seemed not too much bothered by it. Liz reassured him that if he got a year sober she would love to be with him again. Besides she couldn't possibly go through what she'd gone through with Lenny and Johnny. David didn't seem to be the same type, but alcohol did strange things to people. Sadly, Liz hung up the phone. Where was she to go from here? Papa, and now this.

Trail Nestled in the Bottom of a Stone Bowl

Chapter 27
The Reconciliation

It was October, 1986. Liz missed David something terrible, but if he was going to make it she had to stay out of his life. She had to stay strong. He called a few times and eventually came back to A.A. He asked her to marry him, but she smiled sweetly and said not yet, get a year. She was pondering all these things when the phone started to ring jangling her nerves.

"Hello," she answered.

"Liz, it's your mother." Liz knew something was wrong by Alicia's tone.

"Yeah, Mama, what is it? What's wrong?"

"It's your father. He's not good. Jack's boys have been helping me with him."

Liz's brother, Jack and his wife, had moved West just shortly before Liz and the kids and they'd settled right across the road from Alica and John.

Alicia continued. "We've had him in diapers and the boys have had to lift his legs up while I change him. It's been awful. We finally had to put him in the hospital. I don't think he's going to last much longer so I thought you'd better come and see him."

"Oh, Mama!" Liz fumed. "Why didn't you tell me sooner? I would have been there."

"Well, you had to work you just got that new job and all," Alicia stated firmly.

That was Alicia, always practical.

Liz got off the phone and called Bonnie.

"Grandpa's not well," Liz cried into the phone, "And I need to go and see him."

Liz couldn't allow herself to think that he might be dying. She knew since the last time she'd seen him in August he was failing. But now that it was upon her, she preferred to think he was just having a turn for the worse. He'd be okay. He had to be. It was imperative for her to make up with him.

Bonnie agreed to take Liz to Creston. It was a Sunday morning and they could be over the Salmo Creston summit in an hour and a half. Janie agreed to babysit Baillee, and Darren's mother had Wesley and Angelina. The girls left in an all fired hurry.

First, they went to pick up Alicia. Then, they drove to the hospital. Liz was dressed in a grey linen skirt and a turqoise, white and grey plaid silk blouse with a grey velvet jacket, looking every bit the legal secretary.

They slowly walked into the room where John lay moaning. Liz grabbed his hand, tears running down her cheeks. He looked so awful. The bed dwarfed him. Where was the vital man who had been her papa? The man who'd carried her when she was a little girl, the man who'd bought her the turtle book, the man who'd loved her. The man who'd cut her off for no apparent reason. She started to feel the old resentment rearing its ugly head. Then it flew as quickly as it had come as John squeezed her hand in a death grip. She looked at her mama with haunting, helpless eyes. Alicia nodded. She'd been at the hospital with him in this state for a week by herself and she'd developed a hard crust around her heart because losing the man she'd been married to for sixty years was more than she could bear. Alicia was always very stern, but her heart loved John dearly, and she couldn't bear the thought of losing him.

Liz let go of John's hand to seek out a nurse to get some Kleenex. The dam of pent up emotions and love for her papa burst forth and she sobbed deliriously. After getting some Kleenex she returned to the beige prison that her papa was entombed in. She took his hand again and the death grip was back. He moaned. He tried to speak. Liz thought she could hear him whisper, "I love you, Liz." Her heart broke. He really did love her. Why did he wait until now to tell her? Why hadn't her mama told her about his turn for the worse earlier so she could have come to see him before this state.

After some time Liz started to hear funny noises coming from John's chest. She knew then he was dying. Funny how the mind can drift at a time like this. Liz's mind drifted back to when she was a kid. *The Morris boys were teasing her. "When people die they get*

the 'death rattle' and then they grab you with the 'death grip'."
Then they grabbed her and freaked her right out. They had just been playing, but they were right. Now she'd felt that 'death grip' from her papa's hand and she was hearing the 'death rattle'.

"Let's go," Alicia cried jarring Liz out of her thoughts. "I've been here all week. I can't take anymore." She started to hurry out of the room.

"But, Mama, wait. We can't leave papa now," Liz cried.

"NO!" Alicia cried over her shoulder.

Having always knuckled under to Alicia's anger, Liz, once more, caved in. She turned slowly, tears streaming down her face and muttered, "Goodbye, Papa." She gulped back a sob and rushed out of the room. They drove Alicia home, got her settled in and Bonnie said, "Mom, I hate to do this but, I've got to get back. I'm afraid Lillian will be pulling her hair out with the kids. I told her we'd be back before dark.

"Sure," Liz muttered in a daze.

On the trip home Liz was quiet. She stopped crying, making herself believe it wasn't over yet. They arrived at Lillian's around 4:00 o'clock. They no sooner got in the door than Lillian said to call Janie right away. "I hope nothing's wrong with Baillee," Liz muttered as Lillian put the kettle on for tea. It had been a gruelling day and Liz looked forward to a nice cup of tea.

"Hi, Janie, is everything okay?"

Janie was sobbing into the phone, "Grandpa died, grandpa died." Liz dropped the phone and fell to her knees sobbing, great big gulping sobs.

Bonnie grabbed the phone. "Are you alone with Baillee?"

"No, David's here. He was drinking at the bar and he came up to see mom. He was feeling no pain, but while he was here the call came from grandma. He has stayed with me all this time and he's pretty sober now. Grandpa died ten minutes after you guys left."

"Ten minutes after we left?"

"We shoulda stayed! We shoulda stayed! I'll never forgive myself. Papa died all alone. Sob. No one there with him. Sob. I hate Mama. Why did she leave? Why did she make us leave?" Liz cried from the chair Lillian had lifted her into.

Just then the kettle screamed. Liz jumped out of her skin. Everything was so unreal. Was she going to pass out?

"Do you still want tea?" Lillian asked sympathetically.

"No, I have to get home to Janie. She needs me," Liz gulped.

"We'll be right there, Janie," Bonnie said as she hung up the phone.

Lillian and Bonnie had to half carry Liz, one on each side under her arms. Her legs just wouldn't work. The papa that she loved so much was gone. She would never see him again. Why hadn't they made up before now? What a waste of years. Life was so cruel. At least he'd told her he loved her finally. It was a reconciliation of sorts.

By the time Bonnie and Liz arrived at Liz's Gulch home Stacy was there. Stacy and Bonnie helped Liz up the stairs. Her legs were still like rubber and she couldn't walk on her own.

As soon as she got in she hugged Janie to her breast, both of them sobbing. David stood in the background watching. Finally, he put his arms out to Liz. She fell into his arms and he stroked her hair as she sobbed. He was completely sober by this time. "I can't imagine, if I lost my dad, how much it would hurt," he soothed, continuing to stroke her hair. He held her close for what seemed like an eternity. And then Liz spoke.

"What about Baillee? Of course, we'll have to go right back," she uttered in a daze.

"Mom will take her," David said matter of factly. He knew his mom and dad loved Baillee and they would be more than happy to have her. They missed her coming on Sundays.

"Oh, and what about work? I better phone Jeanine."

After talking to Jeanine and being reassured, very sympathetically, that they could get along without her for a week, Liz undertook the huge task of phoning Alicia. Liz wanted to leave right away, but Alicia assured her she was okay, that Jack was there and there would be no sense in coming until the next day because there was nothing that could be done. Liz finally agreed. Sometimes she hated Alicia's practicality and other times it seemed to make a lot of sense. After all, what could she do? What *could* she do? She was five years sober and this was the biggest traumatic event she'd faced in all her sober years. Would she stay sober? *Could* she stay sober? It was a big question. She wanted a drink more than anything else in her life right now.

Chapter 28
The Last Long Ride

Darren's truck sped down the east side of the Salmo Creston summit with Bonnie behind the wheel. It was a beautiful, crisp fall morning. The sun shone through the yellows, golds, and crimsons of the trees warming the countryside. But Liz never noticed. She was in shock. Stacy sat beside Bonnie with Janie on her right and Liz was leaning against the passenger door. The silence in the truck was unnerving.

"A-a-a-m-a-a-zing grace, how sweet the sound that saved a-a-a wretch like me," Liz's voice was haunting as she softly sang the words. The girls, with heads down for fear they'd cry, listened intently.

"I once wa-a-as lost," Bonnie's voice joined almost in a whisper.

"But now I'm found," Stacy and Janie's voices joined in.

The four voices grew louder and louder until there was a resounding crescendo of grief being poured out throughout the canyon as the truck sped them ever closer to the dreaded last long ride for her papa.

****

The front door flew open and Alicia stood on the door step arms open. Liz had never seen Alicia look so lost. She was always the strong, stern one. In spite of their differences, Liz flew into her arms and just sobbed.

After a much needed cup of tea, Jack, Liz and Alicia headed to town to make the funeral arrangements. The funeral would have to wait until Liz's siblings, Alan, Jane, George, and Joy arrived. Lois and Debra would be flying in with them as well. Alica had raised Lois and Debra and they were more like sisters to Liz than nieces.

Picking out coffins, setting a date, making all the necessary arrangements was all a blur to Liz. Thank God Jack was there to take charge. Alicia put on her staunch front, but Liz knew she must be just dying inside. How was she so strong? Liz had never been emotionally strong. She remembered the words she'd read in the Magic Bottle, *alcoholics have a low tolerance to emotional pain.* It was true, boy, she could sure use a drink right about now.

****

The front door flew open and Liz dashed to the entryway. There stood Joy, Jane, George, Alan, Lois and Debra. Liz went to pieces and started to just sob. Joy wrapped her arms around Liz and held her close and rocked her back and forth while she cried. Joy had always been the motherly type. As Joy rocked her Liz's mind reflected back. *She was five years old again. She was playing Ring Around the Rosie with a bunch of kids. She bumped heads with a little boy. Her nose was bleeding profusely and scaring her out of her wits. She rushed home, but Alicia and John were out. All her siblings were on the front porch with their friends laughing and joking and flirting. Joy came to Liz's rescue, took her in, cleaned her up and gave her a big hug.* Now Liz clung to Joy as though she were five years old again. Gradually she stopped crying.

After hugs all around the whole entourage squeezed through the front door and settled in the kitchen. Joy brought out a bottle of whiskey and poured drinks. "Sorry you can't have any, kid," she said to Liz. Liz grabbed Joy's glass before Joy could stop her and took it to her lips. Joy's eyes bugged out and her mouth was agape. Liz's eyes made contact with Joy's and the frantic pleading look in Joy's eyes made Liz freeze. Just for a brief moment. But in that brief moment Liz's mind started to flood with all the pain from her past life, the broken relationships, the broken bones, the abuse to her children, the horrendous hangovers, the struggle to stay sober, the D.T.'s, the stints in the psychiatric ward, and slowly the pain of all that permeated her mind and overwhelmed the present pain of her papa's death. The pain of the one became greater than the pain of the other. And she changed direction. She pulled the glass away from her lips, stuck it under her nose and breathed in deeply of the beautiful, pungent aroma. Oh, how she wanted to take that drink. But she couldn't. Life wasn't fair everyone but her was escaping into a nice stiff drink, and all she could do was smell it. She needed it as much as she needed breath

208

and blood. But she had come a long way. She had the respect of her family back, she had a good job, she had Baillee to care for. She thought about David. What was going to happen there? He had been there for her in her time of grief. He had undertaken to make sure Baillee was taken care of. He was a good man. What good would she be in helping him to stay sober if she took that drink. She handed the glass back to Joy feeling a renewed strength welling up inside her. She would make it. She would get through this sober.

Joy and Jack really liked their booze and were half swacked before the afternoon was out. Jane had had a couple of drinks, but she was in control. Of course, Alan and George, being ministers, both refrained after one drink. Liz was grateful for their sober company. Joy was a happy drunk, but not so with Jack. He always got a little surly when he drank, and that was quite often. That was the reason that John and Alicia had chosen Alan and George to be the executors of their will. Jack, being hurt and feeling left out carried a huge resentment towards Alan and George. He had been there to help Alicia when John was so ill. Where were George and Alan when the going got really tough? His resentment started to fester more and more with every drink he took. Finally, it was more than he could contain.

"So, Alan, I guess you're the white-haired boy, eh?" he slurred.

Alan looked woe begone and Liz felt sorry for him. He tried to remain calm, but as Jack began to badger him more and more, he couldn't contain himself. The emotion was too much and he started to sob.

That's when the proverbial shit hit the fan. Jane, being the one who always protected the underdog and being a wild cat at heart, started to scream at Jack. "Shut up you stupid drunk. This is enough of a bad time without you making it worse."

Jack gave Jane a shove and the war was on. Grief did strange things to people. Liz and Debra grabbed Alicia and led her to her bedroom. "You don't need to listen to this right now," Liz cried. They sat in Alicia's room, Liz rocking Alicia back and forth as she cried. George and Alan were finally able to break Jane and Jack apart. They headed Jack towards the door and pushed him out and told him to come back when he was sober. Liz was appalled. Why did John and Alicia not include Jack. Liz knew his feelings were hurt.

He was often left out the same as she had been and she understood
his grief. George and Alan would have kept Jack under control. Liz
was sure Jack would have been happier to be a part of it all. And all
this could have been avoided.

Once Jack had gone things seemed to settle down. The girls
sat around the dining room table sipping tea and reminiscing. The
whiskey was put away after the tumultous storm. Liz had weathered
it in one piece, and she was grateful for the training she'd had in A.A.
As everyone relaxed the afternoon turned into a giggling session.
Jane and Liz laughed about the time Liz had peed her pants when
they were both still living at home. She and Jane had been moving
furniture around in their bedroom and had been laughing so hard.
There was something about moving furniture that always made the
sisters go bolistic with laughter or maybe it was just the combination
of the two together. Anyhow the laughter made Liz need to go pee
really bad, but they had placed a huge armoire across the door way
and she couldn't get out to go to the bathroom. So the inevitable
happened. And Jane roared all the more.

Then they recalled the time Jane was driving her yellow 55 Chevy
hardtop down the side road from Brian's parents' farm where they
had been visiting. The car had filled up with flies from the barn and
Jane was trying to swat them out of the way with a hand towel. She
lost control of the car and careened toward the deep ditch. Instead
of hitting the brake she hit the gas so they ended up flying over the
ditch and landing nose down in the mud on the edge of a pond. The
accident scared Lois and Debra so bad that they flew out the doors
and starting running up the road, dust twirling and flying behind
them. Jane and Liz just roared at the sight of the girls scurrying
up the road, legs and arms flailing out with dust eddies flying all
around them. Fortunately no one was hurt, but the sisters nearly
died laughing.

Lois, Debra, Jane and Joy bunked in the spare bedroom while
Alan and George slept on the floor in the living room on foamies.
Bonnie, Stacy, and Janie headed back to Trail until the day of the
funeral. Liz slept with Alicia because nobody else wanted to. She
supposed it was because they didn't want to sleep where their papa
had slept. But Liz didn't care. She loved her papa dearly, and now

he was gone. She lay there thinking about it all as the lights slowly went out one by one in each of the respective sleeping quarters. She was so sad in the black velvet darkness, and then echoing from the other bedroom she heard voices.

"Good night, Mary Ellen, Good night John Boy," followed by more giggles. And her heart was warmed. Finally, she felt a part of her family.

The next day Cora and Jimmy arrived. All the girls decided to go on a shopping spree. Jimmy was the designated driver in his old winter beater. Liz had never had such fun with her family. It was a pleasant distraction from the grief they were all suffering. It did her heart good. Jane, Lois and Debra just loved Jimmy and his antics. He was very amusing and witty, and he could tell funny little anecdotes in any dialect, Scottish, Southern drawl, Indian, you name it, he could do it perfectly. He kept them all in stitches for the most part of the day. Another day in. Tomorrow was the funeral and the last long ride.

Everyone came. The coffin was carried by friends of Alicia and John. The family procession followed the coffin. With Alan and George on either side of Alicia, Jack following close behind. Then Joy and Jane with Liz following.

"I can't do this!" Jane exclaimed and started to come apart right before Liz's eyes. She tried to turn around and head back out the door. Liz grabbed her by the arm firmly, and whispered in her ear.

"Yes, you can. I'm right here with you. I'll stay right by your side." Jane seemed to calm down and Liz couldn't believe the strength that she herself had mustered together. She was sure it had to be coming from her Higher Power. She had prayed intensely for Him to help her get through this day and the last long ride.

After the funeral ceremony, the casket was carried out and everyone sniffed and dabbed their noses with Kleenex. Alicia, Jane, Joy, George and Alan rode in the family limousine following the hearse. Liz rode with Jack. Once again the two were left out because there wasn't enough room. They followed the big black family limousine and the hearse to the resting place.

Everyone gathered around the hole in the ground while the last words were said. A bird whistled a cheery song from a nearby tree. Liz couldn't believe the strength she was exhibiting. They each threw a beautiful Iris in on top of the coffin then a shovel full of dirt was thrown down on top of the papa that she loved so much. She gave one last gasping sob and rushed to Jack's car with Jane. As they looked back at the grave site, they saw Jimmy fall to his knees at the grave side while Cora held his head close to her stomach. His shoulders shook with sobs.

"Is he okay?" Jane asked. Liz couldn't answer because she was crying so hard. The hard veneer shell had shattered at the look of her son grieving for the grandfather that he loved dearly. But the last long ride was finally over. Now what?

Liz's sisters Jane & Joy

Chapter 29
The Last Carousel Ride

Liz returned to Trail with Bonnie, Janie and Stacy. She headed right for Rossland to see David. She was spent and she desperately needed to ride the Carousel. Besides she had to pick up Baillee.

"Well, how did it go?" David asked with eyes full of sympathy.

"Hard. It was really hard, but I don't want to talk about it. I just want to love and be loved right now." The two retired to the bedroom where Liz escaped for two glorious hours in David's arms.

"There's an A.A. Halloween dance in Castlegar tonight. We can pick Baillee up in the morning if you want to go." David didn't dance and he didn't particularly like the gatherings. It was still hard for him to party without a drink, but he knew Liz loved to dance and loved a good party. He wanted to cheer her up.

Liz and David walked into the upstairs hall where the dance was being held. They didn't dress up. Liz wasn't in the mood for that, and David never would have anyway. Most of the people weren't in costumes so David and Liz felt better.

After half an hour or so, people started to just pour into the little hall, with a capacity of one hundred and fifty people. Liz was flabbergasted. There had to be three hundred people, as a matter of fact, Gene took a count and there was three hundred and two crammed into the small one hundred and fifty capacity room.

Liz was thrilled. She always liked to be in the middle of the parade and three hundred and one people all around her having a good time was exactly what she needed. Everyone was on a high and when they danced she could feel the floor bouncing, actually rising and falling about an inch. In the back of her mind she was a little frightened, but she swallowed hard, and kicked up her heels and lost herself completely in the night. David sat watching her, smiling to himself. He loved her so, but he knew in his heart it couldn't last.

After an exciting evening Liz reluctantly left all her friends to head home to David's trailer and reality. After a blissful evening of love making, Liz rolled over and whispered in David's ear.

"I love you,"

"I love you too." he answered wistfully. That's why I gotta leave you."

"What?" Liz said as she bounced upright in the bed.

"Liz, I know you don't want a drunk. And I know I can't quit. It wouldn't be fair to lead you on. I can't stand this body that I live in and it's not going to get any better. I'd like to take that son of a bitchin' arm and leg and cut them right off. Too bad they weren't cut off in the accident or too bad I didn't conk out completely."

"David, don't talk like that. You can get sober. If I did anybody can."

"That's the problem. I don't want to. What's in the future for me? I'll never work again. I'm not smart enough to get an office job or a job in a bank. All I know is manual labour and who's gonna hire half a man?"

"Oh, David, let's not talk about this right now. You're just coming down from your last drunk. There's always depression after a drunk. You're just going through a bad time right now."

"Okay," he said reluctantly. He knew he wasn't going to stay sober, but he didn't want to pile more grief on her at this time so he stopped talking about it.

Liz laid down and cuddled under his good arm and fell fast asleep. She was exhausted after her gruelling week. David was awake for a long time watching her sleep. Her face looked so peaceful. He pulled her close. He did love her, but it was going to be his last night with her. He couldn't hurt her anymore.

Chapter 30
Family Album

After the break-up with David, Liz's Carousel seemed to grind to a halt. She had always been at the mercy of the men. She *needed* them. She began to see the difference between needing a man and wanting one. *Needing* one definitely meant being at their mercy. The concept that Bart had tried to teach her was finally sinking in. Enough was enough. A funny thing too was that she had absolutely no animosity towards David like she'd had with the other men in her life. She was just filled with sorrow because she did love him, and it wasn't that he had rejected *her*, he loved her too, but he couldn't stand to hurt her with what he felt he needed to do to go on living.

Liz didn't know if it was the final reconciliation with her papa or if she had finally matured, but she was feeling so strong. She knew she could lick the Carousel. She had to! But when a person gives up something, they always have to fill it with something else or they will revert back. Liz decided to fill her life with her beautiful family. She had done better since she had quit drinking, but she was sure she could do even better still. Especially now that Baillee was starting to need so much attention. No more running off and leaving her with Janie. She had to work, true, but she would have to get a sitter so Janie would be free to pursue a career for her own life. And it was time to leave the Gulch which was filled with drinking establishments. Time for a proper home.

Liz and Janie started looking the very next weekend. They found the neatest little house in East Trail in a very respectable neighbourhood. The house was empty so they gazed through the windows that were bare. There was a huge sunken living room, all carpeted, steps led up to a dining room with a huge opening looking down over the living room. Oak wood spindles stretched across the opening making the room look for all the world like a quaint little tea house. They couldn't see the rest of the house, but Liz was sure it was probably just as nice as what they'd seen.

"It's perfect, mom. I just love it," Janie cried.

"Yeah, it's great," Liz answered sadly. Her mind raced with thoughts of how she wasn't good enough for such a beautiful place.

"But it's not for us. It's too nice. You know how we are, a real orangoutang bunch. Remember how the tree went flying last Christmas. And the kids are always spilling things. I wouldn't want to ruin those beautiful carpets."

"But, mom," Janie whined.

"No let's keep looking."

They drove up to Glenmerry where they looked at a little house that was a ramshackle mess. It was dark and dingy inside and the walls and the floor of the bathroom were made of cement painted a creepy blue color, no tub just a rickety old shower.

"Well, it's food for thought," the owner muttered as Liz glanced around, politely, trying not to show her distaste.

Janie and Liz drove away in fits of laughter. "Food for thought," Janie roared.

"Like Kraft dinner compared to steak," Liz roared and they tittered all the more. "You know it's funny, though, I would probably feel more comfortable there than in that beautiful house we saw in East Trail. If the kids spilled or broke anything I really wouldn't care."

"Oh, mom, we couldn't possibly live there. Please, let's go check out that other house. We could ask the neighbours who owns it."

"Well, okay, but I'm not comfortable, I'm tellin' ya."

They found out who owned it and rented it right away. Liz was nervous, but it turned out to be the best move she'd ever made. Eventually, she ended up buying the house. The landlord wanted to sell and gave her first option, being as she was already living in it. There was a suite in the basement as well, and if Liz bought, she would actually be a landlord. How could this possibly be happening? From a drunk to a legal secretary, to a home owner, to a landlord. She laughed to herself. *You've come a long way baby. Sobriety is good!*

The only drawback was leaving Baillee with a sitter. Janie had gone back to school, which pleased Liz greatly, but Liz had tried several different sitters, and was getting really discouraged. Baillee would just scream and cling to Liz's leg every time she had to drop her off. The women seemed nice enough and Liz couldn't figure out what the problem was because Baillee wasn't old enough to tell her. Liz drove to work every morning with tears running down her cheeks, but she had to work. She cursed the welfare system for forcing young women out to work so they had to leave their babies with strangers.

In the meantime, a new neighbour moved in beside Liz. A really nice lady named Kim. She had two young girls, one Baillee's age and a two year old. She, also, was struggling like Liz had done on welfare. She'd been left by an alcoholic husband as well, so understanding Liz's plight, she offered to sit for her. It was magic. Baillee loved going to Kim's. Because Kim was so kind and had a wonderful way with kids Baillee took right to her. No more screaming and clinging to Liz's leg when she left her. Liz was ever grateful for Kim's magic formula. Kim's daughter Jenny was the same age as Baillee and after a very short time it was as though the two were joined at the hip. One never went anywhere without the other.

A year passed by quickly, Liz and Kim became the best of friends. Kim was so good to Liz and Baillee so Liz grew to love her like a sister. In September Baillee and Jenny started kindergarten together. For Liz it was just like starting over again. She sobbed her heart out when she had to leave Baillee at the school, just as she did with Jimmy in 1968. Where had the years gone? It was twenty years later and it seemed nothing had changed. But, actually, some things had definitely changed. Liz was alone and sober and doing just fine. Jimmy was doing fine too. At first he hadn't been because he and Cora had split up, and he'd been at a loss as to what to do with his life. Liz suggested he talk to the pastor who attended A.A. He'd helped a lot of young people get a start, and Liz figured he could help Jimmy too. The pastor suggested Jimmy try the army as he had no training in any specific field. He did and Liz was so proud of him in his uniform. After that Jimmy did great except that it still haunted him that he had no idea where Jasmine was. She was six years old now, and Jimmy was just sick wondering where she was, how she was.

Then the phone call came. Lotus was in Creston visiting Gary and Susan, old friends of Jimmy and Lotus', and she was going to allow Jimmy to see Jasmine while she was there. Jimmy was ecstatic and so was Liz.

Liz drove Jimmy to Alicia's and when they arrived, Alicia was so glad to see them. John had been gone for two years and Alicia was so lonely. She was pining away in their country home. The wind had certainly been taken out of Alicia's sails after John died and she was more compassionate and understanding. Liz was feeling closer to her mama than she ever had. She genuinely felt sad for Alicia.

Jimmy called Gary's as soon as they arrived. Liz was biting at the bit to get to see Jasmine. Jimmy hung up the phone, head hanging.

"What's the matter?" Liz asked.

"She says I can come and see Jasmine, but she doesn't want you to see her."

"What? That's outrageous! I *will* see my granddaughter and she can't stop me. I'd like to see her try."

"Please, mom," Jimmy pleaded, "Don't. She might get mad and not let me see Jasmine either."

"Well I have to drive you there, anyway."

"I know, but she said you could park at the end of the lane and wait."

How hard was that going to be? Sitting at the end of Gary's lane knowing that her precious Jasmine, that she hadn't seen for five years, would be just a few yards away. How could she do it? She had to! She had to put herself out of the way for Jimmy. It was more important that he get to see his daughter. Lotus was crazy. Liz was sure of it now.

They pulled up to the lane of the secluded farm house. Trees all the way up the drive made a living green canopy. In the background Liz could see the Creston bluffs, so much beauty, and yet she was so sad. She stopped at the end of the lane as she'd promised and Jimmy got out and ran towards the house, eager to see the daughter he missed so much.

Liz sat in the car, tears streaming down her face. She craned her neck trying to get, at least, a glimpse of Jasmine, and lo and behold, there, skipping down the lane towards her, was a happy little girl with black curly hair bouncing all over the place. She had beautiful olive skin and eyes that were not quite Chinese, not quite Canadian.

Liz knew instinctively who she was. There was no question. Jasmine had snuck out of the house to see her grandma and Liz was ecstatic. The door of the old red car with the white racing stripes flew open and Liz ran towards her and scooped her up in her arms and held her tight as though she'd never let her go. Finally, they had found Jasmine. But it was to be the last time they would ever see her. In the years that followed Jimmy met another girl and had little Brian and Alex. He loved them dearly but he would never stop wondering where Jasmine was.

****

And as for Stacy, she finished her nursing course and was now a full-fledged registered nurse. Liz was so proud of her. She had graduated at the top of her class. The girl was brilliant, and she would eventually go on to achieve much, much more. But she'd had quite a struggle, working at a little pizza shop up the Gulch in the evening, going to school in the day time, and caring for Jason all at the same time. She had a sitter just up the Gulch from her little apartment and many times she'd carried a sleeping Jason all the way home, and he was getting to be quite a size.

Finally, Stacy met Raymond and a whirlwind romance was underway. Eventually, they married, combined resources and ended up with a beautiful home. Liz was very happy for Stacy, having come out of the quagmire she'd grown up in. The wedding was like a scene from a fairy tale. Janie was one of the bridesmaids along with Layla and another girl Stacy worked with and Baillee was the flower girl. They were all dressed in pale blue satin. And Stacy looked like a fairy princess in a gorgeous gown of white satin overlaid with white lace. Cora, being a hairdresser, did everyone's hair. Raymond's nephew was the ring bearer and Janie's new boyfriend Richard was one of the ushers.

Janie had met Richard while hitchiking with her friends, Teri and Anita. He had come along in his little red sports car. "Would you look at that!" Richard said to his friend. It was love at first sight. He screeched his tires and pulled a U turn and was immediately on the opposite side of the road where the girls stood with their thumbs stuck out going in the other direction. Liz had been a little worried about Janie after her drinking shenanigans with Teri and Anita, but she totally approved of Richard and when he asked Janie to marry him, Liz breathed a big sigh of relief. Theirs turned out to be another fairy tale wedding and Liz's dream of seeing her daughters married in beautiful white wedding gowns had come true.

After a few years Cody and Tyler were born so Richard and Janie had to move out of their small trailer. They ended up purchasing a beautiful home in Fruitvale. Even though it was in town, it was like a home in the country surrounded with huge maple and pine trees. It was totally secluded from the neighbours and had a hot tub and a huge deck overlooking the spacious back yard. The whole family spent many a happy time at Janie's. Liz would sit in the hot tub with the gang, steam pouring up in puffy white clouds all around them with the sparkling white snow just a few feet away. She felt like she was at a rich winter spa. As a matter of fact the quaint little house had pine cathedral ceilings just like a country spa.

And of course, Bonnie had already married Darren a few years back and they had Wesley and Angelina. And Stacy gave birth to Bryant a year after she and Raymond were married, making nine grandchildren for Liz. Liz was finally content. She was sober, the Carousel lay still and dormant, and a beautiful happy family had arisen out of the swamp she'd lived in.

The years quickly flew by with more joy than Liz could ever have anticipated. The family had grown in leaps and bounds and Liz was growing older, but she still had nine year old Baillee at home to keep her hopping.

"Come to my room and see this," Liz called to Baillee who had just gone to bed.

"What?"

"Look, when I turn the lights out and roll around on this nylon bedspread in my nylon nightgown sparks just fly."

"Mom, you're magic."

"I know."

"Can I try that?"

"Yeah, I've got another nylon night gown in my drawer."

Liz dressed Baillee up in her other gown and they proceeded to roll around and around making static electricity, and then Liz sat up, pulled her hands slowly up from the blanket and sparks flew out of her finger tips. "Do this," Liz cried with glee and Baillee did it too.

"Mom, I'm a fairy godmother! Look at the sparks coming from my finger tips. It's just like Cinderella" Baillee cried all excited. It was, indeed, a magic moment that Liz shared with her beautiful daughter.

Another habit that Liz had gotten into was taking Baillee and her friend Skye to Silverwood in Coeur d'Alene, Idaho every summer. Silverwood was a theme park, kind of like a mini Disney Land. Liz could never have afforded to take Baillee to Disney Land, but Silverwood was the next best thing. There were all kinds of rides, and a small village with a Victorian House that sold candy. And the High Moon Saloon sold lots of drinks like the Huck Up, a combination of Seven Up and Huckleberry syrup that was sublime. There was also an airplane museum with old planes and even a stage coach. An old locomotive train chugged through the surrounding forest and actors, dressed up like train robbers from the old west, would actually hold up the train. And on one occasion when Liz's whole family had gone for a weekend, Liz had to convince little Cody that it wasn't real because he was freaked out by the train robbers.

Even without the Carousel and the alcohol there was always some kind of excitement in Liz's life like the day the 44th Engineer Squadron had open house at the armories. Jimmy phoned Liz to bring Baillee and her friend Skye up to see what was going on.

"It sure is noisy," Liz yelled as a huge green army tank turned into the yard.

"Can we have a ride?" Baillee asked as the back door slid down and a myriad of passengers stepped out.

"Sure," Jimmy answered

"You too, Mom," One of Jimmy's army buddies said to Liz.

"Oh, no not me, I'm claustrophobic," Liz cried.

"Oh, come on." Before Liz could make a move, two young army men surrounded her, one on each side, and took her under her arms. They lifted her until her feet were off the ground and carried her bodily into the open back of the tank. She was plunked down on the wooden bench. Baillee and Skye were all excited, but Liz wasn't. She was petrified. The metal door was pulled up on chains and secured shut. Baillee and Skye were delighted as they stuck their heads out through the hole in the top. Liz was freaked. It was sooo loud and clanked along the pavement. She had never been so uncomfortable and she wondered how the men stood it when they had to ride in the tanks in war times. They went down the Fifth avenue Hill and on down to Noran street where they turned around to travel back up the hill. Liz could see tree tops passing by and the girls waving to all their friends. What a thrill it was for them. Liz had to admit afterwards that, in spite of her misgivings, she had enjoyed the ride as well. After all, it wasn't every day you got to ride in an army tank.

A few years prior, Liz had moved Alicia over to Trail. Alicia had been so lonely after John died and was ready to give up so Liz thought it best to move her closer to the family. Now Alicia lived just two doors down from Liz on Noran Street. And when Liz phoned her to tell her about the army tank ride, Alicia was all excited and said, "The army's in town and they brought a tank right down our street. Where were you? You missed all the excitement."

"No I didn't." Liz stated with a big grin on her face.

Another gathering that pleased Liz no end over the years was the family reunions. Bonnie had started it off by inviting everyone to her new home in Sicamous. Even though there were five bedrooms in the house, there were bodies sleeping all over the place on air mattresses. Bonnie, being the shutter bug in the family, snapped over two hundred pictures and made CD's on her computer for everyone. The young ones even took Gramma Liz out to the bar where she had so much fun watching them perform. Wesley and Jason, just wooed all the young girls. And Angelina could knock the socks off any guy with her movie star looks. Of course, none of them had inherited her alcoholism which Liz was truly grateful for.

Liz was in her glory when year after year the family carried on the tradition. The second year they all went to Stacy's in Calgary where she'd moved in order to go to medical school. She wanted to be a doctor. And the year after that it was Janie's turn to play hostess, and on and on. Liz did, indeed, have a very beautiful family. Beating the Carousel had been well worth it.

The years flew by and there were, indeed, many joys, but a few sorrows as well. Liz sat at her dining room table when the phone started to jangle off the wall. "Hi, Liz, this is Dr. Bob," a solemn voice stated. Dr. Bob had been the drummer from A.A. who played in the Trail Pipe Band. Liz hadn't heard from him in years and wondered what he was about. "I have some really sad news. There's no easy way to say this. Val passed away yesterday."

"Oh, my gawd! What happened?" Liz asked as tears started to flood down her cheeks. She hadn't seen Val since Stacy's wedding, but she had kept in touch occasionally by phone. She was still in Nelson working at Willow Haven.

"She had a massive heart attack right at work. They rushed her to emergency, but she died en route."

"When will the funeral be?" Liz asked.

"There isn't going to be one. That's the way she wanted it," Dr. Bob related.

After hanging up the phone Liz went to her bedroom and sobbed her heart out. She picked up the gold ring with the heart and diamond in it that Val had given her years ago. Her heart was wrenched.

And then a couple of years later, she got a phone call from Reg, Carol Simpson's new husband, in Edmonton. Carol Simpson and her sister Dar were Liz's best friends. They had travelled life's road with Liz for fifty years. Liz had been in touch with Carol and Dar, by phone, over the years, and after she'd been sober for awhile she travelled, at least, once a year to see them.

"We lost Dar!" Reg croaked into the phone and then a big sob escaped his lips. I gotta go," he said, and Liz knew it was because he couldn't talk anymore. Reg had been a close friend of Arnie's, who was Dar's ex-husband, so he had known Dar for years. He'd grown fond of her, and the news of her death was killing him. Carol had called him from the hospital and asked him to let Liz know. It was a hard task for him.

The phone clicked on the other end and went dead. Liz collapsed. She fell right back into her chair as an enormous sob escaped her throat like a giant bubble. Dar had been her sister through all the years of hard times. They had lived together with their babies in the early years. Dar was like an aunt to her children. Liz fumbled with the phone and through crystal tears she dialed Janie's number. "I can't understand you, Mom," Janie stated.

"I-I-It's Dar. She's gone," Liz cried into the phone.

"Oh, my gawd, Aunt Dar!" Janie wailed. "I'll call Stacy and Bonnie."

"And I'll call Jimmy at the armories," Liz wailed. "Of course, we'll all go." Liz never gave a thought to the fact that it was February. She'd been invited to Carol's kids' weddings, and Dar's wedding too, but they had all been in the winter time and Liz absolutely refused to travel in the winter. She had developed an aversion to travelling due to her anxiety disorder and especially in the winter. But this time she *had* to go!

Liz and Janie travelled with Jimmy in Liz's new silver car that she'd purchased after being established at her job for a few years. Stacy and Bonnie travelled together, and Sherri, Liz's tenant in the basement, opted to keep an eye on Baillee who was now in her teens Baillee didn't even remember Dar so she didn't want to go. Hearing about Dar's death was the saddest day of Liz's life, even sadder than her papa's death. She loved her papa dearly, but Dar had been like a sister and had always been there for her in her worst and best times.

After Liz saw Dar laid to rest she began to wonder what was going to happen next. Baillee had graduated elementary school, receiving several awards and a plaque with her name engraved on as best citizen of the year and would soon finish high school. After that she would be leaving home. Liz sat swirling her coffee around in her cup and drifted in her mind. *Where is my life taking me? I am eighteen years sober, my family is all grown up with families of their own. Baillee will soon be leaving. Then where will I be? Will I still be able to hold the Carousel at bay after Baillee is gone? Keeping busy with the family really helped but soon I'm going to be alone. And I've become so tired of late.*

Carol Simpson

Darlene Simpson

Chapter 31
The Paperlady

Looking after eighty-eight year old Alicia, living with a daughter who was dying to leave home, running a household, and working full time in a law office were beginning to wear on Liz. She would work all day, rush home, make supper and take a plate of food over to Alicia. Alicia had taken to eating chips, cookies and candies for all her meals. Liz had to make sure she was getting enough nourishment. Not only that Alicia was forgetting to take her medicine so Liz bought a plastic container for her pills with the days of the week on them. Liz would put out the pills for the week so she could always tell if Alicia had taken them or not. She knew Alicia was getting worse and worse and it was killing her. She and Alicia had never gotten along in their earlier years, but Alicia had changed since John died and Liz was actually beginning to be very fond of her. Finally, mother and daughter were reconciled. Liz was sad, though. She was just getting to genuinely feel her mother's love, but was it too late?

Then one day Liz came home from Safeway with all her groceries in tow as well as Alicia's. She was exhausted and just sat in the car while Baillee and Skye, who were inseparable by this time, took Alicia's groceries in to her.

Baillee and Skye came running out of the house a lot faster than they went in and Liz knew something was wrong. She bounded out of the car and said, "What is it? Is Gramma okay?"

"She has no clothes on," Baillee cried. Skye looked aghast.

"Oh, my gawd!" Liz wailed and raced into the house.

Alicia sat there totally naked from the waist up, smiling sweetly at Liz. This was so out of character for Alicia. She would *never* have gone around like that.

"Mama, what's the matter?" Liz cried.

"Oh, I guess the girls just aren't used to seeing me like this." Alicia retorted.

Liz made an appointment with Dr. Trent right away. Alicia was given the Alzheimers test and failed miserably. Liz was beside herself. She tried desperately to keep Alicia at home and to take care of her, herself. But when she went over one day after work, and Alicia came rushing towards her with her underwear down around her ankles, her dress held up high with feces all over her, looking for all the world like a small child in trouble, Liz knew she had to do something. It nearly broke her heart to have to put Alicia into an old folks home. In spite of working full-time Liz visited Alicia every day for a year. Alicia was like a little girl, so frightened. No way could Liz have abandoned her. But the frequent visits were taking a real toll on Liz. And after a year she had to quit going everyday. She visited only twice a week. On the Saturday night Liz, Baillee, and Skye would take movies and goodies to the home to watch with Gramma. Alicia was like a child and would get so excited. They took movies like Mrs. Doubtfire and Forrest Gump. Alicia was in her glory and it was the highlight of Liz's week. Then came the call. Once more the angel of death visited Liz's life. It was September, 1998. Her heart broke at all the wasted years. She had only just gotten to know her mama, and to truly love her, and it was too little, too late.

Alicia's affairs were settled and the estate distributed. Of course, Alan and George were the executors once again and Liz and every one of her siblings received a small portion of the estate. Liz opted to do some updates on her house with her share of the money, and that's how she came to break her leg. To save money she was doing the revisions herself. She had built a utility shed out in the yard and was siding it. She only had one piece left to put on, just one piece. It was getting dusk and she could smell the snow in the air. Light fluffy snowflakes started to fall. "Oh, man, I've just gotta finish. There's only one piece left. Then it's done for the winter." There was a light skiff of snow accumulating on the back lawn as she went to grab the last piece to cut it. She didn't notice the scrap piece of vinyl siding under the snow and stepped on it and down she went twisting her ankle at an odd angle. Blackness surrounded her then a terrible, permeating cold. She tried to get up and couldn't. Baillee was over at Skye's. Liz was all alone, and it was dark. She started to yell, "Help me! Please help me!" She lay there for what seemed like an eternity in excrutiating pain.

Finally, Baillee came running, "Mom, mom, what are you doing? What's wrong?"

"Get help, get help," Liz squeaked out.

Just at that time Gino and Dolly, her neighbours on either side, came running to the fence. When they saw Liz's dilemma they ran into the yard and carried her between them to her car and Dolly drove her to the hospital.

Corrective surgery was necessary and pins were put in by Dr. Chrisfield. That was it for Liz. She couldn't work because the office was on the second story and there was no elevator. She got sick pay, but it was barely enough. She had to go on assistance. And then after recovering from the fall and the broken leg, things were never the same. She was so tired. She kept going to see Dr. Trent. She had a battery of tests, but nothing showed up. She was chronically fatigued and no one could figure out why. Finally, it was discovered that she had fibromyalgia, and chronic fatigue, along with severe depression. All that together with her anxiety disorder was just too much. Liz had to give up her job at the law office and go on a Disablitiy Pension through the province. She was devastated. She was right back where she had started. She fell into a deep depression, and the only thing that kept her going was her love for Baillee. How could her life turn out this way. Hadn't she had enough. She started to wonder just what this life was all about. She had a lot of time on her hands so she started to read the Bible looking for answers. She couldn't make head nor tail of it. But, eventually, she started to study it indepth and it started to come together for her and give her some hope. She learned there really was a God who cared and that he had a plan for everyone. There really was a purpose to this life.

Slowly, she started to come out of her depression, only to discover that everything in her beautiful yard had become an overgrown mess. It seemed that Liz could never do things in half measures. If she couldn't do it all, then she would do nothing. Another trait of an alcoholic, all or nothing. She had to learn to do things a little at a time, just whatever she was capable of and she soon learned that if she edged one boulevard at a time she would soon have all three done. It was a slower way of doing things for her, but it worked.

Pretty soon she was feeling a whole lot better and her lush green yard was looking the best on the block. But it wasn't enough. She needed more money to get Baillee the extras she needed for her last year of high school. There would be graduation, the Prom, a Prom dress. Those things would cost big time. A paper route became available in Liz's neighbourhood so Liz decided to give it a try. Dr. Trent had told her she needed to walk for her fibromyalgia so this job would be perfect.

Her first day on the route, she was feeling a little sheepish doing a kid's job. Then while going down the alley off Fifth avenue, she encountered two little tots, three or four years of age. The little girl asked shyly, "Are you a paper girl?"

"Yup!" Liz stated proudly.

"Awesome," the boy stated.

That was all she needed to hear. Liz proudly carried on. To her surprise she found that Val's daughter Danielle was one of her paper customers. Danielle's daughter, nine year old Melanie, would hang around the gate everyday when Liz came. Finally, she shyly said, "My mom says you knew my gramma."

"Yes, I did. Your gramma and I were best friends for a long time. She was a beautiful lady."

"I know. I really miss her," Melanie stated.

Liz thought immediatlely about the gold ring with the heart and the diamond and knew exactly what she was going to do with it. Melanie would just treasure it.

The years went quickly by and Baillee graduated high school and left home to go to the big city and make her millions. She moved to Calgary with a schoolmate. Liz was devastated. Now, what was left? Her family was all gone. She was a person with disabilities delivering newspapers. True, she had a beautiful home and yard that she had made her own little castle, but it was so empty.

Then one day she noticed a young man. He was terribly good looking. He waved to her in passing and smiled sweetly. That was it! The Carousel slowly started to spin. "Oh, my gawd," she said aloud. "Now what's happening to me?" It was true she had taken very good care of herself in the last few years. The walking had done her the world of good and she had created her own modern spiky hairstyle. She had been told by several people how good she looked and that she was looking younger every day, but why would a gorgeous young man be interested in an old grandmother. She was sure she was losing it. She put the notion out of her mind.

But as time went on and she saw the young man over and over again, her heart began to take over her head, and she was totally smitten. She decided to go and see Dr. Trent. She was really worried about herself. Was she getting senile? Was this the start of it?

Dr. Trent laughed right out loud, "You've got empty nest syndrome," she stated matter-of-factly.

"It's not funny," Liz stated. I'm really smitten and I don't know what to do about it. I feel embarrassed. The guy would think I'm nuts, although there does seem to be some chemistry working there. Oh, what am I saying. He's gotta be thirty years younger. I used to know when a guy liked me, but now I don't trust my instincts. He's probably just being polite. Anyway I sure can't act on it."

"Just keep yourself busy, get involved in something. A club or something. Volunteer work."

"Are you kidding? I can hardly keep up with my paper route, my house work and my yard as it is. You know I think it's just the old Carousel calling again, now that my family is all gone, and I have nothing to focus on. I guess it's just like the alcoholism. I'll die being an alcoholic and I'll probably die with the Carousel, but I've learned one thing over the years, I can control them both. And that gives me such a feeling of power. Speaking of power, you know, I am so so tired lately. It seems like there is more wrong with me than the fibromyalgia. I've been feeling a lot sicker lately too."

As time passed Liz was struggling more and more. She felt like giving up. She was beginning to feel that if she just drifted off to sleep and never woke up that would be quite alright. Her kids were all grown up and had done well for themselves and she would just like to go to Edmund, her first and dearest love who had died years ago. She hadn't thought about him in a long, long time. She had been too busy fighting her own demons, alcohol and her Carousel. It sure took a lot of energy to fight those demons and she was tiring out. How long could she last?

Chapter 32
The Death of Liz

"What's wrong with her?" Jimmy asked from Liz's bed side.

"We don't really know. It's acting like cancer, but it's hard to tell. She just keeps getting sicker and weaker.

Liz had been in the hospital for a week and they couldn't seem to find anything wrong with her so they just put it down to being cancer. Jimmy had called Bonnie home from Sicamous, Stacy, Baillee and Jason came home from Calgary and they were all staying at Janie's in Fruitvale and visiting Liz's bedside daily. She could hardly recognize them. But she was pleased inside herself when she sensed them all being there.

The doctors had moved her to the family room because they had no hope. She was sinking fast and they just couldn't figure out what it was. She was dying right before their eyes.

The family room in the hospital was dimly lit because the light bothered Liz's eyes. Jimmy, Stacy, Bonnie, Janie, Jason and Baillee were all huddled around her bed, hugging each other with tears streaming down their cheeks. As Liz looked at them, she reflected on the happy years of sobriety she had enjoyed with them.

She coughed and with great effort she whispered, "I love you all with all my heart." She looked at her babies, content that they had finished what she had set out to do, even though the outcome was not the same as her dreams had been. With the aid of government loans, each of the girls had realized their own dreams. Stacy went to nursing school, Bonnie took a course in child care and Janie became part owner of a popular restaurant chain, Jimmy was a master corporal in the army. Liz was so proud of how handsome he looked in his dress uniform. And Baillee was a cashier in a large grocery chain.

She was neither unhappy nor frightened. Yes, she was ready to go. They would be alright now. She tried to comfort them. "Try not to be too sad. In the twinkling of an eye, I'll be where I've always longed to be."

She was so weak she could hardly lift her right arm. But she made the effort, reached over and with her fingers gently caressed the fading white scar tissue on her left upper arm. She looked down. They were still there after all these years, the initials E. B.

"Oh, look the wind is coming up. Quick open the window. I've always loved the wind. It's free and goes where ever it wants," Liz whispered. A warm breeze caressed her face, oh, so gently and then very faintly she thought she could hear the lilting music of the carousel. With that her eyes closed, her body went limp and she died with a peaceful smile on her face; her babies were okay and she was on her way to Edmund.

"Do something, do something," Janie screamed.

Stacy rang the buzzer, lights flashed, buzzers sounded, nurses came running. "You have to try something, do something, anything, Baillee cried desperately. She was only twenty. She needed her mom, her unborn children needed a gramma.

The nurse took her stethoscope, and it was there, just a very faint heart beat, but it was there. She had merely slipped into a coma.

An old doctor came into the room. His white hair hanging down loosely over one eye. Dr. Trent was away. "I've got an idea," he said. "I haven't seen a case like this in years, but if we can keep her alive a little longer. I'd like to run some tests."

Liz was hooked up to all kinds of apparatuses and removed from the family room under this substitute doctor's care.

A battery of tests were run and it was discovered that she had a severe ear disease in the cauliflower ear she was born with. No one had been able to detect it because there was no outward signs. The disease had eaten away all the little bones inside her ear and her ear drum as well and was now poisoning her whole system. She was slowly dying and no one knew why. The disease was very rare, indeed, in this day and age, but, fortunately for Liz, the old doctor, having seen so much in his time, had followed up on a hunch.

An ear specialist was called in from Ontario, Dr. Matt Salla, who performed a five hour operation. He cleaned out all the disease, put plastic bones in her ear, and grafted an ear drum from her jaw muscle.

After the surgery, Liz came to groggily. She was very weak, but her system was already responding to the poisons having been removed from her body. Her throat was so sore, and she couldn't swallow. She wasn't even sure where she was. She'd thought she'd gone to Edmund. "A drink, I need a drink," she croaked out. The nurse brought her a tall cold glass of pineapple orange juice. She would never forget that taste. It was absolutely glorious. She'd been so sick and nothing had tasted any good for months.

After a few days, Dr. Matt Salla, came to her room to take her to emergency to take out the dressings and check on his handiwork. She was even able to walk behind him down the hallway. Quite a feat after being on her death bed. The nurses all wrinkled their noses up at her. Dr. Matt Salla just happened to be the best looking man they'd seen in years. "How do you rate?" one of the nurses whispered to Liz in passing. "He's in love with my ear." Liz whispered back smiling. He was, indeed, in love with his handiwork. And a handiwork, it was. It had saved Liz's life.

Edmund & Ben

Chapter 33
Edmund's Tribute

Liz had nearly died, but now she had a new lease on life. Everything seemed brighter, newer, cleaner, freer. She hadn't thought about Edmund in years and her near death experience brought him back to her reality, and she realized just how much she had truly loved him. How much he had haunted her over the years. How often she had tried to replace him. With Brian. With Norm. With Lenny. With Johnny. And, finally, with David. How often she'd failed.

Thinking of him had stirred a longing to go home. She had to go. She had to go to his grave. She had to go to the old haunts. To Coffee's barn where they spent the night in the hay wrapped around each other, to the tenth line where they fished in the springtime with the snow melting, the long dead grass poking through, and the warm sunshine smiling down on them, warming their hearts. Liz's thoughts raced to Edmund. *He was leaning down over her, then kissing her lips, then raising his head and looking down at her, with his eyes all atwinkle and that silly half-grin, half-smile pasted on his beautiful face.*

****

Cora, needing some distraction after the break-up with Jimmy opted to drive Liz home. Cora and Liz had weathered the storm of the break-up and still remained friends. The plans were made. Cora would meet Liz in Calgary and drive her to Ontario to Jane's. Then she would continue her journey on to New Brunswick where her sister lived, and then Cora and her sister would travel on together to NewFoundland where they had been born and raised. Cora was as excited about the trip as Liz. It was a homecoming for her too.

The trip was long, but pleasant for the women. They talked their way across Canada and hardly noticed the miles. As soon as they got into Northern Ontario, and Liz saw the landscape, the thousands of lakes nestled right next to the flat ground, the tears filled her eyes, spilled over, and streamed down her cheeks. She'd come home. It wouldn't be long and she'd be seeing her sister, Jane and her nieces, Lois and Debra. She carried gifts for all and Alicia's diamond rings for Jane's granddaughter, Julie. She had been Alicia's favourite, and Liz knew Alicia would have loved for Julie to have her rings. And it wouldn't be long until she would be visiting Edmund's grave. She had been so emotional and so upset the last time she'd been there because her husband Brian had just been sent to jail. This time her focus would be on Edmund alone and what their short time together had meant to them.

****

"He still has no stone, not even a corner stone," Liz lamented to Jane as they stood by Edmund's grave. The grave yard was filled with grave stones with the names of many, many people that Liz knew. There was Vera, Carol and Dar's mom. Carol's brother Tommy. Jane's husband Gord Bowman who had died of MS. Sheryl Morris' mom and dad and her brother Clancy. And many more Liz had known from school. They all had nice grave stones to be remembered by. Liz had to do something for Edmund, but she didn't have any money.

"I have an idea," Jane said, "Let's go to Lois'. She has a ton of stuff in her garden shed. Lois donated a round garden stone, and Liz and Jane went to Bradford and bought a set of stencils and some black paint. Liz's brother, George, who was visiting, and who was a minister suggested putting a scripture on the stone and said, "I know just the right one, too. Luke 23:43" Liz grabbed a Bible and looked it up. The scripture read, "Truly I tell you today, you will be with me in paradise." She was ecstatic. It was perfect! She was going to wait for Edmund. No more Carousel for her. Edmund would be the necessary deterrent to stop the constant tugging of the Carousel.

Liz lovingly painted "In Memory Of Edmund Brooker, born 1944, died, 1963, Luke 23:43" on the stone with the black paint. When it dried she painted the whole thing with shelac to keep it preserved in the wild winter weather. After painting the stone she got a terrific idea. She couldn't wait to get home to start.

In the meantime she went to all their old haunts and she spent a couple of days with Sheryl Morris and Brad Peterson who now had three grown children and a couple of grandchildren. Liz asked

Sheryl about Edmund's son who he'd had with Gail. Sheryl was taken aback, "What son? Edmund never had a son, He was always faithful to you, Liz. He was like a brother to me and I knew him really well. He was always faithful to you until he died."

Liz's heart sunk. She'd always thought he'd gone with Gail after her mother made her marry Brian. Edmund's sister had told her about the baby and obviously, she'd lied, probably to hurt Liz because Liz had hurt Edmund so bad. His sister, obviously, didn't know the extenuating circumstances.

After accomplishing everything she'd set out to do Liz left Jane's for the long trek home with a bag full of gifts. One of which was a Johnny Mathis CD with her and Edmund's songs, "The Twelfth of Never", and "Wonderful, Wonderful". Lois found the CD for her. She knew Liz had been searching all over for it and had never been able to find it. Liz bawled like a baby when Lois presented it to her. And she cried all over again when Cora's CD player in the car resounded with the words, "You ask how much I need you, must I explain? I need you, oh my darling, like roses need rain. You ask how much I love you. I'll tell you true. Until the twelfth of never I'll still be loving you." She loved him with all her heart, still, and she was going to make a tribute to him. Her idea was set in her mind like it was carved in stone.

Upon returning to Trail, Liz began her monumental task. She gathered all kinds of information and jotted down tons of notes. She started to type on the old typewriter she had at home. Finally, she had several pages of scrawly typewritten notes. Janie came to stay overnight with Liz and grabbed up the notes and started to read. She was up until two in the morning and the next day she stated, "Mom, this is a really good story!"

That was all Liz needed to keep going. She re-wrote, got books from the library on publishing and writing, and continued day in, day out. Finally, she had a finished copy. She sent it to Carol Simpson. Carol called her back immediately upon finishing the manuscript. "It's excellent. It would make a good movie." More encouragement. Liz had originally called the book "Looking for Love in all the Wrong Places". But somehow it didn't ring true. Then while lying in bed one night, it flashed on like a neon sign. Carousel. The Carousel her papa had ridden with her. The attraction to men was like riding a

Carousel. She'd spin with delight when a man would pay attention to her She had it! It would definitely be called Carousel.

She gave the manuscript to a friend who was also a writer and her friend came back with it and said with an amazed look on her face, "This is a *powerful* story. It has to be told!" Even more encouragement. "But it needs some work." Liz wasn't insulted. She'd never written a book before, and she agreed it needed work, but didn't quite know how to go about it.

"Will you help me?" Liz asked, scared that her friend wouldn't want to take on such a monumental task.

"I was hoping you'd ask."

Liz's face beamed.

So Linda had Liz over to her place one whole winter while Liz rewrote and downloaded it on to a disk. Linda would say, "Now, tell me what happened. How did it feel, how did it look, how did it smell." Liz would tell her and she'd say, "Now, write it like that."

They laughed, they cried, they shared secrets all through that long cold winter. And voila by the spring time it was done. Liz sent it off to an editor in Vancouver, and got it back all hacked to pieces. She wasn't disappointed though. It was what she needed.

Now she had to revise again, but in the meantime, Linda had moved away and Liz didn't have a computer. Liz lamented her problem to Cora. Cora was in the midst of moving up North to Atlin. She'd finished University and had landed her first teaching job. Cora donated her old computer to Liz's project. After all she needed a new computer if she was going to be a teacher. Liz was thrilled and forever grateful. Everything was coming together. Her tribute to Edmund.

Finally, Liz got published. She was a success She was ecstatic. She went on a book tour across Canada with a brand new grave stone made from sparkly black granite with Edmund's name on and her own. Yes, she got permission from the funeral directors to be buried with her beloved Edmund. Her near death experience had awakened her to the reality that she only wanted to be with her beloved Edmund. The Carousel had made it's final turn.

Liz had been an abused child, a tenacious teen, an alcoholic, had ridden the Carousel of her addiction to men, had recovered, rubbed elbows with the elite in the field of law, had become a writer, had almost died several times because of her addictions, but in spite of it all she had lived, she had *really* lived!

The End

Note to My Readers

It was not my intention to go public with my story in the beginning. I didn't care about myself. I had done everything recorded in the pages of my book, CAROUSEL, a long time ago and it was all over, but I didn't want to humiliate or embarrass my family. Thus I decided to kill off the main character so that people wouldn't try to figure out who she was.

It was always my hope to help other young girls with addictions like mine to not feel so alone, and in order to get my book out to them I would need some media coverage. I soon found out, though, that the newspapers wouldn't do an article about my book without my real name. I had run into a brick wall. But my family came to my aid and said, "Go ahead mom, It's a long time ago. It's over now." So with their blessing I went public.

The problem was, though, I had already killed myself off, and CAROUSEL was already going to print. Of course, my readers in my home town knew I wasn't dead and they teased me by saying, "So, how are you going to ressurect yourself in your next book?"

The solution came to me when I read James Frey's book, *A Million Little Pieces*. I read that he had the same ear disease as a child that I had. So in CAROUSEL - THE MISSING YEARS, I wrote in the ear disease as my supposed death-dealing illness. Even though the events of that part of the story happened much earlier in my life they are true and the account is accurate. I was very ill and the doctors couldn't figure out what was wrong with me. I was hospitalized for quite a while, and I could easily have died as a result of that disease.

Kimberley Rose Dawson

About the Author

Kimberley Rose Dawson, author of CAROUSEL, resides in Trail, British Columbia. CAROUSEL and CAROUSEL - THE MISSING YEARS are actually based on her own life story. All the names have been changed to respect the privacy of the characters. Kimberley was born in Scarborough, Ontario and attended Regent Heights school on Pharmacy Avenue. In 1957 she moved, with her parents, to Bradford, Ontario and attended Bradford District High School.

After several anguishing years, she moved to British Columbia in the hopes of effecting a geographic cure for her alcoholism. She finally sobered up with the help of Alcoholics Anonymous and settled in Trail where she lives now with her two cats, Brody and Kitty. She has twenty-six continuous years of sobriety.

Printed in the United States
76555LV00003B/106-126